Speakeasy Secrets

A JAZZ AGE THRILLER

JUDITH A. BARRETT

WOBBLY CREEK, LLC

SPEAKEASY SECRETS, A JAZZ AGE THRILLER

Published in the United States of America by Wobbly Creek, LLC

2025 Georgia

wobblycreek.com

Cover by Wobbly Creek, LLC

ISBN 978-1-953870-92-6 eBook

ISBN 978-1-953870-93-3 Paperback

Dedication

Speakeasy Secrets is dedicated to the colors deep red and sparkly black and to readers who love to dive into a particularly offbeat story.

Chapter One

Nettie pulled back the white lace curtains in the sitting room to peer at the model Ts as they rolled up the driveway then parked in front of the large home on the family estate.

She turned to her husband's cousin who was two years younger than she was and her best friend. "Flossie, our visitors are here a half hour early, as usual. We'll need the appetizers in the living room for our dinner guests; I'm certain Willis has the bar ready for our speakeasy patrons."

Flossie patted her short, dark brown curls and adjusted her bandeau with its rhinestones and a fashionable ostrich feather. "I love this; I'm ready. You manage the important patrons downstairs in the speakeasy, and I'll dazzle our regular guests and collect their monthly subscription dues for the supper club, just like always."

Nettie smiled. "Just like always unless you want to switch."

Flossie snorted. "You gotta be razzing me. I enjoy being Flossie the floozy; not that anyone would say that to my face. I'd say they're too polite, but the truth is, they're too afraid of you."

"Me? I'm a pussycat." Nettie chuckled.

"Sweetie, you're a shark in pearls." Flossie sashayed to the foyer to greet the guests and patrons.

Percy, Nettie's husband, wheeled into the sitting room. "She's right, you know. Who are we expecting this evening?"

He wore his black tuxedo jacket and vest with a crisp white shirt and a red bow tie and had a black silk lap quilt thrown over his legs. Percy walked with a limp from a combat injury in France during the Great War and normally used a cane, but he couldn't stand for long periods.

His wheelchair allowed him to enjoy the reputation of being attentive and approachable at their supper club parties, which added to his natural charm and increased his popularity. Percy had the unique advantage of listening to selected conversations without being intrusive.

"If the head G-man shows up, he'll beeline for the governor's brother. He's been angling for a political appointment and has been trying to impress the governor. You might pick up a little advanced notice on a raid." Nettie furrowed her brow. "We may have an uninvited guest."

"You're never wrong, so I'll be on the lookout," Percy said. "Be safe and enjoy yourself, darling."

"You too." Nettie bent down and kissed Percy then chuckled. "Your mustache tickles, and you have lipstick on your mouth."

"I'm a marked man." He licked his fingers then rubbed his mouth. "How's that?"

"Not a trace of smooching." Nettie pulled out her bright red lipstick from her small bag and artfully repaired the smudge.

Percy leered. "We'll fix that later, won't we, love?"

Nettie smiled and blew him a kiss.

When she strolled into the living room where the appetizers were being served with coffee and nonalcoholic fruit juice cocktails, a young woman stood next to the mayor's wife.

The mayor's wife waved her lace handkerchief. "Yoo hoo, Nancy, dear. It's so nice to see you."

"Nettie," the mayor mumbled.

Nettie narrowed her eyes when the young woman sniffed and rolled her eyes.

"Oh, of course." The mayor's wife slurred her words. "Nellie."

Flossie appeared and slipped her arm through the woman's arm. "Let's twenty-three skiddoo to the porch and chat a while. I'm ready for some fresh air, aren't you? Please tell me who did your hair; it's absolutely stunning."

The mayor stepped close to Nettie and glanced around before he spoke in a quiet voice. "I apologize for my wife. She's been seeing that new doctor; he's pricey, but she likes him, and she does seem to be in better spirits. He said there may be some side effects to her new medicine, but she'll adjust."

Nettie smiled. "I'm sure she will."

She extended her hand to the young woman who was chewing on her thumbnail while she glanced around. "I'm Nettie Wyndham."

The woman mumbled as she quickly wiped her thumb on her dress and tentatively shook Nettie's hand.

"Helen is my new assistant," the mayor said as he side-glanced at Helen.

"Nice to meet you, Helen." Nettie raised an eyebrow at the mayor whose face reddened.

"If you'll excuse me." Nettie strode across the room to greet a friend who stood near the appetizers and was the wife of the second in command of the local mob. "What a pleasant surprise to see you, Marian. How's your mother doing?"

Marian smiled. "Much better. Thank you. She'll be tickled when I tell her you asked about her. She wants to come to dinner with us as soon as she's strong enough."

"I would love that."

After Nettie spoke to several other guests, she slipped out of the living room to go to the kitchen. On her way, she overheard a woman whisper, "Nobody knows this, but Nettie is the chef."

Another woman gasped. "You don't say, but it makes sense, doesn't it? I'll bet she's a terror in the kitchen." She tittered. "She's such a perfectionist."

Nettie shook her head. *There must have been some speculation about where I go when I disappear, and Percy dropped in a hint; he's the best.*

When Nettie hurried into the kitchen, Estelle was placing deviled eggs on a platter. Her once-blond hair had darkened but was highlighted with wide streaks of silver.

After Nettie patted her chef's shoulder, Estelle turned and smiled.

Nettie returned her smile and signed, "Going downstairs."

Estelle nodded and continued with adding garnishes of caviar to the deviled eggs.

Nettie opened the door next to the pantry and went down the stairs. She pulled her embroidered silk shawl tighter around her shoulder against the cool underground air as she unlocked a heavy wooden door then pushed it open.

Willis, the bartender, nodded as he continued to set up his station. "We may pick up a few new patrons next week. Word has it there's a raid in a town near here tonight."

"As long as it's not us, Willis."

"Not yet, but I hear we're on the list."

"All we need is an hour's notice, but twenty-four would be nice," Nettie said. "Are you ready for customers? I'll test the warning light when I go upstairs."

"Yes, ma'am."

"Don't call me ma'am, Willis. I'm only twenty-two."

"Shall I wait until you're a quarter of a century old, Boss?"

"Boss is worse," Nettie grumbled, and Willis chuckled.

After Nettie went upstairs to the kitchen, she pushed the button for their warning light.

Estelle smiled as she glanced up when the light came on above the stove.

"Light's on down here," Willis called out.

Nettie turned off the light and signed, "We're ready for business."

A gangly, thirteen-year-old girl with fine blond hair tapped Estelle's elbow. Estelle pointed to two platters on the counter and then to the dining room. The young girl picked up a platter and held her head high as she marched out of the kitchen.

"Bella's growing up so fast," Nettie signed.

Estelle beamed as she signed, "She's smart like her mama was. She wants to learn how to run a business. Her teacher gave her a book on bookkeeping."

"You and Oliver are doing a wonderful job raising her."

Percy rolled into the kitchen. "The senator is parking his car."

"Thank you, honey. I'll get to work."

Estelle tapped on the counter with her spoon then raised her eyebrows and pointed to a small plate with a deviled egg, a mushroom stuffed with crabmeat, and salmon mousse on rye bread.

Percy signed, "Thank you."

While Percy dug into his appetizers, Nettie signed, "You spoil him, Star."

Estelle beamed.

Nettie hurried to the foyer and opened the door as a portly man with perfectly coiffed, thick, gray hair and wearing a custom-tailored suit strode toward the house. The state senator, who was highly regarded locally, stepped onto the porch.

Nettie smiled. "It's nice to see you, Senator. How is your wife?"

After the senator offered his arm, they strolled toward the kitchen together. "She's finally recovering from her bout with the influenza and felt well enough to tend her flowers today. At lunch, she talked about coming with me sometime soon. Her friends have been urging her to visit that new doctor that's supposed to be a miracle worker. Have you heard of him? What do you think?"

"I've heard mention. I must be old school because I don't see how new means better, and I can't think of anything more healing than digging in the dirt."

The senator chuckled. "That's just what my wife said."

As she led the way down the stairs, she said, "Tell her I've missed her; nobody can match her biting wit. Willis has your favorite this evening."

"He was in the Marines in France with my boy, but I probably already told you that. I guess I just like saying it."

"And I enjoy hearing it," Nettie said. "I'll bring you a plate of hors d'oeuvres. Estelle has outdone herself."

He chuckled. "Someone asked me if you were really the chef, and I said, of course. I must have been feeling ornery."

The senator stopped at the door and cleared his throat. "You might want to give Willis the evening off tomorrow."

Nettie smiled. "That's a wonderful idea, thank you."

When she returned to the kitchen, Estelle had the senator's appetizers ready.

Before Nettie picked up the plate and napkin, she signed, "Willis will not be working tomorrow evening. Tell Oliver no trips tomorrow."

Estelle narrowed her eyes as her fingers flew. "Willis could help Oliver with the mules. What about Bella?"

Nettie signed her reply, "You're right about the mules; I'll tell Willis. Bella can bring her school books if she wants to study. Flossie can manage the appetizers, and Bella and I will help you set up the buffet in the dining room."

After Nettie led three more patrons downstairs and replenished the appetizers, she found Percy in the dining room in a corner near the door.

She smiled at the diners who were returning to the buffet for seconds and glanced at Flossie who listened intently to a political conversation while she appeared to be fascinated by a heated discussion about the best breed of cat to own.

"Busy night," Percy said.

"You've kept us hopping in the kitchen, and we'll have a little extra housework to do tomorrow, but isn't Flossie amazing?"

"She wears me out just watching her. How can anyone follow two conversations at once?"

"She complained three is her max. Can you imagine? After our family devotional, we'll turn in early."

"I'll let Flossie know," Percy said.

"Back to work." Nettie kissed Percy's cheek and whispered, "The senator said we should give Willis the evening off tomorrow."

Percy smiled. "Nice kiss; thanks."

Nettie strolled to the kitchen while Percy shifted his attention to the two women near him.

Nettie carried full platters of food downstairs and chatted with her patrons before she returned to the kitchen with empty ones.

After Nettie helped Estelle serve up desserts, Flossie and Bella carried trays of desserts to the dining room. While Flossie filled a large carafe with fresh coffee to refill the urn in the dining room, Nettie went downstairs and announced coffee was being served, which was the signal for the speakeasy patrons to join the guests upstairs for coffee or to slip out quietly to their cars.

After the last patron left, Willis washed the final few glasses and wiped down the counter.

Nettie said, "We'll be closed tomorrow. Would you be available to help Oliver with the mules?"

Willis dried the glasses and put them away. "I can do that. So, we don't bring any stock from storage, right?"

"Not tomorrow."

"What about next Friday? Same as usual?" Willis removed all the bottles from the back bar and put them into wooden boxes.

"I honestly don't know. Ordinarily, I'd say yes."

"Oliver and I have plenty to keep us busy. Do you want the boxes locked in here, or should we take them to storage?" Willis asked.

"They might as well stay in here." Nettie furrowed her brow as she scanned the room. "This place looks like a bar."

"How worried are you?"

"Super worried. He wouldn't have said anything if it was just a normal raid."

"Yeah, he told me. Oliver and I can build a second root cellar first thing in the morning, or maybe a storm cellar would make more sense. Is that too extreme?"

"Maybe, but let's do it," Nettie said. "What do you need from me?"

"We have everything we need. We set aside extra materials from our projects when we added electricity and indoor plumbing to Estelle and Oliver's cottage and put in this room at the same time. I'll talk to Percy; he's a great design guy. We'll come up with something. I'll finish up here then lock up, and we'll start working first thing in the morning. I'll give Percy a heads-up before I leave, so he'll have a little time to think about it."

Willis handed Nettie a bank bag with the monthly subscription receipts for the speakeasy he'd collected that evening. As she turned to leave, Willis added, "I got the feeling the senator thinks this raid is personal. Rumor has it there's a group that wants Percy to run for lieutenant governor because you could swing the newly franchised women's vote for him."

Nettie snorted. "Percy wouldn't need my help; he's been a charmer since the day he was born."

Willis chuckled. "You're right."

Nettie stopped at the doorway and gazed at Willis. "Sometimes there's truth in rumors. I'll check with Percy; if anyone has approached him about running for lieutenant governor, he may have thought they were joking."

"If he wants to take it seriously, I'm ready to go over the top."

"I'll let him know," Nettie said. *And I'll ask him what going over the top means.*

Nettie went into the root cellar and placed the bank bag into the safe that was buried under the floorboards.

After Nettie blew the air kiss and went into the kitchen, Percy shifted his attention to the two women standing close to him when one of them glanced around the room then whispered, "Did you meet that so-called assistant to the mayor?"

"I didn't even know he had an assistant." The second woman peered at the mayor and the young woman at this side. "I wonder what his wife thinks?"

The first woman tittered. "She only pays attention to that new doctor, and you know he's not about to rock the boat. I heard Helen only got the job because she went to school with Nettie, but I'm sure they weren't friends because Nettie didn't recognize her. I only know her name because I overhead the mayor tell Nettie."

"That doesn't sound like Nettie; she knows everybody and their families."

"Now that you mention it, I don't believe I've ever seen Helen before." The woman sniffed. "She's not from around here."

The women drifted away to join a group, and Percy raised his eyebrow when Helen casually strolled alone to the hallway. Percy watched as Flossie stormed out behind Helen.

When Helen returned a few minutes later, her face was red. Percy propped his chin in thought with his thumb and covered his mouth with his first knuckle to hide his smirk. *Flossie must have caught up with her.*

Helen peered around the corner of the doorway into the hallway behind her then quickly joined a group.

After Flossie returned to the living room several minutes later, one of her friends waved for her to join them.

Helen watched Flossie for a few minutes then slowly made her way toward the door. Percy followed Helen after she sneaked into the hallway. He watched while she glanced toward the kitchen then turned toward the staircase. Percy stayed close behind her.

As she reached for the banister, Percy asked, "Can I help you?"

Helen jumped and whirled around.

Her face was pale as she growled, "Who do you think you are, sneaking up on people? I don't need your kind of help; I'm looking for the senator." She flipped her hair. "I have an important message for him. Somebody told me he was in a meeting, so he must be upstairs."

She sniffed as she pointedly stared at the wheelchair. "So, you obviously can't help me."

"What's your name?" Percy asked. "I don't believe we've met."

She snorted as she took two steps up the stairs.

"Helen, where are you going?" the mayor asked as he strode to Percy's side.

"I was looking for the ladies' room."

"That's not actually correct, Mayor; Helen told me she was looking for the senator," Percy said.

Helen crossed her arms. "He's obviously a gimp and doesn't know what he's talking about."

The mayor growled, "Young lady, you just insulted our host. It's time for you to leave."

Helen's face paled as she whined, "I can't leave. I came here in your car with you and your wife."

"The walk will be good for you, or if you wait by the car until we're ready to leave, you can ride back to town with us."

The mayor took her arm and firmly walked her to the front door.

"You'll be sorry for this," Helen hissed.

"I seriously doubt that," the mayor said. "I'll apologize to our hosts for your rude behavior, but in case you missed it, you're fired."

After the mayor slammed the door, he said, "I am so sorry, Percy. She told me she was one of Nettie's best friends in college, but it's my mistake. I should have checked."

"It would be interesting to know who she really works for," Percy said.

"You're right; I'll discreetly check around, but I can guess."

"You and I are probably on the same wavelength. I'll drop by your office on Monday, and we can chat."

While their guests migrated from the living room to the dining room, Nettie gently encouraged the lingerers in the living room to find their seats for dinner.

When the last guest left the living room, Nettie joined Flossie in the dining room. "I'd like to meet this new doctor. Is there someone who would be eager to invite him to dinner sometime?"

"I know just the person; it will be interesting to see him in action, won't it?" Flossie smirked.

"Exactly my thoughts."

After dinner, the guests congratulated Nettie on another pleasant evening with a wonderful meal before they strolled to their cars. When the last guest left, Nettie locked the front door.

"Family meeting in the living room?" Percy asked.

"I'll grab glasses and the flask Willis left for us," Flossie said.

"I'll bring the platter Bella and I prepared and meet you there," Nettie said.

After the three of them gathered around the fireplace in the living room, Nettie sighed with relief as she sat in her yellow chair that always relaxed her. Percy sat next to her in his chair and squeezed her hand. Flossie carefully measured the contents of the flask into their three glasses.

After their toast, Flossie said, "Your meeting, Nettie."

Percy said, "Right, but first, I have the latest juicy gossip to share before I forget. The senior bookkeeper at the bank suddenly quit this afternoon, and our gossipers are certain she eloped with the electrician from the county north of us."

"Good for her; I heard he was the bee's knees," Flossie said.

Nettie snorted. "Let's get down to business. We need to prepare for a raid tomorrow. Willis and Oliver will repurpose the patrons' room to a storm cellar or maybe a second root cellar. Willis told me he'd discuss it with you, Percy."

"He did, and we tentatively decided on a storm cellar. I told him I'd have the design plan for him first thing in the morning. It has to look like it's always been there. Honey, did you see the mayor's new assistant, Helen? The mayor told me she went to school with you, and that's why he hired her."

"The mayor was pretty upset when he realized I didn't know her. I wondered why he'd bring someone here who hadn't been invited," Nettie said. "Did you talk to her, Flossie?"

"Did I ever. She's a slippery character," Flossie said. "She sneaked out of the living room, but I caught her as she opened the door to the sewing room. When I asked her if she was looking for someone, she told me she had a message from the mayor for the senator, and someone told her he was probably in a meeting."

Flossie took a small sip from her glass then coughed.

After she caught her breath, she said, "This is great batch. It's downright potent, isn't it? I told her he was in a board meeting upstairs, and I'd be happy to convey the message, but she needed to go back to the dining room before Nettie caught her in the hallway. I went into a long explanation about Nettie's family space and the consequences of violating that privacy. Her face turned a gorgeous crimson, and she stomped back to the living room. After I returned to the living room and told the mayor what happened, he must have been confused, because he just nodded. When I caught the senator and gave him a condensed version..."

Percy snort-laughed. After he regained his composure, he said, "Sorry, but sometime I'd like to hear one of your condensed versions."

Flossie's eyes flashed. "Why? So you could bombard me with questions because you have to have all the details?"

Percy held up his hands. "So, what did the senator say?"

"He said he was glad I was on his side." Flossie exhaled.

"Smart man," Percy chuckled. "The mayor gave Helen the bum's rush after I stopped her from going upstairs. I love how invisible I am in my wheelchair. Helen didn't hear me follow her and in fact, didn't know who I was."

"That has to be a story," Nettie said.

"Sure was; I'll tell you later." Percy side-glanced at Flossie as she squirmed in her seat. "What else do you have, Flossie?"

"The mayor's wife said she heard Helen tell some people there was supposed to be a raid tonight; but since there wasn't, the mayor's wife wants to sit on our porch tomorrow night to watch for raiders who are planning to rob us and all our guests. She said they'd be here at eight o'clock and half of them would sneak in the back door, and the other half would break down the front door and make a lot of noise. It took me a while to settle her down, but I promised I would lock the back door and have someone guard the front, so we'd be safe."

Percy raised his eyebrows. "Wow, those are very specific details. What do you think, honey?"

"We have to be ready for anything," Nettie said.

"So, here's my plan," Flossie said. "Percy, while you're working on the storm cellar, Nettie and I can rearrange the furniture in the upstairs storage space to look like a meeting room, so if we are raided, Miss Helen's friends will have something to look at. She had to have been a stoolie sent here to scope out the house."

"She sure had all the markings of a stool pigeon, didn't she?" Nettie furrowed her brow. "Why the upstairs storage space and not one of the spare bedrooms?"

"It will be faster just to rearrange the furniture that's already in the storage room. We can make it look like it's always been a meeting room. You'll see."

"Could it be an actual meeting space?" Percy rubbed his chin. "After we're cleared by the raid party, I wouldn't mind having somewhere to chat with friends that isn't in the public area."

"Let's do it, then," Nettie said. "Flossie, if either of us gets pinched, you have to be Flossie the ditzy floozy."

"You're right, babe," Percy said. "Flossie, you can't get caught up in a raid because we need you here to keep everything running. Too many people count on the

Wyndham family for a stable income to feed and clothe their families. We can't let the business fall apart."

"Then don't get arrested," Flossie said. "I'm going to bed."

Nettie shook her head. "She has a solution for every problem, doesn't she?"

Percy rose from his wheelchair and took her into his arms. He snuggled her neck. "Yes, and she goes for the most obvious, which may or may not be practical. Are you ready to get comfortable?"

"Absolutely. I'll take the platter, plates, and glasses to the kitchen then meet you at the stairs."

Percy pushed his wheelchair to the closet under the stairwell and removed his cane from its holder on the back of the seat. When Nettie joined him, he counted each step in French.

She giggled. "My Cajun mother would be proud of you for using your French."

"I probably should practice more often; the little I did know came in handy overseas. Maybe we should speak in French when we're alone, so I won't embarrass myself."

"I'd like that. We always spoke French at home when I was growing up. I knew enough English thanks to my father to get by when I started school."

After they were in their bedroom, Percy carefully hung up his tuxedo vest and jacket then changed into pajamas.

While Nettie changed into a silk nightgown, she asked, "What does over the top mean? Willis said if you wanted to run for lieutenant governor, he was over the top."

"He said that?" Percy asked. "In the Great War, the trench was the only safe place during an attack. When a man went over the top, he put himself in a position to be shot. Only a brave or reckless man would go over the top to save a friend or his unit. Willis isn't reckless."

Percy furrowed his brow. "The senator mentioned I should run for lieutenant governor a few weeks ago, and the mayor brought it up tonight. I didn't think they were serious. What about you? Wouldn't it put the spotlight on us and possibly the speakeasy?"

"What if it's the other way around? Couldn't the purpose of the raid be to smear you as a bootlegger, so you wouldn't be a viable candidate for lieutenant governor? Even if we put the speakeasy on hold for a while, we'd still have the income from the supper club for our guests. If Willis is ready to go over the top, so am I. I'm certain the senator would support you, but it might be worth knowing whether the local mob would support your candidacy or you'd be a threat."

"That's a good point. I'll talk to Willis about that tomorrow; he might have an idea, but what do you think?" Percy asked.

"I love Marian and her mom to pieces, but I'm concerned the local mob wouldn't want you in office at the state level because they couldn't control you."

"It's not me they're afraid of, love; you're more of a powerhouse than you realize." Percy smiled. "Ready for lights out?"

"Sure." Nettie giggled as she slipped into bed while he turned off the light.

When Percy climbed into bed, he reached for Nettie then spoke in French. "Aren't you going to be cold without your nightgown?"

Nettie snuggled close and responded in French, "Probably not."

Chapter Two

When Nettie woke, she patted the empty spot on the mattress next to her then inhaled the enticing aroma of coffee. She jumped out of bed and quickly dressed before she dashed down the stairs and into the kitchen.

"Coffee woke me up. How do you get up so early without an alarm?" she grumbled.

Percy poured her a cup of coffee and set it on the counter in front of her. "Magical husband powers. Do you want a roll?" Percy winked.

Nettie snickered. "Just coffee's fine for now."

She cleared her throat. "What's your schedule for today?"

"As soon as I finish my coffee, I'm going downstairs to stare at the walls until I decide how to design our new storm cellar and still have access to my lovely bride's little hobby."

Nettie raised her eyebrows. "Little hobby?"

"Yes, do you want to be known for your little hobby of crocheting or cooking?"

"I'm sure you have a point in this question, but I don't cook or crochet. What are we really talking about?"

"Your hobby."

When Nettie continued to stare at him, he said, "Take another sip of coffee. We might need Flossie to interpret. I might be using the wrong word."

"She's a bear to wake up; you owe me cinnamon sugar on toast."

Nettie dashed up the stairs then pounded on Flossie's door before she opened it.

"Are you awake?" Nettie smiled as Flossie struggled to open her eyes.

"Better be important," Flossie grumbled as she sat up and blinked to focus.

"Get dressed. Percy has an idea, but he needs your help."

Flossie continued to grumble as Nettie closed the door then hummed as she returned to the kitchen. "She'll be here in a minute."

Percy pointed to the plate on the kitchen table at Nettie's usual spot.

She smiled at her freshly refilled steaming coffee and the cinnamon toast Percy had cut into four triangles for her.

When Flossie stumbled into the kitchen, she glared as Nettie ate the last quarter of her toast then rose to refill her coffee cup.

"Why does she get cinnamon toast?"

While Nettie poured a cup of coffee for Flossie, Percy set a plate of cinnamon toast on the table.

Flossie sat at her place and sipped her coffee. "What's so danged important that I had to get up before ten o'clock? Thanks for the toast." She took a big bite.

Percy said, "We need to have a product stored in boxes in our new storage room. Flossie, we need yarn, and a lot of it immediately, so Nettie, Estelle, and Bella can crochet items and have them look like they are ready for sale by lunchtime."

Nettie stared at him. "My coffee just kicked in, and I think I finally understand what you had in mind. Your plan is to have the overabundance of my little hobby supplies stored in boxes in the new storage room, right?"

"Yes, so it will be obvious you've been working on your hobby for a while."

Nettie side-glanced at Flossie. "Do we tell him?"

Flossie grinned. "This makes getting out of bed worthwhile. You tell him."

"Tell me what?" Percy stared at them.

"You know I sew all my clothes, right?" Nettie said.

"Yes, and I always know when you wear something new because our women guests gush over your latest dress with envy that borders on outright jealousy."

"So, your idea is I've had this little hobby for a while, and it's gotten out of control, and you needed a storage room to store all my supplies." Nettie's mouth quivered.

"That's right." Percy cocked his head as he examined Nettie's face. "Am I missing something?"

"Do you have any idea how much fabric and fabric scraps our seamstress has? The upstairs storage room is packed," Flossie said. "Why don't we just haul all the boxes of fabric downstairs?"

Percy exhaled. "Remind me the next time I have a good idea to mention the problem I want to fix."

"If you recall...never mind. It's actually a magnificent idea. We'll get on it as soon as Flossie's coffee kicks in too," Nettie said.

"I think I heard Willis' old truck drive up, but if I didn't, he'll be here in a minute." Percy said. "I'll fill him in on my brilliant idea, but I'll leave out the yarn version."

Percy limped with his cane as he went out the back door.

Flossie giggled then drank the rest of her coffee. "After we pull the storage boxes into the hallway, I'll show you what I meant about a meeting room."

After they pulled out a dozen medium-sized wooden boxes of fabric, Flossie said, "I thought you had more."

"I take the scraps into town along with the baby and little girl patterns I create so the ladies in town can make pretty dresses for their little ones. Let's carry the boxes down to the kitchen, then we can rearrange the storage room."

After they had carried down the boxes, the sound of hammering from the cellar greeted them when they went into the kitchen.

"I need a water break and a cookie, but let's sit in the dining room," Flossie said.

While Flossie munched on her cookie, she said, "A woman asked me last night why we didn't have a telephone because almost everybody in town did. I told her the lines don't reach this far. Is there actually a reason we don't have a telephone?"

"You're right about the lines, and that's the best answer when anyone asks. We'll get a telephone when we can have a private line because right now, three or four households share a line. We don't need anyone listening in on our calls."

"That's how it works?" Flossie's eyes widened. "Do people know that?"

Nettie shrugged. "They should, but they forget."

Flossie added, "Or they're listening in themselves."

When they returned upstairs, Flossie said, "Now I want to get a telephone, so I can listen in on everybody else."

Nettie snorted. "You listen to people while they flap their jaws every Friday and Saturday night."

Flossie giggled. "I guess I do; so maybe I'm not missing out after all."

After they removed the dust covers from the furniture, they repositioned the soft chairs into a conversational area and the round table with its chairs in the middle of the cleared area.

Flossie disappeared into the dark recesses of the eaves and returned with a floor lamp with tassels circling its lampshade. "How's this?"

When Nettie pushed the wall switch near the door, the attic was bathed in the glaring light of a bare bulb as it dangling at the end of a cord attached to an overhead truss.

"Not very snazzy, is it?" Flossie giggled.

Nettie wrinkled her nose. "Looks a warehouse. I'll ask Percy to see what he can do about our colossal flop."

Flossie bit her lip. "If there isn't anything else for us to do, I'd like to go into town and get a few things. Do you mind driving me into town them picking me up later?"

"That sounds great; I have a few things to do in town too," Nettie said.

When Flossie's face switched from joyful anticipation to intense disappointment, Nettie added, "I have several shops to visit to drop off fabric. You don't need me to stick close to you, do you?"

The twinkle in Flossie's eyes reappeared. "It would be more efficient if we separate to do our errands, wouldn't it?"

"Just what I was thinking," Nettie said. "After I talk to Percy about the meeting room and pick up my large tote of fabric scraps and patterns, I'll be ready to go. I'll meet you at the car in twenty minutes."

"That's good." Flossie dashed to her room while Nettie turned off the offensive overhead light.

After Nettie found Percy in the kitchen, she said, "Flossie wanted to go into town, and I have a feeling it would be worth my while to check in at my usual stops. We set up the meeting room in the attic, but it needs a better lighting solution than a bright overhead light."

"Willis and Oliver are busy in the cellar, so I'll look at it."

"I appreciate it. I think it's important for our patrons to have a meeting place tonight, so there won't be any speculation. Anything I can do for you in town?"

"If you hear any rumors about a raid, squash them. We need to have everyone assuming tonight will be a normal

Saturday night at the Wyndhams." Percy peered at Nettie. "Do you have your derringer?"

"All the time, love. A few dollars, my lipstick, my small folding pocket knife, and my derringer are always in my favorite beaded bag with the skinny shoulder strap."

After a hug and a sweet kiss, Percy patted Nettie's bottom. "Be safe."

"Always." She picked up her tote bag of fabric then hurried to the car where Flossie waited in the passenger seat.

As she drove to town, Nettie said, "It's time you learned to drive."

Flossie pointed to an upcoming driveway. "You can't see the house from the road. It's been abandoned for a long time. Do you know if it's for sale?"

"I'm sure it is; you aren't thinking about moving out, are you?"

"I was more thinking it would be a worthwhile project. We could buy it and fix it up," Flossie said. "Although if it's too much work, I wouldn't mind fixing up the shack that's close to our house for practice. It's on the same property as the barn except it's closer to the road. Have you seen it?"

"I don't think so."

"It's in the trees, so it's a little hidden from the road. When you're coming from town, it's on the right after you pass our driveway. Percy and his friends pretended it was a pirate ship and played there all the time when they were boys. I hid outside where they couldn't see me and pretended I was a spy for the Royal Navy. I don't think they knew I was there because I was a superior spy. It was fun until that big snitch Arnie told on them, and Percy was grounded. He's still a big snitch, if you ask me. Like another time..."

Nettie interrupted, "We can look at the abandoned house sometime if you like to see how much work it needs, but you'd have to learn to drive if you took on a project like that."

Flossie sighed. "Did you know you have a one-track mind? I'd be too nervous on the road. What if I hit someone?"

"We'll practice in the driveway. You won't have to drive on the road until you're ready."

"I guess I could do that." Flossie stared out her side window. "After all, I might have to be your getaway driver sometime."

Nettie rolled her eyes. "You never know."

As they neared the town limits, Flossie said, "You can park wherever you like. I have several places to go, so I'll make my rounds and meet you back at the car. Is a half hour okay?"

"That's more than enough time for me. I don't want to be gone from the house too long in case there's more we need to do for tonight. Percy said if we heard any hint of a raid, we should stop the rumor. The quickest way would be to make it old news and laugh it off with a remark like, 'Is that still going around?' We don't want our guests and patrons to be nervous about coming."

Flossie raised her eyebrows. "Because it would look like we'd been tipped off."

"Right." Nettie parked. "So, gather some gossip while you're running your errands, and I will too."

When Nettie strolled into Theresa's fabric store, Theresa asked, "New patterns, Nettie?"

The four customers in the shop gathered around while Nettie laid out fabric and patterns on the cutting table.

While the customers discussed each pattern and decided which fabric they liked for the patterns, Theresa and Nettie slipped into the back storeroom.

"I was hoping you'd make it into town. I'm getting that big shipment for you tomorrow morning," Theresa said. "It wasn't supposed to be here until Monday, but somebody got spooked along the way, and I suspect meddling Helen is at the bottom of it. I'm worried the shippers might get careless."

"How can I help?"

"I need the shipment to be diverted. Hi-jack them, if that's what it takes."

"Where?"

Theresa pulled out a pattern for a baby's bib and marked it with a pencil. "If this is the county north of us, the best place is here, about a mile away from the county line."

Nettie nodded. "I know where that is. How open would they be to a man and a woman taking over their shipment?"

"I can get word to them that my driver and I will meet them on the road; they'll know where. I've never met with them, so tell them you're Theresa and wear this shawl to cover your hair. I'll mention the shawl too."

Theresa gave Nettie a pale yellow silk shawl. "Tell them they will get their money next week, as usual.

They might load the shipment into your car for you, but more likely, they'll dump and run if they're as hinky as I expect."

"Do you anticipate trouble here in the morning?" Nettie asked.

"Absolutely, and I'm convinced seizing the product is a bonus. Do you know Helen?"

"Do I ever. Percy caught her snooping around the house last night."

"I'm not surprised. According to people at the boarding house where she lives, she's been reading those new pulp fiction books and got it in her head that she's destined to be one of Al Capone's molls and is trying to work her way up. She approached the local mob and offered to gather information for them, but they turned her down. I think she went fishing somewhere else and got a nibble from a group that isn't as picky as our locals are. She told a woman in the grocery store she has important connections, and everybody will be surprised when a raid busts a well-known merchant. Nobody takes her seriously, but she's been hanging around the shop most afternoons since last week looking at the same fabric."

"Why would anyone raid you?"

"I'm insignificant; the real purpose would be to embarrass the locals when word got around about finding bootleg whiskey in a raid at the fabric store on a Sunday morning during church."

"That's a pretty specific detail."

"Sure is, but that's what I'm hearing."

"So, who do you expect to raid you? The feds or the Atlanta mob?"

"I'm not sure; it could be either one, but I'm more concerned about a rumor there is a ruthless group from out of state that is trying to move in. If it's true, I think their plan is to cause more tension between the feds and the local mob when they blame each other for the raid."

Nettie narrowed her eyes. "Do you want me to give either group a heads up?"

"No, the raid has to be a complete surprise to all because we don't know who to trust."

"What about you, Theresa? It seems like you're in the middle."

Theresa peered at her. "I'm just a small town shop owner. Nettie, you're the flamboyant fireball. You're not just in the middle; you're in the spotlight."

"I'm not sure I understand why." Nettie furrowed her brow then smiled. "There has to be a way we can use that."

Theresa returned her smile. "I love the way you think; let me know what I can do."

"I have more shops to visit, so you won't be targeted by association with me."

After Nettie cleared the cutting table of the fabric and patterns that were left, she headed to the general store.

When she was inside, the elderly shopkeeper came out from behind the counter. "It's good to see you, Nettie. I was hoping you'd drop by this morning. Somebody said there might be some problems out your way, but I told them they were wrong, and you'd be here today if they had any questions."

Nettie raised an eyebrow when two women bustled into the shop then froze when they saw her.

"Y'all here for some of Nettie's fabric and patterns?" the shopkeeper asked.

One woman side-glanced at the other. "Yes, of course. Nice to see you, Nettie. We appreciate the fabric and your patterns."

While the other woman gushed about the last dress she'd made for her niece, the shopkeeper interrupted her. "Nettie, I know you have more fabric to deliver. Thank you so much for dropping by."

Nettie smiled as she put fabric pieces and patterns on the counter near the cash register then left.

When she stopped at the drug store for a new lipstick, she was greeted by more stares and sputters. Nettie hurried back to her car and was soon joined by Flossie.

After they were on the road, Flossie said, "A woman asked me how I got to town, and when I told her we came together, she looked confused, then chuckled and told me I should go to the beauty shop. When I went inside, I asked if you had stopped by, and the owner laughed when two of her customers' faces went red."

"It worked out really well for us to go into town; that was a brilliant idea," Nettie said.

"I just needed to pick up a few things; the brilliant idea was Percy's because I'm not sure I would have gone to the beauty shop if he hadn't warned us."

"We'll give him credit then. You tell him."

Flossie giggled. "Are you kidding me? He'd be full of himself for a week."

Nettie smiled. "You aren't wrong."

After a few more miles, Nettie asked, "So, what's his name?"

Bright red spots popped out on Flossie's cheeks. "What's whose name?"

"The guy you're stuck on that you don't want Percy to know about."

Flossie exhaled. "He's a swell guy, but he's got the heebie-jeebies about you and Percy."

Nettie side-glanced at Flossie. "Cop or mob?"

Flossie clenched her teeth. "What is it always cop or mob with you and Percy? Why can't he just be a regular farmer?"

Nettie shrugged. "You tell me."

Flossie stared out her window as she grumbled, "I should learn to drive, so I won't be harassed."

"So, would this fella with no name give you a ticket or steal your car?" Nettie asked.

"You will not let it go, will you?" Flossie growled.

"Nope."

Flossie shook her head. "It's none of your beeswax."

Nettie nodded. "Copper it is, then."

"How do you figure that?" Flossie's voice was shrill.

Nettie chuckled. "I saw you talking to the cute young deputy sheriff with the wavy brown hair and muscles. Isn't his name Laird?"

"I'm mad at you for the rest of the day for torturing me." Flossie crossed her arms.

Nettie smiled.

After they were home, Percy met them at the front door. "Check the meeting room. I found a second lamp and two outlets."

Nettie and Flossie raced upstairs. When the two of them smacked the meeting room door in unison, they collapsed with laughter. After they caught their breath, Nettie threw open the door. They gawked at the matching floor lamps that lit up the room with warm, soft lighting and the Spanish art déco area rug. The folding screens of multi-panel Japanese artwork hid the extra furniture in the darkened portion of the room and gave the meeting room a touch of old money.

"This is perfect," Flossie said. "I'll polish the furniture and run the carpet sweeper over the wool rug." She ran her fingertips along an old mahogany sideboard. "They even found a sideboard, so we can store glasses and plates."

"If you'll put your finishing touches on the room to highlight its hospitality, I'll host our patrons up here. They'll understand why we won't be serving their usual beverages," Nettie said.

"We should have thought of these ages ago. It's much more than a meeting room; let's call it the hospitality room," Flossie said.

Nettie scanned the room. "You're right; maybe we could come up with an important status like VIPs with a subscription that costs more than a guest, but is not quite inner circle like our patrons."

"I know several people who would jump at the chance."

"It's a perfect topic for our family meeting tonight." Nettie headed downstairs to her office.

Nettie recorded the receipts Flossie had collected the night before by listing half of the total. After she put the weekly wages for Estelle, Oliver, and Willis into her office safe, she lifted the floor boards under her desk and put the remaining cash in the large floor safe. She returned her ledger to the file cabinet and locked it before she set off in her search for Percy.

When she went into the kitchen, Estelle smiled as she signed. "The men are proud of their work. Lunch is ready if you can get your husband to come to the table."

"They've finished already?" Nettie signed.

Estelle motioned toward the stairs for Nettie to check for herself.

Nettie stood at the top of the stairs and called out, "How's it going down there?" Nettie called out.

Percy appeared at the bottom of the stairs. "Come see."

When Nettie joined him, he opened the door, and Nettie peered into a crowded storage room.

"Is this all my fabric?" Nettie stared at all the boxes.

"No, we found more boxes and trunks upstairs filled with old clothes, blankets, and linens. Moving them down here gave us more room in the meeting room and helped fill up the storage room. We left two boxes of fabric pieces and scraps for you in your sewing room."

"So, how long does it take to move the boxes to get to the speakeasy?" she asked.

"It's magic." Percy pointed to a medium-sized box. "Move the box then push the button behind the sea trunk on its right."

When Nettie pushed the button, a section of boxes on the back wall slowly swung backward, and Nettie saw the speakeasy in the opening.

"Wow. I never expected anything like this." Nettie inspected the new door. "What if someone accidentally finds the button?"

"We only turn on the circuit to operate the door when we plan to use the room, and that lever is behind us in the root cellar."

"Good, then we're ready for tonight, and Estelle said lunch is ready."

While they ate, Nettie said, "I'm glad we went into town. We completely deflated the rumor of a raid here last night, and I picked up what I hope will be a minor job for us in the morning. I'll be Theresa, and we'll pick up our shipment for her on the road. She's expecting a raid at her shop during church."

"During church? What kind of ne'er-do-wells are these bad guys?" Percy's eyes twinkled. "What are we supposed to do with the shipment?"

"Maybe you and Oliver could store it at the barn with the rest of the hay for the mules until we need it."

"We could do that. What time do you want to leave in the morning?"

"Early. I'd like to meet them on the road at sunrise. I'll show you where on the map later."

Percy reached over and squeezed her hand. "You come up with the most interesting ways to spend a lazy Sunday morning."

Before they finished eating, Flossie joined them.

As she sat at the table, Flossie nicked a handful of grapes from Percy's plate. When Percy raised an eyebrow, she shrugged. "I couldn't resist."

After she ate all the grapes, including the remaining ones on her cousin's plate, Flossie said, "When we were in town, I overheard a gossipy group carrying on about Helen who had used the boarding house telephone to call a lawyer in Atlanta because she planned to sue the mayor for firing her. Makes your point about the telephone, doesn't it, Nettie?"

Percy raised his eyebrows. "I would think it was a bluff because nothing is private in the boarding house, and using the telephone is like broadcasting on the radio."

Flossie snorted. "I don't believe Helen is that smart."

Percy nodded. "While we were poking around upstairs, we found a dumbwaiter."

Nettie and Flossie laughed.

Percy rolled his eyes. "That was an accidental play on words, but I'll take credit for the laugh, anyway. It wouldn't take much to get it back into service, and it might make serving food in the meeting room easier. Oliver will look at it more closely this next week so we can have it working by next weekend."

"Where does it come out down here?" Nettie glanced around. "In the storage closet?"

"We're not sure because it may have been started and not finished or boarded up, but it's worthy of investigation."

"Old houses have lots of secrets, don't they?" Flossie giggled.

"Lucky for us." Percy shoved his last bite into his mouth and rose. "Oliver heard our neighbor, Mr. Evans, was having some trouble with the bank. I'd like to drop by to see if there's anything we can do to help. Would you like to go along, honey?"

"I'd love to. I'll check in with Estelle before we leave. You'll be okay, won't you, Flossie?"

"I have plenty to do. After I finish with the room upstairs, I'm going to tackle the living room, so it will shine too."

After they were on the road, Percy said, "Sylvester Evans got a bank loan a few years ago when he wanted to expand his pecan orchard and put in peaches. I'm not clear on what kind of loan and terms he got, but it may have been a balloon loan with some escalating interest charges and fees. Oliver said someone told him the new bank owner called Mr. Evans' loan and ordered the bank manager to foreclose immediately on the property. The bank is obviously trying to take over all the property they can, but despite all the wild speculation, nobody really knows why."

"Were you planning on offering Mr. Evans a loan?" Nettie asked.

"That's tricky. Mr. Evans is a proud man and doesn't have any family left since his grandson didn't return from the war. I thought we'd kind of put out some feelers to see how we might help."

When Percy parked in front of Mr. Evans' house, Nettie frowned.

"The yard isn't in very good shape. Mrs. Evans was always proud of her flowers, and they're overrun by weeds. That's not a good sign."

"Maybe he can't take care of the flowers anymore," Percy said.

"It's more than that." Nettie picked up the sack she'd brought before she climbed out of the car.

When Percy knocked on the door, a voice from a radio inside was silenced.

Percy knocked again and then side-glanced at Nettie.

She reached for the doorknob and opened the unlocked door.

"Mr. Evans, it's Percy and Nettie," she called out. "Estelle sent you cookies. Do you want me to put them in the kitchen?"

Mr. Evans came out of the kitchen. "You were supposed to take the hint and go away."

Nettie rolled her eyes. "When have you ever known me to take a hint? Do you have any idea how much trouble I'd be in with Estelle if I returned home with your cookies?"

Mr. Evans snorted. "She is a force, isn't she?"

"Do you have any coffee? Or do you want me to make some?" Nettie didn't wait for an answer; she hurried into the kitchen.

Mr. Evans sighed. "Do you want to sit down, Percy? My leg's bothering me."

Nettie came out of the kitchen a few minutes later with the cookies on a plate and a cup of coffee. "I added cream and sugar because that was how you used to like your coffee."

"Still do," Mr. Evans mumbled. "Didn't think anybody was around who remembered."

Nettie returned to the kitchen and brought out two more cups of coffee.

Mr. Evans bit into a cookie and sighed.

Percy picked up a cookie. "Estelle's a talented..."

Nettie interrupted him. "So, what's the bank's problem?"

Percy sipped his coffee to keep from smiling.

Chapter Three

Mr. Evans stared at her and then laughed. "Was that your version of subtle, Nettie?"

"It's the best I can do. Tell us about the bank."

After Mr. Evans confirmed what Oliver had told them, he said, "Before you even ask, there's nothing you can do to stop the bank."

Nettie raised an eyebrow. "Is that a dare? Because I can stop them."

"I'm not taking your money," Mr. Evans growled.

"Well, that clears the air because I don't want you to. I have a much better idea."

Mr. Evan's face paled. "You can't shoot the bank owner or the manager, Nettie."

Her eyes sparkled as she sighed. "Well, in that case, why don't we become your partners? Percy will pay off your loan, and we'll have a thirty percent interest in your property. Is it okay if we use Keith Fielding as the lawyer? Percy will drive us to the lawyer's office to draw up the papers, and then you can wait for us there while Percy and I go to the bank and pay off the loan and all its fees."

Mr. Evans stared at her before he turned to Percy. "Should we become partners?"

"My unbiased opinion is my wife is as brilliant as she is beautiful, and anyone who argues with her will lose."

Mr. Evans narrowed his eyes at Nettie who raised her eyebrows.

Percy covered his mouth with his hand to hide his smirk.

"Keith Fielding is an old friend; I wouldn't trust anyone except him." Mr. Evans rose with the help of his cane and put on his hat before he grabbed a thick file folder from his safe. "Let's get moving before the bank closes."

After they were in the lawyer's office, Percy explained their plan. Mr. Fielding smiled as he drew up the papers. His clerk disappeared with the signed agreement and returned several minutes later with summary pages for Mr. Evans and Percy.

After Mr. Evans and Percy signed the summaries, Mr. Fielding gave a set to Percy, and Percy and Nettie sped to the bank and arrived ten minutes before closing.

After waiting for five minutes, Percy rose with the assistance of his cane. Nettie followed him as he strode to a door with "A. Cartwright, Manager" engraved on the brass plate. Percy opened the door and held it for Nettie as she went inside the office.

"Are you here to plead with me on behalf of that deadbeat Sylvester Evans?" Mr. Cartwright sneered when she walked in.

"Not at all," Nettie said. "We're here to pay our debt."

Mr. Cartwright cocked his head as confusion spread across his face.

He turned to Percy who came in behind Nettie. "Percy, we don't have a loan on your property."

Percy raised his eyebrows. "Arnie, I assume you meant to continue the discussion with Mrs. Wyndham."

Mr. Cartwright's face reddened, and veins popped out on his neck. "I don't do business with married women, only their husbands."

Percy crossed his arms while Nettie glared at the bank manager then marched to his visitor's chair and pulled it close to his desk before she sat down.

Nettie's voice was icy as she put her hands on his desk and leaned closer. "Did you miss the news women have the vote? You actually do have a loan on our property. We're Sylvester Evans' partners."

"It's a lot of money." The bank manager stared at Nettie's hands.

"We agree; that's why we want to pay it off. Give us a final statement of the payoff amount, and we'll transfer money from our account to cover it," Percy said.

"I don't have time to do that today."

Nettie narrowed her eyes. "Yes, you do. You don't want anyone to say the bank might be short on money."

Mr. Cartwright paled. "Give me five minutes."

When he rose from his desk, Nettie rose with him. "I'll watch over your shoulder while you calculate the payoff, so you won't have to waste extra time explaining the details to me before we leave."

Percy smiled. "My wife is a whiz with numbers. You can explain how you reached all your calculations to me if you like after you've come up with the payoff amount."

The bank manager's shoulders slumped as he opened a file cabinet with Nettie at his elbow. She stood on her toes and peered inside the drawer. "Are these the files for all your outstanding loans? How many do you have?"

He jerked out a file folder marked S. Evans; when Nettie reached for a folder inside the file cabinet, he slammed the drawer and locked it. Mr. Cartwright put the key on top of the cabinet and glanced at Nettie then quickly stuck it into the inside pocket of his suit.

After he sat at his desk, Nettie stood behind him.

"I'll let you two work; I need to stretch my legs." Percy wandered out of the office.

"Do you have to stand behind me?" Mr. Cartwright growled. "You're making me nervous."

"I can fix that." Nettie moved the chair around the desk, slid it against the left side of his chair, and sat down. "I can actually see better here, anyway. Thank you."

The banker's hand shook as he calculated the payoff.

"Oops. That should be a five, not an eight." Nettie chuckled as she pointed to a line on the form. "It's a good thing I'm helping you, isn't it?"

Percy returned and winked at Nettie.

Nettie nodded. *He's good at picking up tidbits no one else notices.*

Cartwright glared at her then he continued with the final calculations. When he finished, he shoved the sheet across the table to Percy. "This is the payoff amount."

"Two final adjustments," Nettie said. "You used Monday's date. You need to change that to today; otherwise, we'd technically owe two days' accrual of interest. We need the actual payoff amount. Also, we need two copies of the transaction so we can give one to Mr. Evans for his records."

Percy nodded. "I'll want a paid in full receipt for me and for Mr. Evans, too."

The banker sputtered and then rewrote the payoff sheet to include the date correction.

Percy read over the updated sheet and then glanced at Nettie, who nodded. The two of them intently watched Mr. Cartwright as he completed two more documents with the payoff information.

After Percy signed all three copies of the document, the banker signed them.

"Add 'paid in full' to our copies and initial and date them, please," Nettie said.

After Cartwright complied and gave the two copies to Percy, Percy rose and put out his hand. "Very good. Thank you for taking the extra time and saving us a little money."

The banker reluctantly shook hands with Percy and avoided looking at Nettie. He walked them to the front door and locked it behind them when they went outside.

After they were in their car, Percy leaned over and kissed Nettie. "You're a marvel; I love watching you in action. Let's pick up Mr. Evans."

"Flossie told me you and your friends used to play pirate ship in the shed until Arnie snitched. Is that the same Arnie as Mr. Cartwright?"

Percy smiled. "I'd forgotten about that, but yes."

"What did you learn at the bank?" she asked.

"A new owner bought the bank, and Cartwright plans to leave town at the end of next week. The two bookkeepers, who were women, of course, were in a huddle whispering about finding new jobs before the new owner takes over. The two male tellers glared at them. I got the impression they thought the women were being hysterical."

Nettie frowned. "I'm glad we paid off Mr. Evans' debt. Should we check with Willis and Oliver so we can run down the bank account on Monday?"

"That wouldn't be a bad idea. I'll talk to them."

When they went inside Mr. Fielding's office, his eyes widened. "Did you have a problem? You weren't gone very long."

Percy handed Mr. Evans his copy. "All done and marked paid in full as of today."

Mr. Evans' eyes welled up. "I guess you better take me home, because I've got work to do."

The lawyer smiled. "Good move, Sylvester. I wouldn't want Nettie catching me slacking off either."

"Tell them," Mr. Evans said.

Mr. Fielding nodded. "Mr. Evans doesn't have any living family, so to keep his property intact, he's leaving it to you in his will, although he will probably outlive us all. He's actually been stressing over how to keep his land from being chopped up, and you've given him the perfect solution."

Mr. Evans cleared his throat. "The thought of everything I've worked so hard to build my entire adult life being ripped apart has been dragging me down more than I realized. I can't imagine anyone who loves the land as much as I do except you two."

"We're truly honored, Mr. Evans," Percy said.

On the way to his house, Mr. Evans said, "Nettie, I started putting in a peach orchard. I have a lot of room to expand it, and I know people who need jobs. What about more peach trees?"

"I love peaches. We'll pitch in extra for the labor to get the trees planted," Nettie said.

"I might take you up on it; we can plant a lot more trees in a shorter amount of time, if you do that."

"We know people are looking for work, so we'd be pleased if we could help them," Nettie said.

After they dropped off Mr. Evans, Percy asked, "Wasn't it a pleasure to do something without..."

Nettie shouted, "Shooters ahead."

Two men with shotguns appeared on opposite sides of the road.

Percy gritted his teeth and jammed his foot down on the accelerator. "Grab my deer rifle from under our feet and start shooting."

Nettie snatched up the rifle and exhaled as she aimed at the man on her side of the road and pulled the trigger.

When the man dropped, Percy said, "The man on this side jumped into the ditch for cover."

Nettie scrambled into the back seat and leaned out the side window. The man in the ditch stood up and aimed at Percy, but before he fired, she shot him.

Percy sped down the road. When he slowed a few miles later, Percy asked, "Are you okay?"

Nettie exhaled and her hands shook as she laid the rifle on the back seat.

She climbed over the seat to sit next to Percy. Her breathing was ragged. "I can't believe someone tried to ambush us. My hands are still shaking."

Percy brushed away the hair from her face then put his arm around her shoulders and pulled her close. "Darlin', you were steady when you fired, so you're entitled to be rattled after the fact. You don't know how much my combat soul wanted to grab up the rifle, but I knew I had to focus on driving; we were a team, and you handled it."

Nettie sighed as she laid her head on his shoulder. "You always know the right thing to say."

She straightened her back and peered at him. "No one would know we were unsuccessfully ambushed except those who were involved in the planning."

"You're right, and somebody is bound to slip up."

"Stop," Nettie shouted.

Percy slammed on the brakes and reached back for the rifle as Nettie leaped out of the car before it came to a stop. When she raced into the weeds, then knelt down and lifted a handful of fluff, Percy exhaled as she hurried to the car.

"You scared me half to death. One minute we're talking about being ambushed, and the next minute you jumped out of the moving car to scoop up a...what have you got?" Percy asked as Nettie climbed back into the car, hugging a furry brown animal in the crook of her arm.

"It's a puppy; hold it for me while I see if there are any more or a mama nearby."

When Nettie returned, the puppy whimpered as it snuggled against Percy's chest.

"You can't drive and hold the puppy," she said.

"You drive, then. My leg aches."

Percy climbed out of the driver's seat. He exaggerated his limp while he crossed in front of the car to open Nettie's door, and she rolled her eyes.

After she stepped out of the car, he sat in the passenger seat and cuddled the puppy to calm him.

"We'll have to see if we can find her owner," Nettie said.

"The puppy is a boy, and he's ours. What are we going to name him? He's all brown except for his black muzzle."

Percy stroked the puppy as it settled down and whispered, "What's your name, buster?"

The puppy licked Percy's hand then yipped.

Nettie chuckled. "I think he just told you his name is Buster."

"I knew that," Percy muttered as he stroked the puppy.

Buster snuggled against Percy's chest and went to sleep; Nettie smiled and sped to their house.

When she slowed to turn at their long driveway, Percy and Buster opened their eyes.

Nettie smiled. "You two knocked each other out."

Percy returned her smile. "I relaxed my muscles and slowed my breathing, so he would feel safe."

"You accomplished your mission."

Nettie parked, but before she opened her door, Percy said, "I was surprised at how quickly the man on your side of the road went down. Where did you shoot him?"

"I wanted him to drop immediately, so I aimed for his knee. I must have been close enough."

"What about the other guy?"

"He made me mad when he hid then tried to shoot you, so I aimed at his heart."

Percy's face paled.

"Don't worry; I changed my mind and shot him in the right shoulder."

"You waited a split second to be sure he was right-handed, didn't you?" Percy opened the car door and set Buster on the ground then climbed out.

"Of course I did." Nettie hopped out of the car then smiled as Buster trotted along behind Percy to the house.

When they went into the kitchen, Bella was sitting at the kitchen table reading a book. She squealed when she saw Buster and knocked over her chair in her excitement as she jumped up. Buster scrambled across the wooden floor to her.

Nettie tapped on Estelle's arm and pointed at Bella and Buster.

Estelle's eyes lit up as she signed, "New puppy?"

Nettie nodded and signed, "His name is Buster."

While Bella rubbed Buster's belly and cooed, Estelle filled a bowl with water and put it next to the puppy.

Buster rolled to his feet and drank his fill of water.

After Estelle opened the refrigerator and pulled out the chopped chicken she had cooked earlier for croquettes, she dropped two tablespoons of chicken into a small bowl and added chicken broth. When she set down the bowl next to the water bowl, Buster yipped then gobbled down the chicken and lapped up the broth.

Percy signed, "Where are Willis and Oliver?"

"Working on my house," Estelle signed her reply.

"I'll check in with them then return in time to dress for this evening." Percy leaned down and rubbed Buster's chest. "Good boy."

After Percy left, Nettie furrowed her brow. "I'll be right back."

She dashed up the stairs to the hospitality room and opened a box of fabric pieces. After Nettie found what she wanted, she raced back downstairs with a square of olive green paisley fabric.

When she returned to the kitchen, Flossie was sitting on the floor with Buster.

"Buster is such a sweetheart, but he needs a collar," Flossie said.

"We'll get him one as soon as we can." Nettie folded the square into a triangle and tied it around Buster's neck like a cowboy's bandana. "There you go, Buster. I think we've found your signature style to impress our guests."

"Perfect," Flossie said. "Do we still expect a raid?"

"Oh, yes; we should probably have a family meeting before our guests arrive."

"I need to get all gussied up if we're having visitors. Do I charge them for a full month's membership?"

Nettie chuckled. "Not a bad idea; do whatever you like."

"At a minimum, I'll make them sign our guest book."

"We don't have a guest book," Nettie said.

"Yet." Flossie hurried to the stairs.

When Percy joined Nettie in the kitchen, he said, "We need a family meeting."

"You're right; let's get dressed first." She led the way up the stairs to their bedroom.

After Nettie put on her sleeveless, ankle-length, black silk dress with a modest neckline and a bare back that plunged to a point below her waist, she buckled her T-strap heels.

Percy pulled on his tuxedo pants then whistled as he buttoned his tuxedo vest when Nettie turned her back to him to brush her hair. "Your latest creation nearly exposes your derriere and certainly won't hide the fact if you're packing heat, darling."

"We're both going formal. You haven't worn your tuxedo pants in ages; you usually sneak and wear pajama bottoms then hide them with your lap quilt." Nettie smiled as she picked up her black sequin evening bag and slipped the long, slender strap over her head and across her chest then threw her red silk shawl over her shoulders and let it drape across her back.

She patted her evening bag. "I've got my derringer, and I'm ready when you are."

"I'm with you." Percy put on his tuxedo jacket and grabbed his black cover for his legs.

They stopped in the hallway for Percy's wheelchair. Percy wheeled himself to the kitchen, and Nettie walked alongside him.

When they went into the kitchen, Estelle was putting pinwheel sandwiches on a tray, and Bella was reading her new book to Flossie with Buster at Bella's feet. Flossie wore a bright green, short satin dress with a plunging neckline, sequins, and tiers of fringe.

Nettie said, "I wish I knew the purpose of the raid. Are they here to smash and intimidate or to find incriminating evidence to shut us down?"

"We're ready either way," Percy said. "Willis and Oliver will be here as honored patrons and will bring a few of our old friends as guests."

"We don't know how many there will be. If they don't break into more than two groups, Flossie and I can entertain them to keep them from breaking anything or planting any evidence."

"I'll let Willis and Oliver know you might need back up," Percy said.

Nettie furrowed her brow. "Flossie, you're good at dazzling. See if you can get the scoop on what their purpose is, and I'll do the same."

Flossie's eyes twinkled. "Want to make it a competition?"

Nettie smiled. "You're on, and I hear cars coming up the driveway."

The fringe on Flossie's dress gently undulated as she strode to the window and peered out. "Two guests and a patron. Are you going to relocate the patrons to the meeting room upstairs?"

"I thought I would. What do you think, Percy?"

"You should, because it's your usual routine. The meeting room is a little farther from the kitchen than the cellar is, but you'll be fine. Estelle has olives, cheese, hot mustard, and fresh bread for the patrons, and I asked

Willis to pick up sparkling apple cider and pastrami so they won't feel completely neglected."

"You and Estelle are sneaky but brilliant. Thank you." Nettie followed Flossie to the front door. "If you'll escort these folks and cover the living room, Percy and I will answer the door."

When Willis arrived, he and Nettie agreed on a signal of two taps on the floor if he needed her. After he carried the trays of food upstairs, Nettie gathered the patrons one at a time and quietly explained the new hospitality room then led them upstairs.

As the senator and Nettie went up the stairs, he asked, "How long do you expect the hospitality room to be in operation?"

"I'm thinking about a new membership class that could take advantage of the hospitality room."

The senator chuckled. "You're always thinking a step ahead."

When they went into the hospitality room, the senator smiled as he scanned the room then headed to the sideboard. "Nice work, Nettie. I might want to sign up for dual membership."

"You're always welcome in the hospitality room, Senator," Willis said. "Would you care for sparkling cider, coffee, or tea?"

Nettie slipped out of the room and went down the stairs.

Flossie stood at the window near the front door. "Two cars with three men in each car. They're wearing fedoras and suits with bulges at the waistline, but their hands are empty. The men from the first car are going to the back door; I'll greet the men coming to the front door."

"Back up Flossie, Percy. I'll greet our backdoor guests," Nettie said.

Percy glared at her. "No."

Nettie raised her eyebrows. "You can't cover the front and back."

"Watch me," he growled.

Nettie tapped Estelle's shoulder then signed, "Raiders are here. Keep Bella and Buster close to you."

Estelle nodded.

Nettie said, "Stay close to your granny and look after Buster, Bella. When I come in here with the men, I'll sign, so don't react to anything you hear."

Bella signed, "Will do."

"Thank you," Nettie signed.

Nettie wrapped her silk shawl around her shoulders then hurried to the back door and went outside. As she rounded the corner of the house, she stopped near the front and smiled at the men who were walking toward her.

"Welcome. Are you here for dinner or the appetizers?"

The men stared at her.

"We're here for an inspection," one man said as they strode past her.

Nettie narrowed her eyes as she caught up with the man in the lead and walked alongside him. "I didn't think our inspection was due for another month. I'm Nettie Wyndham. What agency are you with?" She held out her hand.

The man raised his eyebrows then shook hands with her.

"I've heard of you, Nettie Wyndham. You can call me Johnny. We're with the state office."

"Oh, my mistake; excuse me. I thought you were the county health department. Well, let's get busy. Do you have a checklist?"

"No, we don't. We're just supposed to look around."

"Aren't you going to start with the roof before it's too dark to inspect it?"

Johnny growled, "That's not what we're here for."

Nettie nodded. *Thought so. I'll make sure you don't find what you're looking for.*

"Well, our guests are in the living room enjoying appetizers; they'll be moving to the dining room soon for dinner. Do you mind starting in the dining room first, so we won't have to delay their meal, or do you want to start with the kitchen?"

"We don't need to inspect the kitchen or the dining room. We're just here for the private room."

"Oh, is that all? Not even the kitchen? That won't take you long." After they were inside, Nettie said, "Follow me. It's upstairs."

When they went past the living room, Flossie was flirting with the men who came in the front door. One man cocked his head and raised his eyebrows at Johnny who shook his head then motioned for the man to stay where he was.

As Nettie led the men past Percy who was chatting with a man in a suit, she raised her eyebrows in surprise at Percy's old marine buddy. *I've never seen Cliff in a suit.*

She smiled. "Honey, these gentlemen are here to inspect the hospitality room."

Percy nodded at the men, and Johnny returned his nod.

As Nettie and Johnny preceded the other two men up the stairs together, Cliff followed them.

She said, "Our hospitality room is for our patrons, whose membership dues are more costly than our guests. We serve them gourmet appetizers and meals that rival any five-star restaurant. Our clientele expect fine dining and attentive service, and we strive to exceed their expectations."

When Nettie reached the top of the stairs, she glanced back at Percy, who put his fingers near his mouth and signed, "Atlanta mob."

Chapter Four

When Nettie and the men reached the door to the hospitality room, she paused with the key in her hand before she unlocked the door. "I assume you will respect the confidentiality of the identity of our patrons."

The leader narrowed his eyes then turned to the other two men. "Wait here. I'll let you know if I need you."

"Thank you," Nettie whispered as she led him into the hospitality room then closed the door behind them.

Willis smiled at Nettie and signed, "Mob."

Nettie nodded and returned his smile.

Johnny strode to the sideboard and spoke quietly to Willis. Willis nodded as he poured a glass of sparkling cider then handed it to Johnny.

While the two men chatted, Nettie picked up a silver tray with small crystal cups that contained a small salad of crabmeat, caviar, and avocado in each cup and offered the tray to her patrons, one at a time.

"Are you okay?" the senator whispered.

Nettie pulled out a small bottle of hot sauce from her beaded bag and giggled as she set it on the table next to the senator's chair.

"Of course, I remembered. Is there anything else?"

The senator smiled. "You're the best."

When Nettie returned the tray to the sideboard, Johnny finished his cider. "Nice operation, Mrs. Wyndham. Do you have a basement?"

"No basement, but we have a root cellar."

"Show me."

Nettie nodded. "We need to talk."

When they reached the door, Nettie pushed it open.

After they stepped into the hall, she closed the door to the hospitality room behind them.

Johnny said, "It takes a key to go into the room but not to get out. Good security in every sense of the word, Mrs. Wyndham."

The two men with Johnny stood near the stairs. When Johnny narrowed his eyes, both men stared at their feet. Cliff scowled as he stood in front of Nettie and Percy's bedroom with his arms crossed.

"What's going on?" Johnny asked.

"He wouldn't let us search the bedrooms," one man whined.

"Why did you want to search my bedroom? Are you here to rob me and my guests?" Nettie's eyes flashed with fury.

She turned to Johnny and stomped her foot. "I have bent over backwards to assist you with your inspection. If your men need to see lacy underthings, I'll pack up a box, and you can take it with you, but they are not welcome in my home."

"Guess you bums have been kicked out by the lady. Go wait in the car," Johnny growled.

Cliff followed the two men to the front door then out of the house.

"Show me that root cellar, Mrs. Wyndham."

As they went down the stairs, Nettie said, "I still don't know who you work for or why you're here, but I have the distinct feeling you're looking for something very specific. I could help you if you tell me what it is; is it small or large?"

Johnny exhaled. "I'm here to see what I could find if I was a G-man."

"I'm not interested in a partnership or in expanding my business. It was nice to meet you, but my small town operation isn't for sale, lease, or open to the most amazing deal I'd be a fool to pass up."

"Show me your root cellar."

Nettie crossed her arms and glared at him. "And then you'll leave?"

Johnny sighed. "If you wish, but..."

Nettie raised an eyebrow and interrupted. "There will be others. I'll take this as a quality check and show you the root cellar."

When they went into the kitchen, Estelle was whisking a pan of gravy, and Bella was working on her homework. Neither one of them glanced up as Nettie picked up the flashlight on the counter, opened the door next to the pantry, and turned on the light for the stairs.

"Watch your step; these stairs are steep," she said.

When they reached the bottom of the stairs, Nettie opened the door to the root cellar and turned on the flashlight then handed it to Johnny. "It has a low ceiling, and we added more shelves this summer. The weather cooperated, and we had a bumper crop of peaches this year; our vegetable garden did well too."

He ducked his head as he went inside. "You're right; it is cramped." He removed all the jars of canned peaches from a shelf and set them on top of a case of strawberry jam that was on the floor.

After he inspected the wall behind them, he returned the jars to their shelf. "How long has the root cellar has been here?"

"I really don't know. I suspect it was dug before the house was built."

Johnny nodded. "Let's go upstairs. You said we needed to talk, and you're right. Wyndham is a common name; I didn't realize you were married to Percy Wyndham. Would it be possible for him to meet me out back for a few minutes?"

Nettie narrowed her eyes. "After you."

When they were at the top of the stairs, Nettie turned off the light to the root cellar. "You can wait outside the back door while I find Percy."

After Johnny left the kitchen, Nettie strolled into the living room as their guests filed into the dining room.

When Percy was the only person left in the room, he said, "Our front door visitors didn't stay very long. I think Flossie scared them off when she asked them if they were married. How did the inspection go?"

"Nothing found as far as I could tell, but Johnny wants to talk to you privately. He's waiting for you outside in the back. I'll stay near the door in case you need me."

Percy furrowed his brow. "Any idea what he wants to talk about?"

"No, but I have a feeling he has something he wants to share with you. Whatever it is, I'm certain it's something you'll want to hear."

Percy rolled to the back door then pulled out his cane from its holder and stepped outside.

When Percy scanned the area, the bright moon lit up parts of the yard, but the branches of the large oak trees cast deep shadows. The dead leaves on the ground crunched under his feet, and Percy inhaled the earthy aroma of the chilly fall night air.

Johnny stepped out of the shadows near the trees and strode toward Percy with his hand extended.

After they shook hands, Johnny said, "I told your wife to call me Johnny. My name doesn't matter, but your father covered for me when I got into trouble as a teen. He didn't have to do that; anyone else wouldn't have noticed or walked away. I'll always be grateful because he didn't condemn me or expect anything from me, which is more than I can say about my old man."

Percy nodded. "He had a kind heart, but no head for money at all."

"I came here to determine Nettie's vulnerability to a raid to shut down her business operation. I wanted you to understand I owe your father, which is why I'm telling you your wife is caught in the middle of a power war. You want to ask her to join us?"

Percy strode to the back door and opened it.

"Everything okay?" Nettie asked.

"Johnny wants you to hear what he has to say."

After they were outside, Percy said, "Johnny was telling me there is a power war."

Johnny nodded. "This corner of Georgia is relatively untouched in terms of what some call protection and others call extortion partially because of the vigilance of your local mob, but more because Nettie has tremendous political clout at the state and national levels."

"Nettie? Seriously?" Percy furrowed his brow.

Nettie scowled. "Are you sure about that, Johnny?"

"I'm not high enough in the organization to have all the details, but I'm smart enough to fill in the blanks. My bosses and their greedy bankers control forty percent of the state's politicians and the wealth, specifically cash and property. Nettie either controls or significantly influences this corner of the state, which is another twenty percent. She's pivotal in a power struggle."

Percy narrowed his eyes. "I'm not as sharp as Nettie with math, but who has the other forty percent?"

"Thirty percent of it is in the hands of an unknown individual in Georgia who may be out of New York, and ten percent is in the hands of a variety of individuals."

Nettie nodded. "I see where I fit in and understand conflict would be inevitable. So, what about the feds?"

Johnny rolled his eyes. "They're the wild card because some of them are on the take, and others are on a prohibition crusade for the notoriety or bounties. There aren't many what you could call good cops these days, except for the few county sheriffs here and there."

"No change for us, then." Percy exhaled. "The month before Nettie and I were married, my family estate was in foreclosure. In less than three months she had negotiated a settlement and paid off the entire debt."

"I didn't know that, but I'm not surprised."

Percy furrowed his brow. "I hadn't thought about it before, but there haven't been any foreclosures in our area since then. Is that Nettie's influence?"

Johnny chuckled. "She obviously has a knack with both money and people. Nettie, you have a rare combination of skills, and it's easy for people to underestimate you because you're young. I came here to assess the vulnerability of your operation to a raid that would then be used as leverage to gain your cooperation. The assumption has been by everyone that the Wyndham business was easy pickings. I'll report back that your value has been inflated, and you are not as influential as everyone has assumed."

"Will that stop your boss?" Percy asked.

Johnny shrugged. "It might, but it isn't my boss I'd be worried about. He'd try to talk Nettie into joining them, and if that didn't work, he might ante up to buy her out, or he may decide she's not a threat after all. I think the kicker is the unknown crowd. I've heard their style is the rough stuff. Your advantage is my boss isn't a fan of the unknown interloper trying to bust his way into Georgia."

"That's where I come in," Percy said. "We'll be ready."

Bella opened the back door and signed, "Granny has to talk to you, Miss Nettie."

Nettie turned to Percy. "My help is needed in the kitchen."

After Nettie went inside, Johnny said, "I understand your friends are encouraging you to run for lieutenant governor, Percy. As a friend of your father's, I'd tell you it will be dangerous, but I'd advise you to gather your staff and have Nettie plan your strategy for your campaign because your esteemed opponent will play dirty." Johnny smiled. "I almost feel sorry for him."

As Johnny strode down the driveway to his car and his waiting henchmen, Percy hurried into the house.

While Percy and Johnny talked, Nettie went into the kitchen, Estelle signed, "Bella told me Willis tapped twice on the floor."

Nettie dashed up the stairs then unlocked and slowly opened the hospitality room door. She waited a moment then peered inside before she casually strolled in. Willis glanced up and tilted his head toward the senator.

Nettie stopped at the senator's table.

"Oh, there you are, Nettie. I was just getting ready to leave. My wife asked me to be home early."

"I'll walk downstairs with you. I have a few things to do in the kitchen."

After they were downstairs, she asked, "Shall I walk with you to your car?"

"I'd enjoy your company, but it's chilly now that the sun's gone down."

Nettie smiled as she slipped her arm into his. "My wrap is warmer than it looks."

As they strolled down the walkway to the senator's car, he said, "What would it take to convince Percy to throw his hat into the ring for the office of Lieutenant Governor?"

"If he knew he had your support, I think he'd be open to the idea."

"Well, tell him he has it. Let me know when you want to meet to map out his campaign strategy."

Nettie smiled. "You know me only too well."

The senator chuckled as he climbed into his Model T. "I know Percy's smart enough to leave the strategy to his in-house expert. Bring our next lieutenant governor to my office on Monday morning at nine. I'll provide coffee."

"We'll be there."

After the senator headed down the driveway, Nettie dashed back to the house with her teeth chattering.

When she went inside, Percy's eyebrows raised. "I was looking for you. Your lips are blue." Percy rose from his wheelchair and wrapped his arms around her.

"I claimed my wrap was warmer than it looks." Nettie snuggled against him.

Percy chuckled. "I can't wait to hear the rest of that story."

"We have a lot to talk about."

Nettie wriggled free then hurried to the kitchen and picked up the large platter of desserts for the hospitality room. "Come with me, Bella. I can't carry the platter and unlock the door at the same time." She handed the key to Bella.

When she reached the top of the stairs with her platter, she mumbled, "I can't hold the platter with one hand so I can open the door. We need a table next to the door."

"I'll tell Miss Flossie," Bella said.

Nettie smiled. "She'll find the right table for us, won't she? I'll get the key from you when I come to the kitchen."

Bella nodded then raced down the stairs.

After she served the desserts, Nettie joined Willis at the sideboard; he poured her a small glass of sparkling cider.

She sipped her cider and scanned the room until she was certain their patrons were deep in their own conversations. "Any problems?"

"The senator recognized our visitor, but no one else seemed to notice him," Willis said. "We had a short but in-depth chat; his message was we should expect trouble next week."

Nettie exhaled. "Was it a threat?"

"That wasn't how I took it."

"I'm interested in why you think so, because I'm inclined to agree with you. Do you think we could get together tomorrow and talk?"

"If we want to meet in the morning, it will have to be early because my wife and I take the kids to church on Sundays."

"I don't want you to feel rushed. What time's best for you?"

"How about right after church? Around noon?"

Nettie smiled. "That's gives us time to get a few things done in the morning."

Willis nodded as Nettie left the hospitality room then joined Estelle, Bella, and Buster in the kitchen.

Bella was sitting at the counter reading a book, and Buster was asleep under her stool.

Estelle pointed at two large trays and signed, "Desserts for the dining room."

"I'll take them. Are you and Bella leaving now?" Nettie signed.

Estelle smiled as she signed, "Soon."

"I'll open the door for you," Bella said.

When she stepped into the dining room from the kitchen, Flossie was chatting with three middle-aged women; Flossie glanced at Nettie, and signed, "Someone wants to meet you."

Nettie nodded; Flossie turned her attention back to the conversation.

Nettie placed the trays on the sideboard then announced, "Anyone ready for dessert?"

She smiled and nodded as guests helped themselves.

Flossie stood in the doorway while she chatted with a woman who had been recently widowed and a slightly overweight, middle-aged man with a ruddy face. She motioned for Nettie to join them.

The man stepped forward and put out his hand. He grasped Nettie's hand with both of his as they shook. "Mrs. Wyndham, it is such a pleasure to meet you. I've heard quite a few unbelievable things about you."

"This is Doctor Doughtery," Flossie said.

"It's nice to meet you, Doctor Doughtery," she said.

"Everyone calls me Doctor M because they say I'm magical with medicine." He chuckled as he continued to hold her hand. "I understand you are the chef. The meal was delicious, but frankly, from everything I've heard about you, I expected you to be much older."

Nettie smiled as she disengaged her hand. "People are kind, but they do like to exaggerate."

"I suppose, but one can't help but wonder why Mr. Wyndham prefers to hide his accomplishments by claiming such a delicate young woman could actually stop a bankruptcy." Doctor Doughtery guffawed.

Flossie stared at him and then raised her eyebrows at Nettie as she signed, "Are you going to slit his throat now, or is it my turn?"

Nettie smiled. "Few have guessed our secret; you're quite perceptive."

"That's what they tell me." Doctor Doughtery beamed and reached for her hand, but Nettie put it on her hip; her raised eyebrow dared him to touch her. He cleared his throat as he quickly dropped his hand to his side.

She motioned toward the dining room sideboard. "You may want to select your dessert before our guests who are particularly fond of sweets go back for seconds."

Flossie linked her arm through Nettie's as Doctor M joined the widow in the line for dessert.

"He's been like that all night," Flossie whispered. "Arrogant, judgmental, and practically begging to be neutered. Are you going to the kitchen to wash your hands with lye soap now?"

"He definitely lived up to his reputation, didn't he?"

After the guests left only traces of crumbs on the dessert table, a few began their slow exit to the front door as they stopped to thank Nettie for a wonderful meal and chatted with each other.

When Nettie returned to the kitchen, Buster whined as Estelle and Bella prepared to leave.

"You're a good boy." Bella rubbed Buster's belly. "I'll see you tomorrow."

Nettie gently stroked Buster's ears and neck while he sadly gazed at the back door after Bella and Estelle left.

Buster trotted to the oversized towel Estelle had put on the floor for him. He turned in circles then flopped down and went to sleep. Nettie strolled into the dining room, spoke to a few guests, then hurried upstairs to spend some time with the patrons in the hospitality room.

After the last guest and patron left, Willis went outside to check the perimeter of the house. When he returned, he met Percy in the hallway near the dining room.

While the two men spoke quietly in serious tones, Nettie strained to hear what they were saying. She casually moved closer to the doorway and picked up a glass that had been left under a chair.

Her attempt at eavesdropping was interrupted when Flossie pushed the clattering utility cart into the dining room as she came out of the kitchen.

"Are we ready to clear the table?" Flossie asked.

Percy and Willis moved away from the dining room, and Nettie sighed as she nodded.

Nettie and Flossie worked on opposite sides of the table as they raced to collect the glasses, plates, and silverware for the bins on the utility cart.

Flossie tossed a fork and spoon from the midpoint of the dining room table, and they landed in the top bin.

"I win!" She threw her hands into the air in victory and danced the latest dance craze with jazz hands swaying, toes pointing, and feet kicking back and to the side in rhythmic, bouncy steps.

Nettie laughed then copied Flossie's dance until both of them ran out of breath from dancing and laughing.

While they leaned against dining chairs as they gasped to catch their breath, Nettie asked, "Where did you learn to dance like that?"

"One of the girls has a cousin from Charleston, South Carolina, and she gave the rest of us lessons on the porch tonight. She called it the Charleston. We went outside one at a time like we were in high school sneaking outside to smoke."

Nettie chuckled. "I can see y'all doing that. Show me those steps again."

"I wish we had some music," Flossie grumbled. "We need a phonograph, so we can have some tunes in the living room."

Nettie chuckled as she danced. "Good idea; would you offer dance lessons for our guests?"

Flossie giggled. "Can you imagine the shock of some of our more staid ladies?"

Nettie rolled her eyes. "You'd have them dancing and reminiscing about their own glory days of sneaking out back to smoke."

After they were satisfied with their dancing proficiency, Flossie pushed the utility cart into the kitchen while Nettie gathered up the table linens then froze when she heard a creak from the front porch floorboards.

She casually carried the linens into the kitchen and signed, "Someone's on the front porch. Find Percy. I'm going out back and will take the corner."

Flossie nodded and strolled to the stairs while Nettie strode to the back door. She grabbed Percy's wool work jacket that hung on the pegs near the door and put it on. After she stuck her derringer in the jacket pocket, she slipped outside.

Nettie quietly crept to the corner near the front of the house and listened as she waited in the shadows while drifting clouds hid the moonlight.

Percy threw open the front door. "Come on, Buster. Let's go hunting. If you'll flush out that pesky Eastern rattler under the porch, I'll shoot it."

When Nettie heard footsteps running toward the woods, she raced toward the sound.

As she closed in on the fleeing figure, she spotted Flossie racing toward her with Percy not far behind. Nettie dived low and rolled. When she slammed into the back of the intruder's knees, the woman screamed as she crashed to the ground.

Nettie jumped to her feet and pulled out her derringer.

The clouds drifted away, and the bright moonlight revealed the prowler's identity.

Nettie growled, "Don't move, Helen."

Helen was face down and splayed out on the ground as she screamed, "I'm going to sue."

When Flossie put a foot in the middle of Helen's back to hold her down, Helen whimpered, "You're hurting me."

Flossie snorted. "Are you saying I'm fat? You better watch what you say, girlie. What are you doing here?"

Helen's whimpering turned to sobs. "I left my purse; I came to get it."

"Likely story." Flossie removed her foot. "Did it ever occur to you to knock on the door like a normal person? Where did you leave it?"

"I don't remember." Helen groaned as she raised herself to lean on her elbow and revealed a red patent purse.

"Well, look at that," Flossie said. "There's your purse, after all."

"I meant my small purse with my money in it," Helen whined as she clutched her red purse to her chest.

"Sure you did. I wouldn't be moving so all-fired fast, if I were you. My cousin still has a gun pointed at your head," Flossie said.

"I'm wearing a warm, heavy wool coat and can stand here all night until you decide to tell the truth, Helen, and I have a nose for lies," Nettie said.

"Are you going to make her stay on the cold, uncomfortable ground like that? Brr." Percy said. "I'm glad it's not me lying on the ground. Let me know if you need us. Buster and I still need to find that Eastern diamondback rattler," Percy said.

Buster trotted to Helen and sniffed the top of her head, and she flinched and turned her face away from him. "What's that?"

Buster sniffed her ear.

"Buster's been following that snake. I guess it's around here somewhere," Percy said. "Let's go, Buster."

Percy strode a few yards away from the women with Buster on his heels.

"It is getting a little chilly," Flossie said. "We could just tie her and check on her in the morning."

"You wouldn't do that," Helen said.

Flossie chuckled. "Try me."

Helen whined, "I put a flask of whiskey under a chair on the porch, so there would be evidence of a speakeasy at your house."

"Was it good whiskey?" Flossie asked.

"I don't know," Helen said.

"I'll check." Flossie darted to the porch and returned.

"I guess that much was true." Flossie waved a silver flask over her head then opened it.

After she sniffed the contents, Flossie said, "This is vinegar. Those cheapskates didn't even give you a flask of whiskey."

Flossie dropped to her knees and sniffed Helen's breath. "Ah ha. You drank the whiskey and then filled the bottle with vinegar. That's why you didn't want our canine to smell your breath. I wondered why he was alerting. Won't you get into trouble for that?"

"Of course, she will," Nettie said. "Let's go inside; it's too cold out here."

"What about me?" Helen cried out.

"You can get up; just don't come back," Nettie said.

Helen rose to a sitting position. "I can leave? How do I get back to town?"

"You can get back however you got here, but you have one minute to get off my property." Nettie posed in the bright moonlight with a hand on her hip and her derringer in the air. "I shoot intruders."

Helen scrambled to her feet and raced down the driveway.

After they were inside, Percy said, "You two are bullies, and if you scared her enough to disappear, you probably saved her life."

Nettie sighed. "I hope so."

Percy wrapped his arm around Nettie and stroked her cheek lightly with his fingers. "I loved your moll pose, darlin'. I was sure glad I wasn't an intruder."

Nettie raised an eyebrow. "I always wanted to be a gunslinger. My uncle carved a wooden gun for me when I was three and gave it to me for Christmas so I could practice."

Percy laughed. "Your uncle wouldn't have done any such thing, but you stick with your story. I love it, my sweet gunslinger."

When Percy leaned down to kiss Nettie, she pulled him closer and returned his light kiss with more passion.

Flossie snorted. "What about our family meeting?"

Percy ended their kiss with a nibble on Nettie's bottom lip. "I'll lock up then meet you in the kitchen. I brought up a Mason jar from the cellar with a vintage whiskey in it from last week's shipment."

"We have leftover appetizers too," Nettie said.

"Party time," Flossie said on their way to the house.

When Percy returned, Nettie had poured their drinks, and Flossie had put a tablecloth on the kitchen table before she set the appetizers and plates in the middle of the table.

While they sipped the whiskey and munched on smoked salmon on crackers, sharp cheddar and goat cheese, and assorted olives, Percy said, "I'm surprised there was any salmon left."

"Estelle always holds back a little for us," Nettie said. "What did you hear tonight, Flossie?"

After she took a small sip of whiskey, Flossie said, "The three men who came in the front door were supposed to start a diversion if there was any trouble so the important guy they were guarding could get out of the house before any trouble started. They hinted the mayor was the important guy, but I think that was a ruse."

"So, do you think this important guy is the kingpin of the syndicate?" Percy constructed a cracker sandwich as he piled on smoked salmon, sliced black olives, and goat cheese then popped it into his mouth.

"I'm not sure if they were blowing smoke up my skirt, but they left the impression it was someone that no one would suspect, like the high school principal or the librarian."

Percy raised his eyebrows. "The librarian, Miss Charlotte? She's a frail, elderly woman."

"She's not as feeble as she looks," Nettie said. "The last time I was in the library, I watched her lift a box of twenty books without batting an eye. I asked if I could help, and she told me she'd promised her recently departed husband she would retire when she couldn't lift a box of books. He specified twenty books, so she moves that box from one table to another every day. I suggested she could substitute the heavy box with a box of twenty children's picture books because people might want to check out the books she had in her box." Nettie furrowed her brow. "I wonder if she knows who the kingpin is. Maybe I'll ask her next time I go into town."

Buster flopped down on Percy's feet, and Percy reached down and scratched his ears. "We're leaving long before daylight to pick up a shipment, Flossie. We can let Buster out and feed him before we leave, but he's a little guy, and we don't know how long he can go without a break."

Flossie groaned. "Make a pot of coffee before you wake me. Buster and I will keep each other company. How long will you be gone?"

"We hope to be back not too long after dawn," Nettie said.

"Dress warm," Flossie said. "Do I need to know where you'll be?"

"It's probably better if you don't," Percy said.

"Do we want to talk about our VIPs?" Flossie asked.

Nettie nodded. "Honey, we have guest and patron subscriptions. After we have the speakeasy back in operation, Flossie and I like the idea of an intermediate subscription called VIPs that would be more exclusive than guests and would meet in the hospitality room. I envision the VIPs would have the same meals as the patrons, but not the same beverage choices."

"I like it. Talk to Estelle to be sure she's okay with the additional work, and we'll need to get the dumbwaiter in operation."

Nettie nodded. "Can you manage the guests alone? I think Flossie should host the VIP group."

"She's a natural; what do you think, Flossie?" Percy asked.

"I'm a social butterfly. The hospitality room needs someone more anchored."

"Anchored? Do you mean more stodgy?" Percy narrowed his eyes.

"Exactly." Flossie smiled, and her eyes twinkled. "Like you. I'll entertain the guests, and you can impress the VIP crowd."

"I can see it," Nettie said. "You'll lose your invisibility, but you'll be a confidante. That's brilliant, Flossie."

Percy glared at Flossie. "I like confidante better than stodgy."

Flossie shrugged. "Sorry, but it fits you better. Good night, all."

Flossie took her glass with its single sip left up the stairs to her room.

"I'm going to take the jar back downstairs. Do you need a sip more, doll?"

"Go ahead. I'll take Buster out back for a quick break before bed."

"No, that makes me nervous. I'll take him when I return, and you can go with us."

After Percy returned the Mason jar to the speakeasy, he and Nettie took Buster outside.

"Tell me the real reason I'm the host for the VIP crowd," he said.

"You'll be running for lieutenant governor. The VIP group will be your main backers and will be experienced movers and shakers in the political arena."

Percy chuckled. "So, we're going to charge them extra for the privilege of advising me on my campaign because they are the experts. Is that right?"

"Well put, and the patrons will tell us which strategy will be the most successful. Shall we take Buster inside and then head upstairs?"

After Percy locked the back door and checked the front door again, they headed the stairs.

Percy said, "I've been thinking about your three tiers of subscriptions, and you amaze me, darling. So, what is the purpose of the guests? What are they doing for us?"

Nettie chuckled. "Keeping us respectable; if it weren't for them, we'd be bootleggers and train robbers."

"Train robbers?" Percy side-glanced at her.

Nettie stopped and stared at him. "Of course. Haven't you ever wanted to jump off a train with a big bag of money?"

Percy shook his head. "No, I never have, but don't say anything to Flossie. I have the feeling the two of you would do that on a dare."

Chapter Five

Percy whispered, "Sweetie, time to wake up."

Nettie groaned as she turned on the light. "You're already dressed!"

"Are you ready for a cuppa joe? I'm warming cinnamon rolls in the oven. After you're dressed, wake Flossie then come downstairs and have some coffee. We'll take sausage biscuits with us to eat on the road."

Nettie dressed in her warm slacks and a long-sleeved black and red flannel shirt.

When she went into Flossie's room, she said, "Rise and shine. We're going to be leaving soon."

Flossie threw a pillow at her, and Nettie snorted as she ducked. "You missed me. Your coffee is waiting in the kitchen."

Nettie dashed downstairs with Buster at her side.

When they reached the kitchen, Percy said, "Drink your coffee; I'll take Buster outside and then feed him."

Percy and Buster came inside; Buster bounded to his bowl then grinned at Percy.

While Percy fed Buster, Nettie filled their thermos with coffee and put three biscuit sandwiches with egg and cheese into the oven to warm before she started another pot of coffee.

She spread out the road map and pointed. "I was thinking we could take the state road that goes straight north."

Percy glanced at it and nodded. "What's our escape plan?"

"We have two alternatives, depending on what we want to do. If we want to return fast, we can take any of the side roads that go east to the paved county road that parallels the state road. If we're more concerned about stealth, we can use private roads to get to the dirt road on the west that isn't on the map."

Flossie stumbled into the kitchen. "Did you leave me any coffee?"

"I made you a fresh pot. It's on the stove."

Flossie poured a cup and blew across the steaming liquid. "Too hot."

Percy folded the map and stuck it into his inside coat pocket. "Are you ready to go?"

Nettie pulled out the biscuits from the oven and wrapped the egg and cheese biscuits in a napkin and put them in a picnic basket next to the thermos and their tin cups.

She put on her warm coat and hat, and wrapped the pale yellow silk shawl from Theresa around her shoulders. As she carried the wicker basket on the way out the back door, Percy put on his warm coat and his fedora before he grabbed their rifles, his cane, and a lap blanket for Nettie.

"I'll lock the door after you leave," Flossie said

The night air was chilly and damp, and a sliver of the moon hung in the star-filled sky. The frosty grass crunched under their feet as they hurried to the car and loaded up. While Percy started the car, Nettie tucked in her lap blanket and then poured their coffee. When they were on the road, she handed him his first biscuit.

"If we stay on the state road, we should meet up with them in less than an hour," Nettie said.

After he ate his biscuit, Nettie poured Percy a cup of coffee, and he immediately downed it. "I'm ready for that second biscuit."

They ate and drank in silence while Percy sped north.

When they were about three miles from the planned rendezvous point, Nettie hissed, "Turn at the first private road ahead. Someone's on the road ahead of us."

"One is coming up quick; hang on." Percy made a sharp left turn onto a private road that was so narrow it appeared to be a driveway.

"Drive into the brush and park."

After he backed into the brush, Percy turned off the engine and then hopped out of the car with his rifle. Nettie grabbed her rifle and joined him.

He scowled. "Where do you think you're going?"

"We're going to walk the ditch, aren't we?"

"I'm going to walk the ditch; it's not safe for you. Stay here."

"That makes no sense. Why would we split up?"

Percy exhaled. "It's best if we both go."

After walking for a quarter mile, Nettie grabbed Percy's arm.

She whispered, "Voices just ahead; they're arguing."

They moved a little closer until Nettie could understand the words; she held up her hand, and Percy stopped with her while she listened.

A man grumbled, "Are you sure this is the right place? What if she's already gone past here?"

"Then we'll stop her on the way back, but we haven't missed her; she was supposed to meet them at dawn."

"What if she took the county road? It's not that far away." The first man's voice turned whiney.

"It's none of your beeswax, but it's covered."

Nettie raised her eyebrows as she tapped her ear, and Percy frowned as he shook his head. She motioned for them to turn back.

After they reached the car, Nettie said, "I heard two men. They plan to ambush a woman, and they were arguing about whether they missed her. I'm positive they were talking about Theresa."

"We can go around them. We passed a road going east about a half mile back."

Nettie shook her head. "We can't use the county road. One man said it was covered."

"Back roads it is, then, which is actually our favorite way to travel, anyway." Percy peered at the driveway where they turned. "This isn't a driveway; it's too wide."

"Let's see if we hit a road going north; aren't we just a few miles away?"

Percy drove away slowly at first then picked up speed. "How did you know the men were there? I didn't smell any cigarette smoke, and their headlights weren't on. Did you see flashlights?"

"No, it was like a silent movie in a fog on the road in front of us. I saw two thugs with handguns, and their car was parked in the middle of the road across both lanes to block it."

"Is that how you know things? You see them?"

"Not always. Sometimes it's just a tingly feeling that puts me on edge."

Percy muttered, "I had those in France a few times, and they never failed me."

"But not since France?" Nettie asked.

"I don't know; I want to put those days behind me."

Percy slowed as the road came to a Y and stayed to the right. Nettie pulled out the compass from the glove box and put it on the floorboards between her feet.

She peered at the compass. "We're going mostly north."

Percy chuckled. "Mostly north?"

Nettie shrugged. "The compass always jiggles funny when I hold it."

"That's interesting. Is that why you won't wear the wrist watch I bought you?"

"No, that's something different. My arm itched, and I got a red rash when I wore it for very long. I took it to the watch maker, and he said I was probably allergic to gold. I gave it to Estelle; it doesn't bother her at all."

"That was brilliant; I'm glad it's working for Estelle," Percy said. "But why does the compass not work for you?"

"I asked the watchmaker if that was why the compass jiggles funny when I hold it. He said it's rare, but some people have a high level of electrical current in their bodies that interferes with the earth's magnetic pull on a compass."

Percy furrowed his brow. "Sounds like an offbeat theory. Seems like someone would test it."

Nettie snorted. "I don't think anybody cares except people who can't hold compasses. Do you want to check the direction?"

"Mostly north is good enough."

Percy slowed then turned right toward the state road.

Nettie peered ahead. "We're getting close."

He snorted. "I want to tell you to stay down and keep your eyes open. I'm not sure how you'll do that, but I'm certain you'll figure it out."

When they came to the state road, Percy said, "They should be a few yards away, but I don't know whether to go left or right if we want to go around them and come back at them from the other direction."

"I think I hear them; go left," Nettie said. "Then we can head back if we don't find them."

Nettie pulled off her hat and draped the pale yellow shawl over her head to cover her hair.

After Percy had driven two miles on the state road, Nettie said, "We should stop here; make a U-turn, so we're facing south."

When he pulled to the side of the road, Percy turned off the engine. "What now?"

"Theresa told them she would have a driver. If you stand near the car with your cane but have your rifle handy, I'll talk to them. It would be ideal if I could convince them to load the shipment into our car, but we'll have to see how big the shipment is, how stable they are, and what they're willing to do."

Tree frogs and katydids in the nearby woods sang their songs as the clouds that had been scattered in the sky began gathering. The moonlight was soon hidden by the cloud cover.

"They're coming," Nettie said.

"It might be someone else, honey. Stand in the trees until you're certain they have Theresa's shipment."

Nettie pulled the shawl over her head and picked up her rifle. As she made her way across the ditch, she asked, "Where are you going to be?"

"In front of the car."

After she was in place, Nettie listened. "They'll be coming around the curve in a minute."

When the headlights shined on their car, the approaching car slowed then stopped on the road five feet from Percy's bumper.

"You people okay?" the passenger called out.

Nettie stepped across the ditch. "We're fine; thanks for stopping."

"I think I know you," the passenger said.

"I'm Theresa," Nettie said.

"Good; where do you want it?" the driver asked.

"Put it on the side of the road so you don't have to wait. We have a truck not too far behind us that will pick up the shipment."

The two men unloaded the five unmarked cases onto the ground next to their car then turned around and roared north.

"Why didn't you tell them to load the cases into our car?" Percy asked.

"I had a feeling the passenger recognized me; I didn't want him to remember who I was, and I didn't want them to think it was just the two of us."

"It was obvious you had a reason; I'll back up so we can get loaded as fast as we can," Percy said.

"I'll hand them to you," Nettie said. "You're a more efficient packer than I am."

After they quickly loaded the cases, Percy sped to the nearest private road.

He slowed for his turn and continued at a crawl west on the rutted dirt road until they came to a T; Percy turned south.

"This road is a welcome improvement," Percy said as he sped up. "Oliver will be waiting for us at the barn."

As they neared their house, Nettie said, "There's a car coming toward us."

Percy pulled into a driveway that curved to the left toward the house and turned off the headlights and engine. They stepped out of the car and stood near a small stand of trees as the other car continued north.

"Are we clear now?" Percy asked.

"Yes."

Percy started the engine but didn't turn on the headlights. As he backed out of the driveway, an inside light toward the back of the house lit up a portion of the side yard.

Nettie held her breath until they were on the road. "Did we wake someone up?" she asked.

"I don't think so. If we had, they would have turned on the front porch light."

"You're right; I wasn't thinking straight." Nettie sighed. "I'll feel better when we're home."

After Percy turned at the driveway to the barn, he reached for Nettie's hand and squeezed it. "We're a good team. After we unload the hooch, take the car to the house. I'll walk back with Oliver."

Oliver was waiting for them when they reached the barn. He and Percy quickly unloaded the car, and Nettie drove to the house. After she parked, she unlocked the back door and strolled inside.

Buster barked his version of a big dog bark.

"It's me," Nettie called out. Buster scrambled to her and flopped down for a belly rub.

Flossie hurried from the living room and joined them. "Did you hear that bark? Wasn't that amazing?"

"It really was. He's a great guard dog already, isn't he?" Nettie put away her rifle in the gun chest and then cooed at Buster and rubbed his ears.

"Do we have any coffee?"

"Sure do. I made a coffee cake too. I thought you might need a bite of something after getting up so early. Where's Percy?"

"He'll be here soon. I love your coffee cake." Nettie hung up her coat.

While they enjoyed their hot coffee and cake, Flossie said, "It wasn't as bad as I thought it would be to get up early. After I drank my coffee, I laid down on the sofa, and

Buster hopped up and snuggled against my feet to keep them warm. We napped until Buster heard you come in the back door. Did you run into any problems?"

"Not at all." Nettie smiled as Buster's ears perked up. "Percy must be back; look at Buster's ears."

Flossie giggled.

Percy came into the house and rubbed Buster's chin. "What do I smell?"

"Coffee cake. Have a seat, and I'll pour you a fresh cup of coffee to go with your cake," Flossie said.

"In a minute. Honey, Estelle has a nasty headache. Oliver asked if we'd take Bella to church. She sings in the choir, and Estelle doesn't want to be the reason she misses her solo today."

"We can do that; I didn't know Bella sang in the choir, but I'd love to hear her sing."

"I'll let Oliver know; we'll have to leave in an hour." Percy stopped. "I'll have time for that coffee cake after I talk to Oliver and change clothes, Flossie, so don't throw it out."

Buster trotted with Percy to the back door, and they left.

Nettie dashed upstairs and put on her soft blue dress with tiny embroidered pale pink and cream peach blossoms and beige lace in the deep V of the neckline. She smiled. *Theresa's pale yellow silk shawl will be perfect to wear with my dress.*

She met Percy on the stairs.

He smiled. "Bella's excited that we'll hear her sing this morning. I'll change into a suit and then be right down for my coffee cake."

When Nettie went into the kitchen, she poured herself a cup of coffee. "Flossie, if it warms up a bit, take Buster on a short walk with his new leash. If we walk him on the leash every day, it won't be strange to him when we take him into town."

"That a wonderful idea; I'd love for him to go with us into town so we don't have to leave him behind. We'll work on it."

"What are you going to work on?" Percy asked.

"Getting used to a leash."

Percy bit his lip. "Good; how about that coffee cake?"

After he finished two pieces of coffee cake, Percy said, "Ready to go?"

Nettie and Percy stroked Buster's chin before they put on their warm coats. Percy grabbed his fedora while Nettie hurried to the small house behind theirs. When she and Bella joined Percy at the car, Bella climbed into the back seat, and Nettie gave her the lap blanket.

"Wrap up," Nettie said. "The faster we go, the colder the wind is."

"That must be why Granny told me to wear my crochet hat instead of my church hat."

"Probably, but it's also really cute on you." Nettie smiled as she pulled up her collar on her coat and then pulled her shawl over her head while Percy headed down the driveway.

On the way to town, Bella leaned forward. "Where's your church hat, Miss Nettie?"

"I decided I'd like to be traditional today and wear a shawl over my head rather than a modern hat," Nettie said.

"Is my crochet hat modern?" Bella furrowed her brow.

Nettie side-glanced at Bella. "Not at all; is that copacetic with you?"

Bella leaned back and grinned. "It's hunky-dory."

Percy reached over and squeezed Nettie's hand. When she glanced at him, he winked.

They arrived at the church thirty minutes before it was time for the church service to begin.

After Percy parked, Bella said, "I hope I'm not late."

"You aren't." Nettie pointed. "The choir director just parked."

Bella dashed to the side door and went inside with the choir director.

"We have a little time; did you want to cruise past Theresa's shop?" Percy asked.

"I'd love to, but it might make more sense after church so I can return her shawl."

"Do you want to sit out here or go inside?"

"Let's go inside so we can pick where we sit."

Percy opened her door then offered his arm. As they strolled together to the church, he said, "We can sit close to the front so you can hear Bella, but I'd like to be as close to an exit as possible."

"Okay. after we choose our seats, I'd like to leave my coat with you so I can cruise for news."

Percy chuckled. "Nice rhyme."

Nettie smiled. "I'd say thank you, but I didn't catch it until you said something."

After they selected their seats, Nettie took off her coat, folded it neatly, and set it on the pew seat next to

Percy. As she strolled away, a man who had been seated on the opposite side of the church headed toward Percy. She raised her eyebrows when she recognized him as one of Percy's old Marine buddies. *I haven't seen Smitty since he left for Savannah. Wonder what brings him back.*

Nettie continued toward the women's restroom. Before she reached it, a familiar voice called out, "Nettie."

She smiled as she turned. "It's nice to see a friendly face, Marian."

Marian's dark orange felt bowler with a felt rose on the front of her hat complemented her dark green woolen suit and sturdy brown heels. "Thank you; seeing you has made my morning."

Nettie smiled. "Bella is singing in the choir today, so we're here for moral support."

Marian returned Nettie's smile. "Front row seats, I'm sure."

"Pretty close to it; how are you doing?"

"I forgot something in my car. Are you brave enough to walk out with me, or do you want to get your coat?"

"I'll be fine; it's just a little nippy."

As they linked arms and strolled out to the parking lot, Marian said quietly, "We're leaving tonight for Alabama. Ira owns a small farm near the town where his parents live, and the tenants moved out two months ago. He told the children he wanted them to grow up knowing their grandparents, but he's been worried about the rapidly changing political climate. He doesn't want anyone to know where we'll be because he said it wouldn't be long until the children and I wouldn't be safe because of his position. We're not saying anything to anyone, but when he saw Percy's car, he told me it was okay if I wanted to tell you."

"What about your house here?"

"Ira wants to stay here to help Percy in his bid for lieutenant governor."

"Anything I can do?"

Marian stopped when they reached her car and pulled out a key from her handbag.

"If Ira has to leave after all, I'd appreciate it if you'd empty the house and give our things to people who can use them." She pressed the key into Nettie's hand. "I wish I'd had more time to give away a few things, but Ira said I couldn't do anything like that because it would call too much attention to us."

Marian opened her passenger door and feigned picking something up from the floor and putting it into her pocket.

As they headed back to the church, Marian asked, "Is Estelle feeling okay?"

"Oliver told Percy she has a severe headache. It must be bad because she wasn't well enough to come to church. Even though she couldn't hear Bella sing, I know she would have loved watching her."

Marian frowned. "That tonic she brews makes a tremendous difference in the duration and intensity of her headaches, but I still wish she'd see a doctor, except not that quack."

"I'll talk to Percy. Maybe we can come up with a way to encourage Estelle to see a doctor."

Marian smiled. "Turn it over to Flossie."

Nettie chuckled. "It's tempting, but Flossie doesn't drive."

"Really? That's so unusual these days. It's been my impression that all you young women wanted to be independent. I can't imagine that Flossie wouldn't want to drive."

"I've offered to teach her to drive for a while, but I think she finally has some motivation."

Marian side-glanced at her. "Is it that young deputy who falls all over himself when she's around? They are entertaining, but I don't think anyone is supposed to notice. They've been seeing each other for quite a while." Marian chuckled. "Seems like I've seen Flossie in town almost every day for the past couple of months. She must watch Oliver and Willis like a hawk to catch a ride into town."

"I saw Flossie with him yesterday, but she didn't want to talk about him at all."

"If it helps, Ira said Deputy Laird is one of the few good ones, and Ira would know."

When they reached the main door to the church, Marian hugged Nettie. "I'll miss you. Be safe; I'll be praying for you."

Nettie shuddered as she strolled to join Percy in the pew.

After she joined him, he put his arm around her, and she scooted closer to him.

"Put on your coat; you're freezing. Is everything okay?" he whispered.

Nettie put on her coat and pulled it closed. "Marian is going to pray for me. As soon as the church service ends, we have to leave."

Percy squeezed her shoulder. "We'll be okay."

"No, something is going to happen today, and I don't know what it is or how to stop it. Do you think it would be okay if we slipped out after Bella sings and picked her up after church?"

"I'll check with her." Percy rose from his seat and strode to the front of the church then opened the door to the hallway that led to the choir room.

When he returned, he said, "I talked to Bella. She's nervous about singing, but even more worried about Estelle. When she asked if we could check on her grandmother, she told me she would wait for us at the fabric shop if we aren't here when the church service is over."

"I don't like that idea at all."

"Why don't you stay here then, and I'll run home to be sure everything's okay. If I'm not back in time, then you and Bella can go to Theresa's shop or stay here. Bella will be fine if she's with you because you'll keep her safe. I'll find you."

Nettie examined Percy's face. "I can do that; you'll be okay."

Percy took Nettie's face into his hands. "Tell me you will, too, doll. Promise me."

Nettie smiled. "I promise we'll be okay. Both of us."

Percy hugged her and kissed her neck.

She giggled when his mustache tickled her then inhaled the essence of his cologne as she leaned against him and whispered, "You smell yummy, but we're in church, you goof."

He raised his eyebrows. "We were married in this church. Have you already forgotten our wedding vows? Love, honor, and smooches?"

"I seem to remember it differently, but I like your way better."

Percy chuckled as he stroked her cheek. "I'll see you soon."

Nettie rolled her eyes as Percy rose and left the church through the side door seconds before the organist played the first chord of the opening hymn. When she glanced behind her, she narrowed her eyes as she inspected the congregation. *The only men left are the two elderly men in wheelchairs. I wonder if they slipped out to go to the dive that's open on Sunday mornings.*

While the pastor delivered his sermon, Nettie watched Bella who was slowly scanning the churchgoers. Bella cocked her head then stared at Nettie and quickly signed, "No men."

Nettie responded with a quick nod as she signed, "We are okay."

Bella exhaled, and Nettie smiled.

Nettie signed, "We will leave by the side door as soon as we can."

Bella weakly returned her smile then her eyes twinkled as she signed, "Now?"

Nettie covered her mouth to stifle her chuckle.

After the sermon, Bella sang a solo.

Nettie was mesmerized by the clear tones of Bella's voice. When Bella ended the hymn and sat down, the congregation was stunned in silence until a two-year-old in a back pew clapped and shouted, "Yay!"

Everyone laughed and applauded.

The redness that appeared in Bella's cheeks spread to her neck when the woman next to her elbowed her and motioned for Bella to rise. Bella stood then quickly sat. When the noise quieted, Bella hiccupped, and several children giggled.

When she hiccupped a second time, there were more giggles. Nettie rushed to the front. After she put her arm around Bella, Nettie ushered the hiccupping girl to the choir room to grab Bella's coat, and then they left the church by the side door.

Nettie raised her eyebrows. "The cold air seems to have cured your hiccups."

"Am I in trouble?" Bella asked. "I was just so embarrassed..."

"No, you are definitely not in trouble; it was actually a brilliant move. Let's go to the fabric shop to wait for Mr. Percy. Maybe Miss Theresa has some hot tea or hot chocolate."

"I love to sing, but there were more people than I expected," Bella said as they rushed to the fabric shop.

Nettie grabbed onto Bella's arm and froze after they turned the corner. She shuddered at the sight of a lone car parked in front of the shop with a man she didn't recognize sitting in the driver's seat. "Let's circle around and go in the back door so we don't disturb Miss Theresa while she's waiting on her customer."

As they circled around the two blocks to avoid being seen by the driver, Bella asked, "Won't the door be locked?"

"Miss Theresa keeps a spare key in a hidden spot."

After they were at the back of the shop, Bella covered her eyes. Nettie smiled then opened the back door. When she heard a scuffle and a man shouting, she quietly closed the door and bit her lip as she rubbed her forehead.

"Honey, Miss Theresa could use my help, but I don't want to leave you out here by yourself. Will you wait inside by the back door? You'll have to stay there and be as quiet as you can."

Bella's eyes were wide as she nodded. Nettie opened the back door, and she and Bella slipped inside.

Chapter Six

The back room was in shambles. After Bella found a clear spot to sit behind a jumble of boxes, Nettie pulled out her derringer from her beaded bag. Before she reached the curtain that separated the front of the store and the back storage room, the front door slammed.

Nettie waited a moment then slipped through the curtain and gasped at Theresa's crumpled body on the floor. Theresa moaned as she tried to lift her head. Her face was bloody, and her right arm was bent at an unnatural angle.

Theresa mumbled unintelligibly in a panicky voice.

Nettie rushed to lock the front door and peered out the window; the car that had been parked in front was gone.

"He's gone. I'll take you to the hospital. Where are your car keys?"

Theresa mumbled, "My purse. Not hospital."

"I have Bella with me. Give me a minute to talk to her, then we'll take you to Doc Jackson. Do you know the man who beat you?"

"No. He said stop Percy."

Theresa moaned as she tried to stifle a cough before she continued in a stronger voice, "I stand with Percy."

"I'll be right back."

Nettie hurried to the back. "Did you hear what Theresa said?"

"Yes, ma'am. She doesn't want to go to the hospital, so we're going to take her to Doc's house because she's hurt bad, isn't she?"

"She's got a bloody nose and a split lip. I'll have to fashion a sling for her arm because it might be broken."

"Pappy taught me to help him when the baby goats are being born. He says I'm an excellent nurse because I'm smart and strong."

Theresa had struggled to push herself to a sitting position and was bracing her broken arm against her chest. "Ready."

"I'll cut some fabric to make you a sling. Bella, check to see if there's anyone out back. We can see the front door, but I don't want anyone sneaking in on us."

Bella dashed to the back door and peeked out then went outside.

While Nettie cut a large section of fabric, then folded it into a triangular bandage, Theresa said, "He waved a baseball bat in my face and told me to make sure Percy didn't run for office. I've never seen him before. He had a red scar that ran from his left earlobe to the corner of this mouth. I was terrified, but when he swung at my head with the bat, I threw up my arm. After I fell, he kicked me in the face. When he heard you at the back door, he rushed out the front. I know he thought I was dead."

As Nettie tied Theresa's sling, Bella came inside.

"I kind of looked around, and there's a man standing in front of the drug store. When a car with a family drove by, he stepped close to the door and turned his back."

Nettie bit her lip. "We'll get out of here as quickly as we can. Bella, help me get Theresa to her feet. I'll get behind her and lift if you stand in front of her and keep her feet from slipping out from under her."

Theresa bent her knees with her feet braced against Bella's. "Give me your hand, Bella, so we can help Nettie lift me up."

After Bella grasped Theresa's good arm with both of her hands, Nettie said, "On my count; one, two, three, lift."

After Theresa was standing, Bella ran ahead with the car keys to open the doors.

Theresa exhaled. "Can we fight fire with fire?"

"I'd rather blindside them."

"How?"

Nettie shrugged. "I'm not sure yet, but I'll come up with something."

Theresa chuckled then coughed. After she caught her breath, she groaned. "They'll never know what hit them."

When Theresa was in the passenger seat, Nettie held up a key on Theresa's key ring. "I'll lock the shop's back door. Is this the key?"

Theresa nodded.

Nettie locked the back door while Bella climbed into the back seat.

As Nettie headed to Doc Jackson's house, Theresa said, "Take them down. I'm all in."

After they reached Doc's house, Nettie hurried to the door and knocked.

Doc opened the door and narrowed his eyes. "What's wrong?"

"Theresa was beaten; her arm is broken, and she has a bloody nose and facial abrasions."

"Let's get her inside."

Doc and Nettie helped Theresa into the house while Bella held the door.

After Theresa was seated at Doc's kitchen table, Nettie said, "I have a feeling Percy and I need to run down our bank account and could use your help."

Theresa stared at her. "How can we help?"

"Do you either of you have a loan with the bank?"

"I had a loan on the small farm I bought when I moved here after I retired, but I paid it off after I received my retirement money," Doc said.

"I took out a loan with the bank on the shop." Theresa shifted in her seat and groaned.

"Here, Theresa, take this." Doc filled a glass of water for Theresa then handed her the glass and two pills. "It's just aspirin that I take for my lumbago. It will help you."

"Would you consider making Percy and me partners with twenty percent interest in your business so we can pay off your loan tomorrow morning, Theresa? Mr. Fielding can handle the paperwork."

"I heard the bank was being sold, and one of my customers told me she heard new bank owners foreclose on farms and small businesses. A teller asked if I'd hire him. I didn't want to be rude, but I can't imagine a man working in a fabric shop. Was I wrong?" Theresa frowned. "I need a partner."

Doc said, "I went to a conference in Atlanta last week, and an old friend told me a new bank owner in his town offered higher rates on the deposit accounts. Naturally, most of the depositors left their money in the bank because of the higher rates. Do you think that will happen here? Aren't higher rates a good thing?"

"Not always," Nettie said. "I'd rather invest my money in my friends, who are more reliable than any bank, no matter what the rates are."

Doc shrugged. "We'll agree to disagree then, because I wouldn't advise a friend to leave money on the table."

She set Theresa's car keys on the table. "Unless you need us, Doc, we have to go; Percy will be looking for us."

Theresa pushed the keys toward Nettie. "Take my car."

"No, we'll be fine. It's a short walk to the fabric store, and he'll probably pick us up before we get there. I'll check on you tomorrow."

When they were outside, Nettie asked, "It's not too cold for you is it?"

"Not for me. What about you?" Bella asked.

"The exercise will warm me up."

"Did you see that big coffee mug at Doc's house?" Bella asked.

"It was really large, wasn't it? All I could see was 'In Case'."

"I think it said 'In Case of Fire', but I didn't understand it if it was supposed to be a joke," Bella said.

"Maybe you could fill it with water and put out a fire because it's so big."

Bella shrugged.

Nettie chuckled. "I thought it was a farfetched idea too."

After they had walked two blocks, Bella asked, "Do you see the car parked in the next block with two men inside?"

"Yes, and we are going to turn here and head to the church. Feel like running?"

"I'm with you."

When they reached the church, the parking lot was empty. Nettie was out of breath; Bella wasn't.

Nettie groaned. *I need to get into shape.*

"Are you okay?" Bella asked. "We can go in the front door; it's always unlocked."

Nettie nodded.

When they reached the door, she finally caught her breath. "I hear Percy's car."

Bella cocked her head. "Now I hear it. How can you tell it's Mr. Percy's car?"

Nettie shrugged as Percy turned the corner then continued to the church's front door.

When they were in the car, Percy asked, "Everything okay?"

"Is now. When we went to the fabric store, we found Theresa on the floor. A man broke her arm with a baseball bat and kicked her in the face."

"What?" Percy roared, and his face darkened. "Who was it?"

"Theresa didn't really know, but we can talk after we get home. How's Estelle?" Nettie glanced at the back seat. "Bella, wrap up in that lap blanket."

Percy exhaled. "Much better; she was glad you went to the church to hear Bella sing."

"Bella has a beautiful voice." Nettie turned to smile at Bella. "I loved hearing you sing."

"I was really nervous, and I get the hiccups when I get nervous. Thank goodness I sang my solo before I realized how nervous I was," Bella said.

"Very well done," Nettie said.

After they parked, Nettie said, "Tell your pappy about Theresa so he can decide when to tell your granny."

Bella nodded and raced to the small cottage.

"I need to hear what you know," Percy growled.

"Let's talk while we change clothes; I'm freezing."

When they went into the house, Buster greeted them with yips and a wiggly butt. Percy scratched his ears while Nettie hurried into the kitchen.

"We're back. Bella was amazing, and I'm freezing. We're going upstairs to change."

"I'll put on a pot of coffee. I made chicken soup for lunch because I got cold on our walk this morning," Flossie said.

Nettie rushed up the stairs to join Percy in their bedroom. While they changed, Nettie told Percy what Theresa said.

Percy narrowed his eyes. "I know who they are. My guys and I call them torpedoes; they're definitely gangsters. What's your plan? How do we stop them?"

"We'll blindside them and hit them where it hurts."

"Most of their income is from selling whiskey and prostitution."

Nettie's eyes twinkled as she pulled up her trousers and then tucked in her blouse. "What if I dry up their supply of whiskey? That will also directly affect their income from prostitution too."

"How are you going to do that?"

"I'll make it more profitable for the source to do business with me."

"What are you going to do with all that whiskey? You're not opening a string of speakeasies, are you?"

"No, but farmers are having a hard time paying the loans they took out for the equipment and land they bought to help the war effort, and the demand for their products has dropped."

Percy stopped with one leg still in his suit pants then dropped onto their bed to keep from falling. "You lost me."

"We corner the market on moonshine; the farmers use it to create new products, tonics for migraines or manhood issues, and then ship cases of their products to New York, Chicago, and Philadelphia, and make a ton of money."

As Percy hung up his suit pants, he said, "Ship it how?"

"It's definitely up for discussion, but the simplest way I can think of it is to create a transportation pipeline with the bootleggers returning with a load of tonic to drop off for shipping."

"The shipping part needs work; maybe Ira can help us out. Overall, it all sounds good on paper, but how do you keep the goons from going from farm to farm to shut down the operations?" Percy asked.

"Honey, farm boys spend entire days sitting in trees with deer rifles. The farmers will take care of their own."

"I can't argue with that. What about the suppliers?"

"Bootleggers are hard-boiled; they won't be stopped."

"I'm seeing so many pitfalls, but what's our biggest risk?" Percy asked.

"Our biggest risk is that we don't move fast enough, which gives them time to find the holes before we close them. We have to distract them by hitting hard in the political arena. That's where you come in."

"We need that shipping gap filled first, then while you get the farmers and bootleggers in operation, I'll announce my candidacy." Percy frowned. "I was counting on you to run the campaign, but you'll be busy with the tonic operation."

"I thought Willis could work with us on setting up the tonic business then manage it while I run your campaign."

Percy furrowed his brow. "Flossie could easily manage the guest subscriptions, but what about the VIPs and patrons?"

"Flossie will be fine with the VIPs; she just needs a little encouragement to increase her confidence. Willis and I will work out a plan for the patrons."

Percy buttoned up his shirt. "I realize I have a tendency to be overly cautious, but there are too many moving parts for me."

Nettie hugged him and raised her face for a kiss. "I know, but I have more." She told him about her offer to partner with Theresa.

"I've been worried about the bank freezing our funds; this is a brilliant way to empty our accounts quietly." Percy sighed and kissed her. "I'll have a ringside seat while you make it all come together, won't I?"

Nettie giggled. "Nice try, bud. You'll be too busy with your campaign to sit around and stew."

As they went down the stairs, Nettie asked, "Did you know Ira is taking Marian and the children to Alabama this evening?"

Percy frowned. "We talked about it; I told him he'd be calling attention to himself and sending the signal he was afraid. I don't think he'd thought about it like that."

"Do you think Willis and Oliver will be working at the barn? I'd like to talk to them."

"I suspect they are."

"Flossie made soup for lunch; let's sit down with a bowl before we look for them."

Flossie and Buster came inside through the back door and met them in the hallway.

"Are you ready for lunch? The soup is simmering on the stove, and I have biscuits I can throw into the oven." Flossie beamed. "Estelle said she's going to turn over the Friday evening appetizers to me starting this week."

While the three of them ate, Percy said, "I knew you have been helping Estelle out, but it sounds like you've been training too."

Flossie nodded. "I've always hung around the kitchen to keep Estelle company when I wasn't busy. I didn't realize how much I would love cooking until she asked me if I wanted to learn."

After Nettie explained their plan to stop the torpedoes, Flossie raised an eyebrow. "Fascinating; is this all about stopping Percy from running for lieutenant governor?"

"I'm sure it is, but I'm convinced the purpose of a raid would be to keep Percy so busy he wouldn't have time to become as well-known statewide as he is around here."

"So, what do I do?"

"We need for you to manage the house and take over the weekend hospitality for the members and VIPs," Nettie said.

"Can I swap the hospitality room with your sewing room?"

Nettie sighed. "I should have thought of that earlier. Do you want any help?"

"I can do it with a half hour of Oliver's time when he's available. What else can I do?"

"Do you know how to make Estelle's tonic?" Percy asked.

Flossie grinned. "I sure do. I've been dabbling with my own tonic that is more for men. Estelle's tonic is sweet, so I thought I'd try one with coffee. I plan to call it Tough Guy Tonic."

"Does your tonic have moonshine in it?" Nettie asked.

"It's twenty-five percent alcohol, just like Estelle's. We'd like to increase it to thirty-five percent for the extra kick."

"Does anyone else create a tonic?" Nettie asked.

"Yes, but theirs are mostly molasses based because they don't have access to moonshine like we do."

"If we had a decent supply of moonshine, do you think you could recruit at least twenty women who would be interested in making tonic to sell?" Nettie asked.

"Sure; could we order small sized bottles for the tonic? I know we could order them through the drug store. Right now, everyone's using pint jars. We should bottle it into smaller containers, and of course charge a lot more for our products."

Percy stared at Flossie. "Have you been thinking about this for a while?"

Flossie giggled. "We're always kicking around ideas on how to make money. Did you think we just talked about fashion on Fridays and Saturdays?"

Percy shrugged. "I hear a lot of political talk."

"That's because you're listening for it. When can we get started?"

"The sooner the better; can you sketch out a plan for me so we can plan the delivery of more moonshine? How would we ship the tonic?" Nettie asked.

Flossie waved her hand. "That's duck soup; we'd ship by rail. We have already scoped out an empty building close to the train station where we can pack our items. The druggist's sister knows a woman whose brother owns a wholesale business in New York. We'd ship to his business, and he'd take it from there."

Percy shook his head. "What type of product did you have in mind when you were planning all this?"

"We were thinking soaps because we have all the supplies to make it, but tonic is better because it's easier to make, the price can be higher, and it will have a higher demand."

"You will need a name for your business; what were you thinking?" Nettie asked.

Flossie furrowed her brow. "I hadn't thought about that, but Estelle was my inspiration. What about Estelle's Tonic?"

Nettie smiled. "What about Star Tonic?"

Flossie's eyes twinkled. "Golden Star Tonic."

Nettie nodded as she cleared the table. "We'll talk to Willis about increasing our moonshine order. We'll have a better idea of how much more we'll need when we begin production of the tonic."

Nettie and Percy buttoned up their warm coats. When Percy grabbed his walking stick, Buster dashed to the back door and nosed it.

"Buster's going with us to the barn," Nettie called out.

When they were outside, Nettie asked, "Walk or drive?"

"We're dressed warm; let's hike it."

They headed to the shortcut toward the barn. As they strolled along the narrow trail, Buster dashed into the brush then back out a few feet ahead of them. He barked then looked at Percy and barked again.

"That's a big boy bark," Nettie said.

Percy hurried to Buster's side and bent down to pat him. "Good boy, Buster."

Nettie joined them as Percy rose. "Honey, Buster found a purse." He held it up for Nettie to see.

Her eyes widened. "It's red patent leather, just like Helen's. Is there anything in it?"

Percy handed her the purse.

After she carefully scrutinized it and turned the lining inside out, Nettie said, "There's absolutely nothing in it. Now, what?"

"I'll take it." Percy dropped it on the side of the trail. "I'll leave it here to mark where Buster found it so Oliver and I can scour the area to see if we find anything else. I don't want to invite a search of our property."

As they continued to the barn, Nettie asked, "Do you think the purse was a plant?"

"It was close to the driveway and not that far off the path, so it could have easily been pitched from the driveway. If Oliver, Buster, and I don't find anything else, we'll bury the purse unless you come up with a better idea, which you probably will because you always do." Percy side-glanced at Nettie. "Or have you already?"

Nettie smiled. "I love your confidence in me. It's not my style of purse, so you definitely have my permission to bury it."

As they neared the barn, Nettie said, "I've changed my mind; don't bury it. If it's a plant, someone is already planning to call for a search. We're going into town early tomorrow morning. Let's drop it off somewhere it can be easily seen."

Percy furrowed his brow. "I'd rather get rid of it today. Let's go into town after we talk to Oliver and Willis."

"Perfect. We can take some of Flossie's soup to Theresa and toss the purse into the bushes next to the boarding house."

When Percy and Nettie neared the barn, Oliver met them on the path.

Nettie smiled. "Oliver, Bella's solo at church was beautiful, and I appreciated spending some time with her. You and Estelle are raising a remarkably capable young woman."

"Thanks. She scares and amazes me every day."

Percy shook his head. "I'm so sorry to say this, Oliver, but it sounds like Bella is a junior Nettie."

Oliver nodded. "It's no surprise because Bella has studied Nettie since the first day she came to stay with us."

As they continued to the barn, Oliver said, "We just finished expanding the storage area."

"I've been checking around, and we may have access to additional storage in town if we need it," Percy said. "Let's find Willis."

After Willis showed Nettie and Percy the expanded storage, the four of them sat on the wooden crates outside the barn.

Nettie explained her plan to take down the torpedoes.

Willis whistled long and low. "I thought we'd be going to war with the torpedoes. Your tonic could put them out of business in Georgia."

"That's the idea," Percy said.

Willis continued, "I guess I better leave right away to parley with our suppliers to pitch Nettie's plan. I have a feeling they'd rather do business with Nettie, anyway. I've heard some complaints about the torpedoes' strong-arm tactics, which is definitely not the way to approach bootleggers. What are you going to call your new tonic?"

"Flossie is gathering a team to make the tonic that she's named Golden Star Tonic," Nettie said.

Oliver raised his eyebrows. "She's naming it after Estelle?"

"Her tonic inspired the idea."

Oliver turned away to hide his face. "That's a wonderful thing to do; she'll be overjoyed. She could use a boost in her confidence."

"We'll probably go from twice a week to three times a week for deliveries," Willis said. "Do you mind if the suppliers decide to make tonic too?"

"Not at all; the more the merrier," Nettie said.

"You might even suggest it," Percy said. "That's a perfect solution for removing an even more significant amount of moonshine from the supply pipeline."

Oliver frowned. "Won't the tonic need a prescription or something?"

Nettie's eyes twinkled as she smiled. "Probably, but that's up to the sellers. Our sellers are experienced and will know all the ins and outs; they'll proceed accordingly."

Oliver smacked his forehead with his palm. "Sometimes I forget you manage the most successful business in Georgia." He furrowed his brow. "What else is on your mind?"

Nettie raised her eyebrows and then told Oliver and Willis about finding the empty purse.

Percy added, "We're certain it's Helen's purse. We're going to take it into town and drop it off at the boarding house where Helen was staying."

"Why don't I do that?" Oliver asked. "You don't want anyone to see you. I'm virtually invisible compared to you. If you want the purse found today, you shouldn't go into town until tomorrow."

Willis rose. "I gotta go; let Oliver handle the red purse. I'll check in with you tomorrow."

Nettie cocked her head in thought as Willis left the barn. "I wanted to take soup to Theresa today."

"I can drop off the soup and everyone will think Estelle sent it; they've been friends for years," Oliver said.

Nettie nodded. "It's cold, so we were wearing gloves. Be careful."

"Got it. I'll wear my gloves. Don't worry; I'm a shadow." Oliver's eyes darkened. "No one will notice me."

Chapter Seven

Nettie narrowed her eyes as she examined him. "You're right; you have the gift."

After Oliver left, Percy asked, "What gift does Oliver have?"

Nettie raised an eyebrow. "He blends in. We don't see it because we're too close to him."

"Are you ready to inspect the changes we made to the barn's concealed storage?"

After Percy showed off the additional space, he asked, "Is this what you had in mind?"

Nettie furrowed her brow. "Is there a way to double the space? I have a feeling we'll need it."

"I'll talk with Willis; we'll come up with something."

As they strolled back to the house while Buster explored along the path behind them, Percy asked, "Why do we need so much more storage? Tell me more about this latest feeling of yours."

"There seems to be a pattern of escalating events beginning with Johnny's visit, Helen snooping around, and her plan to leave moonshine on our porch, the red purse, and the attack on us and then Theresa."

Percy nodded. "I'd add the sudden foreclosure on Silas Evans' property, and the slimy attempt to cheat us too. I like your plan to run down our bank account as low as we can on Monday."

Nettie slowed her pace to match Percy's as they strolled along the path.

He sighed. "The uneven terrain wears me out."

"Maybe I can come up with something so it doesn't slow you down."

She stopped when Percy did, and he hugged her. "Thank you, but I need to learn to pace myself better."

When they went inside, Buster dashed past them and scrambled to the kitchen.

"I have a feeling Bella's in the kitchen with Flossie." Percy smiled as he headed to the living room. "I'll put up my feet and relax for a bit."

"Good."

When Nettie went into the kitchen, her eyes widened.

Estelle smiled as she kneaded bread dough on the countertop. She stopped to sign. "I feel much better. A friend of Flossie's came by, and she went into town."

Bella added, "I peeked out the window; he was tall and looked familiar."

Nettie cocked her head. "Was it the deputy?"

Bella shrugged. "I've only seen the deputy in uniform, so I'm not sure."

Estelle signed, "Where's Percy?"

Nettie replied, "He's resting in the living room."

Estelle pulled out a snack plate with meat, cheese, and a dinner roll from the refrigerator and placed it on the counter. After she poured a glass of milk, she signed, "For Percy. He needs to keep up his strength."

Nettie picked up the plate and glass and carried them into the living room where Percy relaxed on the sofa while he read a book.

"Estelle sent you a snack." Nettie set the plate on the table next to Percy.

"She's convinced I need more protein." Percy sighed then pulled apart his roll and made a sandwich of meat and cheese.

"Whatever works, darling." Nettie exhaled then paced. "Let's talk strategy for your campaign. We've talked about your military service being an advantage, and your reputation with farmers is untouchable. Is there a way we can pull those two together?"

Percy stretched his legs then propped his feet up on his footstool. "A lot of farms in France were abandoned, seized, heavily damaged, or contaminated by the fighting, but the farmers who survived embraced crop rotation and established innovative practices like co-ops to pool resources."

"That's it. Innovation is your platform, and unless we come up with something better, your campaign slogan is 'Innovative Leadership You Deserve.'"

Percy furrowed his brow. "One disadvantage of having Flossie take over our member subscription dinners is that I won't always be available for gathering information."

Nettie snuggled next to him on the sofa. "I have a secret weapon. Bella hears even more than you do."

"Is that safe? Does Estelle know? What about Flossie?"

"Bella is even less noticeable than you as she slips in and out with platters, and she tells Estelle what she hears. It's been good practice for the three of us, and there has been no reason for me to tell Flossie."

Nettie rose and paced while she muttered, "Your mustache is good, and your cane is a reminder of your war injury. I suppose you could wear a suit to some events, but we need you out talking to farmers in your farm work clothes."

"Aren't we ignoring the cities?"

"That's what your suit is for, except I think you're better off campaigning in your work clothes. Your male supporters are veterans and men who work with their hands like you do. Your female supporters are wives like Marian, businesswomen like me, and flappers like Flossie."

Percy raised his eyebrows. "Sounds like a solid foundation."

"That's what we've all been trying to tell you, honey." Nettie leaned down to kiss him, but he laughed and pulled her close.

When she lost her balance and fell onto the sofa and on top of him, she laughed, and he kissed her open mouth.

When a loud knock on the door frame interrupted them, they broke away and glanced toward the door where Estelle grinned. She signed, "Bella said a car is coming up the driveway."

Percy laughed while Nettie struggled to her feet then tucked in her blouse that had become awry when she fell.

"You're no help." She rushed to the window and peered outside as the car parked. "It's Flossie and the deputy, but he's not in uniform."

"Laird? What's he doing here?" Percy growled.

"I think he might be Flossie's boyfriend, and you'd better be nice to him; they're coming inside."

After the front door opened, Nettie called out, "We're in the living room, Flossie."

Percy chuckled when Flossie whispered, "My cousin doesn't bite, but watch out for Nettie."

Nettie glared at Percy, who winked.

When Flossie and the deputy came into the living room, Percy rose and held out his hand. "Nice to see you, Laird. Is this an official visit?"

"No, sir." Laird shook Percy's hand. "Flossie told me you're running for Lieutenant Governor, and I wanted to volunteer to help however I can."

"Did you clear it with the sheriff?" Nettie asked.

"He told me I could do what I wanted on my own time, and if I wanted to take off extra time during the campaign, he'd approve it because he'd like to see Mr. Wyndham be elected too."

"Laird's an excellent photographer," Flossie said. "We need someone who could take pictures for the newspapers."

Nettie raised her eyebrows and glanced at Percy, who nodded. "We certainly do," she said. "Can you show us some photographs you've taken?"

"I have a folder in my car. Flossie said you'd want to see my work."

After Laird left, Flossie said, "His pictures are fantastic."

When Laird returned, he handed a thick folder to Percy. "I want to record what times are like now, so most of my photos are of people. Some of my photos are posed because people think that's what they're supposed to do, but I like candid shots because they're more natural and tell a story."

Percy pulled out the four by six inches pictures from the folder. "Flossie, Estelle's in the kitchen; why don't you take Laird into the kitchen for a snack while Nettie and I look at the photographs?"

"That's a great idea," Flossie said. "Laird, Estelle would be very upset if we had a guest and didn't offer them something to eat and drink." She grabbed his hand and pulled him toward the kitchen.

Percy and Nettie slowly examined the photographs.

"What do you think, sweetheart?" Percy asked.

"These are excellent. I'd like to hire him. Do you think the sheriff could get by without him until after the election?"

"We can ask; did you want him to travel with me on the campaign trail?"

"That was my thought." Nettie pointed to the next photograph. "Can you believe how well he captured the pure joy of that young boy and his puppy, and how proud the father is? You'll be the darling of the front page every Sunday, and the newspapers will love the candid shots for their dailies. It's free advertising."

"I don't know what it would take for him to develop and print the photos on the road, but I'm sure he would. Let's talk to him."

When Percy and Nettie strolled into the kitchen, Bella was signing while Flossie and Estelle chuckled at a story Laird was telling.

Flossie elbowed Laird and pointed at Percy.

Laird stopped in the middle of his story, and his cheeks pinked.

"Sorry for the interruption, Laird, but we wanted to talk to you about being the photographer for Percy's campaign, which would mean traveling with him," Nettie said.

Bella continued signing, and Estelle smiled.

"Is that possible?" Percy asked.

Laird beamed as he explained how he could process the film on the road and give prints to the local newspapers.

"Could you explain your set up to Oliver for developing and printing on the road after I talk to the sheriff tomorrow?" Percy asked.

Laird nodded. "I bought a wagon from a retired photographer; the wagon's not in very good shape, but he threw in the equipment that he'd always kept up-to-date. I repaired the inside, but it's not set up to be pulled by a motor vehicle because it was horse drawn."

"It probably won't take long for you and Oliver to have it ready to roll. I'd like a list of the supplies you need so I can order them tomorrow when we go into town," Nettie said.

Laird frowned as he cleared his throat. "I'm kind of particular about quality and use only certain suppliers."

"Okay, then tell me how much money it would take to buy what you'd want to have on hand from now until the election," Nettie said.

Laird hesitated and glanced at Flossie.

Nettie felt his silent call for help and smiled.

"If you'll give me your list of suppliers and what you'd need for two weeks, I could get you started," Flossie said. "You'll have a better idea of what you'll need after you see how close your estimate was after the first week, and then I'll order for another two weeks based on your new estimate."

Laird smiled. "I'd feel better adjusting as we go along."

"Good. Nettie, we need a telephone for the campaign if they're going to be traveling around the state," Flossie said.

Nettie narrowed her eyes. "As long as we stick to safe topics; we can't afford to have anyone repeating our strategy or where Percy will be going next."

"That's easy; no one uses the telephone except you and Bella, who will answer the telephone and take messages when you're not available," Flossie said.

Nettie glanced at Estelle and raised an eyebrow; Estelle nodded.

"Okay, that will work," Nettie said.

Estelle refilled the snack platter with sandwiches of biscuits with ham, and Percy popped one into his mouth. Estelle smiled at Laird and pointed at the food.

After Laird ate two ham biscuits, he said, "I have to go home to get ready for my shift. Thanks for everything."

Percy handed Laird his folder. "You're a talented photographer; I'll appreciate having you on board."

"I'll walk with you to your car," Flossie said.

Percy picked up another ham biscuit. "This is the last one for me."

When Flossie returned, Nettie asked, "Did you know Laird was a photographer?"

"I knew he fiddled with his camera, but I'd never seen his photographs until today. We were talking about Percy running for Lieutenant Governor, and I told Laird Percy needed to be recognized everywhere in the state like he is around here, and one thing led to another."

"I have a feeling there's a little more to your story than that, but it was a brilliant idea," Nettie said.

Flossie's face reddened. "Actually, I got the idea from you when you said Percy needed to be known statewide."

"You're still brilliant, Flossie, because you made it happen," Percy said.

Flossie's cheeks reddened, and her eyes welled up; she ducked her head.

Percy picked up the last ham biscuit as he headed toward the door. "These are my weak point, and Estelle knows it."

Percy signed, "My favorite. Thank you."

Estelle smiled and nodded as he left for the living room.

"A car turned at the driveway," Nettie said.

"It's Pappy!" Bella squealed as she signed for Estelle. Estelle smiled.

"You have sensitive hearing for your Pappy just like I have for my Percy," Nettie said.

When Oliver came into the kitchen, he kissed Estelle on her cheek then hugged Bella.

"Grab your snack, then join us in the living room," Nettie said.

When she went into the living room, Percy was sitting in her favorite yellow chair with his feet propped up on his leather footstool. He opened his eyes.

"Are you doing okay?" she asked.

"I took some time with your chair, which is almost like consulting with you, and discovered I have to pace myself; I've been fairly sedentary this past year."

Nettie stood behind him and rubbed his shoulders. "You're doing great, but are you pushing yourself too hard? I realize everyone has been pressuring you to run for lieutenant governor, me included. Give me the word, and I'll clear the way for you to decline."

"I don't want to back out. I'll be fine."

She nodded then kissed him on the top of his head before she sat on the sofa. "I'm glad you're taking breaks. It won't take you long to build yourself back to where you were."

"I know; I just get impatient, so tell me something that will make me smile."

Nettie's eyes twinkled as she glanced around then whispered, "I'm not wearing any panties."

Percy laughed. "What? Seriously?"

"No, but I made you smile." Nettie's mouth quivered as she side-glanced at him.

"That was as wicked as your smile." Percy laughed again.

Flossie followed Oliver as he strode into the living room.

"I had a successful trip into town," Oliver said. "I dropped off that red purse in the bushes next to the boarding house where Helen was staying then went to see Theresa. After I gave Theresa the soup, which she much appreciated, she remembered something she forgot to tell you. She saw the flash of a tattoo that looked like eagle's talons on his forearm when he swung the bat."

"Did she notice any other markings?" Percy asked.

"She mentioned the scar again, so I didn't press her." Oliver exhaled. "She was still shaken up."

Flossie flopped down on her favorite chair while Oliver continued, "Estelle caught me up on what she knew, including our new photographer and a telephone in the house that only Nettie will use, except Bella will take messages when Nettie's not here, which is brilliant. She said I should ask you about Laird's wagon."

"He bought his wagon from a retired farmer who was also a photographer; it was originally pulled by horses," Percy said.

"He got a good deal, and it's still perfect for developing film," Flossie said.

Nettie, Percy, and Oliver stared at her.

Flossie shrugged. "He's been teaching me how to process film and print pictures."

"When has he been doing that? Is it hard to do?" Percy asked.

Flossie snorted. "Of course, it's hard; otherwise, anybody could do it."

She flounced out of the room and stomped up the stairway to her room.

Oliver cleared his throat. "We can convert the wagon so it can be pulled by a truck without too much effort, but we might have other options, depending on how big it is. I'll go into town tomorrow and catch up with Laird to see what we can do. When do you want it ready for the road?"

"I'll have a better idea tomorrow, but I'd like to get Percy and his team on the road before the end of this upcoming week," Nettie said. "We only have four weeks before the election. The senator can help us map out a strategy to cover the state, but Percy will have to take a second pass before the election to touch base with areas that require extra attention."

"Are you going to travel with Percy?"

"No, I'll have to stay home to keep our estate running and to help Flossie with her tonic business."

Percy stretched his legs then groaned as he rose with the assistance of his cane. "I wish you could go along; I wouldn't mind having your insights."

Nettie smiled. "Maybe I can come to some of your key events; the senator can advise us on what those might be. I can see where it might be an advantage to have your wife with you once in a while."

"My preference is as much as possible. Flossie can take care of things around here and the tonic business for a few days without your help, and you can join me during the week."

"I love the idea, sweetheart, but Flossie's just starting out, and I can't dump everything on her; it's all too new to her, and me too. After all, we don't know what we don't know."

"Are you saying we're unaware that we're unaware?" Percy chuckled.

Nettie giggled. "Something like that."

Oliver shook his head. "You're about to get into one of your deep, family discussions that I never understand; I'll see you in the morning."

After Oliver left, Percy asked, "What do you think about the tattoo? Is it significant?"

"Maybe, but it's so generic, it's hard to say. Did you notice Flossie left before she answered your question about when she learned how to process film?" Nettie's eyes twinkled.

"A mere oversight on her part, I'm sure," Percy sniffed then winked. "Ready to go upstairs for a family discussion?"

Nettie fluttered her eyelashes. "I'll race you."

"Only if you'll give me a head start."

Nettie rose. "Okay. Let me know when you're ready for me to beat you."

Percy left the living room and headed up the stairs. Before he reached the next-to-last step at the top, Nettie raced past him and into their bedroom.

After Percy joined her, he growled, "You cheated; I didn't say ready."

Nettie sniffed. "I had a feeling you did."

Percy laughed and grabbed for her, but she dodged him, and he fell on the bed. When she belly flopped onto the bed next to him, they laughed together.

Chapter Eight

The next morning after breakfast, Nettie signed, "We're going into town and will be gone most of the morning. We're going to check on Theresa. I thought we'd take a little of your soup to her."

Estelle smiled as she dished up a bowlful of soup from the pot in the refrigerator and put it into a container.

Estelle signed, "Buster and I will enjoy a quiet morning. Flossie got up earlier and left with Oliver and Bella. Oliver and Flossie will drop off Bella at school then go to see Laird's wagon."

Nettie side-glanced at Percy, and he frowned.

On their way into town, Percy said, "I've been hoping Flossie would find a man she liked, but I'm not excited about the idea of a deputy sheriff hanging around."

Nettie raised an eyebrow. "Does that mean you've changed your mind about Laird being your photographer?"

"That's different," he muttered.

"Do you care to explain to me how that's different?" Nettie's eyes flashed.

When Percy gripped the steering wheel so tightly that his knuckles turned white, Nettie crossed her arms and stared out her window at the frost that still lingered on the fields that were in the shade.

Before they reached the city limits, Percy said, "A photographer won't be invited to family meals."

"Are you worried about our business or about Flossie getting hurt?"

Percy exhaled. "I'm worried a deputy sheriff would dump her when he learned about our business."

"I have an idea he already knows, but all he cares about is Flossie."

"I'm just not interested in finding out whether that's true. Where do we want to go first?"

"Let's start with the senator's office."

When they went into the senator's office, his wife, who was also his office manager, smiled. "We've been expecting you."

After they were seated in the senator's office with coffee and cookies, Percy said, "I'm going to run for lieutenant governor. We're here for any advice you can give us."

Nettie added, "We're thinking it would make sense for Percy to tour the state, and Laird has agreed to travel with Percy as his photographer."

"To take pictures for the local newspapers? That's brilliant. What else are you thinking?"

Percy summarized the discussions they'd had about different types of voters.

"I like your plan so far. You'll want to work with the local politicians. My favorite approach is to let them know I'm coming and invite them to work with my advance team, if they are interested."

"Cliff and his sister will be our advance team," Percy said.

"Good choice." The senator pulled out a folder from his desk. "This is my schedule I follow when I'm campaigning. You're welcome to look it over and change it to suit your purposes. My contacts are also in the folder."

"Do we send out the letters now?" Nettie asked.

"Yes, as soon as you have your schedule; I'd also call them to let them know you were sending a letter so they will have time to clear their schedule or suggest a different date, which reminds me of another tip. I'm not great on the telephone, so my wife wrote me a script; it's in your folder too so you'll have an idea of what I say."

"Thank you for all your encouragement and help." Percy rose, and Nettie followed his lead.

After the senator and Percy shook hands and Percy and Nettie headed to the door, the senator asked, "Did you hear about Ira's house?"

Nettie shuddered with dread at his serious tone.

Percy put his arm around her and said, "No, we haven't heard anything."

"It caught fire last night. The fire marshal is investigating it. Ira and Marian went to his farm for the weekend but left their children with his parents until the first of the year. I heard Ira's mother was a retired schoolteacher and claimed to miss teaching, so she'll be homeschooling the three children. My wife said the grandmother will discover she's not as young as she used to be, but that's true of all of us when we reach a certain age."

"That's terrible," Nettie said. "How much damage was there? Where are they?"

"Their house and everything in it was destroyed; they're staying with Marian's mother until they decide what they want to do."

"I want to stop by to see them before we go home," Nettie said.

Percy nodded. "So do I. Thank you for everything, Senator."

"Call me if you need me."

When they were in the car, Percy asked, "Where do we go next?"

"Let's stop by the telephone office and order our telephone; after that, let's pick up some food at the café for Theresa and see her before we go to Marian's mother's house."

"We may have to take Theresa to Mr. Fielding's office so she can do the paperwork to make us her shop partners."

Nettie nodded. "Our dance card just got punched for every dance the rest of the day, didn't it?"

"Sure did, but you've always been my favorite dance partner, so we'll be fine."

After they left the telephone company and were on their way to the café, Nettie said, "That was nice of the manager to offer me an office to make calls until our telephone was installed."

"I'll come with you; I don't trust any man with a smile that phony."

"You're being a little harsh; maybe he can't help being slimy."

Percy laughed as he parked at the café. "I should have known you thought the same thing I did about him."

"Why don't you wait in the car while I dash inside?" Nettie asked.

"Better yet, why don't both of us go inside and get a large mug of hot chocolate with a peppermint stick?"

While they waited for their order, Ira came into the café. Percy hailed him. "Care to join us?"

"I'd like that. Let me put in my order first."

When Ira came to their table, Nettie said, "Excuse me; I see someone I've been wanting to talk to."

Nettie strode to a table where two of the biggest town gossips sat.

"How are you doing?" she asked when she reached the table.

"You must join us; you probably don't get into town enough to catch up on the news, do you, you poor thing?" The older woman asked.

"Not nearly enough," Nettie smiled.

The server came to the table. "More hot chocolate, Nettie?"

"I'd love it." She sat at the table.

The two women exchanged glances, then the younger woman asked, "Did you ever meet the mayor's new assistant, Helen?"

Nettie furrowed her brow. "I'm not sure I have."

"She was a real piece of work. I've never known anyone so incompetent. None of us understand why the mayor didn't fire her..."

The older woman interrupted, "Some of us thought there was a little hanky-panky going on between her and the mayor, if you know what I mean."

When the server brought Nettie her cup of hot chocolate, the two women glared at her in silence.

The server rolled her eyes, and Nettie smiled. "I love your hot chocolate; thank you."

The younger woman narrowed her eyes as the server hurried back to the kitchen then cleared her throat. "From what I heard, she thought she was the cat's meow; she told a friend of mine that everyone told her she was the spitting image of Mary Pickford. Can you imagine?"

"Well, the cat with the fiddle has evidently run away with the spoon." The older woman chortled at her own joke then motioned for her companion and Nettie to settle down even though neither one of them had laughed. "Anyhoo, Miss Helen has disappeared and left a large, unpaid bill at the boarding house behind her."

The younger woman sniffed. "Well, you haven't heard the latest." She leaned on the table to be closer to the other two and whispered, "They found her red purse in the bushes at the boarding house, and the sheriff is tight-lipped, as usual."

"Nooo." The other woman's eyes widened. "What do you think? Was she robbed?"

The younger woman snorted. "Who would want to rob her? She was dirt poor. I think she was trying to make it look like she was robbed, so she'd have more time to get away."

The older woman chuckled. "Get this. She left...are you ready? A red herring." The older woman laughed so hard her chair tipped, and she almost fell.

Nettie glanced at Percy. "I'd better get back. It was nice chatting with you."

"Red herring." The older woman chuckled. "I should be on the stage."

When Nettie joined Percy and Ira, Percy said, "I didn't catch the conversation at your table, but it must have been hilarious."

Nettie rolled her eyes. "How is Marian, Ira?"

"Shook up, but both of us are glad the children were at camp."

He doesn't want it to be publicly known where the children are. Nettie nodded. "If we have time, I'd like to stop by and see her today or tomorrow; do you think that would be okay?"

"She'd love it." Ira rose. "You can count on me, Percy."

Percy rose, and the two men shook hands.

After Ira left and the server brought their food order to the table in two large sacks, Percy said, "Well, it was a well-deserved break, but we have errands, honey."

While they headed toward Theresa's house, Nettie told him the rumor about Helen.

"That's a relief; no mention of us or the estate, and no one saw Oliver. I have good news too. Ira's going to join the campaign, so we'll have the locals watching our back."

Nettie cocked her head. "Does he think an arsonist burned his house? Was it a warning?"

"He's positive it was intended to be a warning, but now Ira and the locals are determined to stop the torpedoes. If they hadn't torched his home, the locals would have remained neutral."

"It sounds like we benefited from the arson. Isn't anyone suspicious that we set the fire?"

"I asked Ira the same question, and he told me it wasn't our style because no one could match our passion and respect for family ownership of land and property."

When Percy parked in front of Theresa's house, she opened the front door and stepped out onto the porch.

Nettie bit her lip at Theresa's swollen, battered face and her black eyes. *I hate how badly she was hurt.*

Percy said, "I'll carry in the container of soup and the sacks from the restaurant. I have a few things to take care of while you visit with Theresa. I shouldn't be gone very long."

Theresa's eyes brightened when Percy carried the container and sacks inside. "Is this from the restaurant?"

Percy smiled as he left.

Nettie said, "We brought you a container of Estelle's soup, and we stopped at the restaurant and picked up a few meals for you. We knew you'd heal faster with Estelle's magical healing elixir."

"Thank you so much."

After Theresa and Nettie went into the kitchen, Theresa sat at her kitchen table.

While Nettie heated a serving of soup, Theresa said, "I thought about my loan at the bank, and I'd love for you to be my partner. I called Mr. Fielding, and he is drawing up the papers for me to sign so you can pay the loan. His assistant should be here soon with the paperwork; after I sign, she'll take it back to his office, and he'll do all the legal stuff so you can take a copy of the document to the bank."

"That's great; I'd like to get everything taken care of this morning because I have a feeling it will soon be too late."

"What kind of feeling?" Theresa asked as Nettie put the bowl of hot soup in front of her and put the sacks of food in the refrigerator before she joined Theresa at the table.

Nettie furrowed her brow. "It's the feeling you get when lightning is about to strike near you."

Theresa shuddered. "I know that prickly feeling. I'm glad we're moving fast. What else can I do?"

"Open your shop as soon as you feel up to it."

Theresa tasted her soup. "Mmm. Estelle's soup is the best. We need all the eyes and ears we can get in place, don't we?"

"That's exactly right." Nettie portioned the rest of the soup into three bowls then put them into the refrigerator. "Can you organize the shop owners in town? It would be extremely helpful to know how many torpedoes there are."

"Won't they know they're being watched?" Theresa asked.

"By the time they do, we'll know enough about them to know who their kingpin is and to block their plans. If we cut into their profits hard enough, they'll be ready to move on." Nettie exhaled as she rubbed her forehead. "I should have thought of this earlier."

Theresa patted Nettie's hand. "We're on it now."

Nettie rose. "Someone pulled into your driveway. I'll answer the door."

Mr. Fielding's assistant followed Nettie into the kitchen. She put the papers to be signed on the table then sat next to Theresa. "I'll go over the papers with you, and then you can sign them if you don't have any questions."

"After I sign the papers, can you drop me off at my shop?" Theresa asked.

"Of course, if that's what you'd like to do," the assistant said.

Nettie smiled. "I hear Percy's car; I'll talk to you later, Theresa. Please don't overdo."

After Nettie was in the car, she said, "Theresa accepted our offer to be partners. Mr. Fielding's assistant is here with the papers for Theresa to sign."

"That's a relief, isn't it? Did you want to visit with Marian at her mother's house after we pick up the papers from Mr. Fielding and go to the bank? I'm meeting Ira at his office."

"I think I'll visit Marian tomorrow when I feel less rushed, so we can spend a little time together. Can you run me home before you meet with Ira?" Nettie asked. "I want to plan your travel schedule and write your script so you can make calls this afternoon."

"Sounds good to me. Let's get this business taken care of. Ira's going to help a couple of his men like we're doing for Theresa."

"The lawyer needs a little time to pull together all the paperwork. Is there anything you'd like to do?" Nettie asked.

"I'm supposed to drop by the mayor's office sometime this morning. Are you okay with that?"

"Fine with me."

"Are you going in with me?" Percy parked in front of the mayor's office.

"I don't know; is this one of those man-to-man talks?"

"Not that I know of, but you're more in tune with people than I am."

"I'll wait in the car; that will give you an excuse to keep it short."

While Percy was in the mayor's office, a sudden chill hit Nettie, and she had goosebumps on her arms. *Percy needs me.*

She hopped out of the car and rushed into the mayor's office.

When she opened the door, Percy signed, "Thank you."

"I'm sorry to interrupt, but we have an appointment," she said.

"You're right, honey. I'd completely forgotten. The mayor was called away to a meeting."

Percy grabbed Nettie's arm and rushed her out of the office.

"What's wrong?" Nettie asked.

"The mayor's office manager is not a big fan of Doctor Doughtery. Sara thinks the doctor is getting confidential information from women."

"Like what?"

"I couldn't understand her; she went off on a wild rant that was unintelligible, so I don't have a clue."

"Is it okay with you if I see if I can find out what's wrong?"

Percy exhaled. "Only if I go with you."

"Let's do it."

When Nettie stepped into the office, Sara was sobbing. "Oh, Nettie, I'm so worried about the mayor and what's going to happen."

"If you wash your face, Sara, you'll feel better."

Sara wiped her eyes with her handkerchief. "You're right; I will, but you need to know the doctor has been drugging over half of the women in town." She blew her nose. "He's a snake, but he's gathering information for someone else."

"What kind of information?" Nettie asked. She hurried to the small lavatory, dampened a hand towel, and then took it to Sara.

Sara blotted her face with the towel. "Thanks, Nettie. Any dirt on anyone that will frighten them into silence, and he plans to blame the mayor."

She straightened her back. "Percy, I can give you details."

Sara opened a drawer and smiled as she pulled out a notebook and dropped it on the table. "The doctor spoke freely in front of me because I'm a nobody and was invisible to him. I took notes; you can have them, Percy. They're in standard shorthand. They will come in very handy after you're elected."

Percy picked up the notebook.

"What about you?" Nettie asked.

"My mother lives in Birmingham. I've been away from her too long; I'll leave after I tell the mayor goodbye. He's a good man; I owe him that."

"Are you going to be okay if we leave?" Nettie asked.

"I'll be fine; my car is packed, and my landlady is paid up through the end of the month."

Nettie hugged Sara. "Be safe."

"You too, Nettie."

Nettie and Percy left.

As he drove to the lawyer's office, Percy shook his head in disbelief. "You'd think I'd be used to it, but you're amazing, honey. Sara was incoherent when I tried to talk to her, and you waltz in and tell her to wash her face. Why?"

Nettie shrugged. "It was logical; her mascara had run down her cheeks; she was a mess."

Percy rolled his eyes.

When they went into the lawyer's office, Mr. Fielding was in a meeting. His assistant gave them the papers they would need to pay off the loan for Theresa.

On the way to the bank, Percy smiled. "Do you think we won't be welcome at the bank after today?"

"Probably; not that it will stop us, though." Nettie frowned. "Does Willis have any loans with the bank?"

Percy chuckled. "I asked him, and he said he didn't have the time to expand his crops and buy new farm equipment when everyone else did because you kept him so busy with the speakeasy."

Nettie giggled. "It's nice to be useful."

When they went into the bank, the teller paled and hurriedly closed his window. Before he reached Cartwright's office, Nettie beat him to the door.

Nettie flung open the door and raised her eyebrows as the bank manager's assistant jumped off his lap and buttoned her blouse. Cartwright's face turned red, and his neck veins pulsated.

"Now, what do you want?" he growled as the assistant bumped into the door frame in her rush to escape.

"Excuse me?" Nettie glared at the manager.

"Care to rephrase that, Arnie?" Percy roared as he stepped in front of Nettie.

Cartwright's eyes widened, and he swallowed hard. "Sorry, Mrs. Wyndham; what can I do for you today?"

"We're here to pay the rest of our loans." Nettie strolled into his office and pulled a chair next to him and sat down.

Percy closed the door and put the folder from Mr. Fielding's office on the desk as he sat in the visitor's chair in front of the bank manager.

The banker looked through the papers. "I don't know..."

Nettie interrupted. "I had coffee with a couple of lovely ladies at the restaurant this morning and heard the most shocking, juicy gossip. I'm certain they'd be interested in what I just saw, so skip the stalling tactics. Just do your job."

"Yes, ma'am." Mr. Cartwright organized the papers then systematically filled out the appropriate forms with Nettie at his elbow, watching each calculation.

After all the transactions had been completed and confirmed by Nettie, Percy held out his hand. "Pleasure doing business with you."

Cartwright hesitated then exhaled and shook Percy's hand.

When they were in the car, Percy asked, "Are we broke yet?"

"Not quite. We still have twenty large left; feel free to take us to zero if Ira can use our help to pay off any loans."

Percy side-glanced at her. "You don't care if I empty our bank account?"

"Not at all. It will be just numbers on a piece of paper when the bank closes for good."

"You really think that's going to happen? Seems like there's a lot of money floating around."

Nettie nodded. "Bank money floats like soap bubbles; one minor blip, and they'll all pop. It's inevitable."

When they neared their driveway, Nettie said, "Drop me at the road; I need the walk to think. I have to be certain we've plugged as many holes as possible before it's too late."

After Percy pulled into the driveway and stopped, he stroked the back of her neck with his fingertips. "Is there something I should be doing?"

Nettie closed her eyes and sighed while Percy massaged her neck. "You're doing it."

She blew him a kiss then opened her car door. "Actually, the connection with Ira and his group is crucial. When you get back, we'll go over your schedule and telephone script. We can decide whether you want to return to town for telephone calls, or if we need to rework the schedule or the script, then we can make the calls in the morning."

When Nettie reached the house, she hurried to her sewing room that doubled as her office. She quietly closed the door and tossed her coat onto a chair. After she sat at her small desk in the corner, Nettie purposely set her mind to ignore any distractions.

As she studied the senator's schedule and his contacts at each stop and took notes, she briefly paused when she thought she heard a car, but shook her head and continued her intense focus on the schedule.

After she sketched out a draft schedule, she edited it into a final schedule for Percy to review and set it aside.

Nettie rolled her shoulders then read the script the senator's wife wrote. She tapped her pen as she read it again.

"It sounds like the senator," she mumbled. "I need to write a script that sounds like Percy."

She set aside the document and gazed outside at a young squirrel that jumped from the top branches of an old, tall oak to a nearby branch of another oak.

Nettie wrote a script that sounded like Percy was next to her, dictating what he wanted to say. After she was satisfied, Nettie stretched her back and strolled to the living room to check in with Flossie. She smiled when she found the room empty. *Of course, she's in the kitchen with Bella, Buster, and Estelle.*

When she opened the kitchen door, Bella screamed, "You're okay!"

Buster scrambled to Nettie while Bella grabbed her grandmother's arm and pointed at Nettie.

Estelle's eyes widened, and she grabbed onto the counter.

Bella sobbed and put her arms around Nettie's waist. "A man came to the house and told us you and Mr. Percy had been badly hurt in a car wreck outside of town. He told Flossie he could take her to the hospital, and she went with him."

"Did you know the man? What did he look like?"

Bella straightened her back and brushed away the tears. "We didn't know him; he had a scar on the left side of his face that went from his jaw to the corner of his mouth."

Nettie turned to Estelle and signed, "I have to find Flossie."

Estelle signed, "Oliver has the truck; take our car. The keys are on the floorboard."

"I'm going with you," Bella said.

Nettie spoke as she signed, "You have to stay here and be your granny's ears to protect her."

Bella glared at her then sighed and nodded.

Before Nettie left the kitchen, Estelle grabbed her arm and then signed, "How can Percy find you?"

Nettie quickly signed, "I'll head back toward town. I'll leave a note in the car if I see anything."

Nettie ran to her sewing room and grabbed her warm coat and purse with her derringer. When she rushed past the living room to the back door, Bella blocked her way and handed her a pad of pink paper and a pen.

"Granny said you will need a pad and pen to leave a note. We know you'll find Flossie because you'll have a feeling."

Nettie exhaled and stuck the pad and pen into her coat pocket. "Tell your granny thank you, and I'll remember to pay attention to my feelings."

As Nettie hurried to Oliver's car, she listened to the buzz of the cicadas. When she heard a second group of cicadas echo the first, she exhaled. *We'll have rain this evening.*

She smoothed back her hair from her face with both hands and sighed as her wildly frizzled hair stubbornly bounced back into her eyes. *Even my hair agrees.*

On her way into town, Nettie intently scanned the landscape for any signs of Flossie or a car. When she slowed as she came to the driveway of the abandoned house that Flossie wanted to renovate, she frowned as a sudden thought struck her. *Flossie is in an abandoned building.*

Nettie abruptly turned then continued at a crawl toward the old house while she scrutinized both sides of the overgrown driveway.

After she parked, Nettie climbed out of the car to inspect the once-impressive house that was in an imminent state of collapse.

She stroked the massive columns that had been the major support for the now-collapsed roof over the wraparound porch. "We can't rebuild the house, but we can repurpose your magnificent beams and siding in another house so others can enjoy your beauty."

After she continued her inspection by methodically strolling around the house, Nettie narrowed her eyes at the front door. "Flossie isn't here, is she?"

A powerful gust of wind suddenly swept through the tops of the trees, and the old house groaned.

Nettie cocked her head. "I won't find an abandoned shack in town, will I? I'm headed in the wrong direction."

She jumped into Oliver's car and sped toward her home.

Chapter Nine

After Nettie passed her driveway, she slowed to a crawl as she peered into the woods at the side of the road. When she reached the driveway that led to the barn, she slammed her hands on the steering wheel. "I missed it."

She gritted her teeth as she pulled into the driveway and followed the ruts that defined the path to the barn. When she reached the barn, she parked. *The shack would be closer to the road.*

Nettie stared at her flowing skirt and the strappy heels she had worn to go into town and shook her head. *This is not cross-country attire.*

She quickly searched Oliver's car and found a pair of his overalls. When she held them up to herself, she snorted. "I'd have to be at least a foot taller to wear these."

Nettie tossed the overalls back into the car and furrowed her brow. *There has to be a way to get to the shack from the driveway because the sides of the ditch are too steep along the road.*

She trudged down the driveway until she spotted tire tracks that abruptly turned from the driveway into the brush. She exhaled and followed the flattened brush tracks. After she turned her ankle a second time in her attempt to move as fast as she could, she slowed her pace and more carefully picked her steps. When she came to a thick patch of blackberry bushes, the tracks stopped.

She furrowed her brow. *They must have parked here. Now what?*

She examined the ground then saw drag marks going into a patch of blackberries that was between her and the road. She fished out her gloves from her coat pockets and put her arms up to protect her face as she turned toward the road and pushed into the bushes. The thorns snagged her coat and scratched her legs, but she kept moving. *I'm getting close.*

After she broke through the bushes, she stepped into the high, dry weeds and grass that was as tall as she was. *I hope it's too cold for snakes.*

When she suddenly came to a clearing, Nettie gasped at the dilapidated, small wooden building in front of her. She took a step back into the tall grass and crouched as she listened to the wind rustling the treetops. She scanned the area from her hidden vantage point and peered at a shallow hole with the shovel planted in a pile of dirt next to it like a marker. *It looks like a shallow grave.*

Nettie jumped when raucous crows flew overhead in a relentless pursuit of a hawk as it twisted and turned in the air to escape from the harassing birds.

She crept to the building and held her breath as she slid back the heavy wooden bar across the door. When she opened the door, her heart ached at the terror in Flossie's eyes.

"It's Nettie, Flossie. I'm taking you out of here."

Nettie pulled out her small folding knife from her purse and cut the ropes binding Flossie's feet and hands. After Nettie pulled down the gag across Flossie's mouth, Flossie said, "They'll be back any minute."

Nettie helped Flossie to her feet.

"Is there a fast way to get to the barn?" Nettie asked.

Flossie nodded then groaned as she put her hands on her head. "Yes. My head hurts."

"Let's get out of here." Nettie held onto Flossie's elbow until they were outside.

Nettie returned the bar to the door, then put her arm around Flossie's waist to help her walk.

"Can you do this, Nettie? I'm taller than you and outweigh you by at least forty pounds," Flossie whispered.

"I'm strong; we'll be fine."

Flossie pointed toward the tall grass behind the shack. "That's our path. It parallels the driveway."

"Okay, take a step, and I'll match you."

Flossie lost her balance on her first step. Nettie clutched Flossie's belt and grunted as she kept Flossie from falling.

"Told you," Nettie said. "I'm strong. It's not a race; take it slow."

Flossie exhaled, and they moved forward.

Nettie exhaled in relief when the grass thinned so she could see her feet and watch her steps.

After they had staggered through the weeds in what Nettie estimated to be halfway, Flossie stopped. "I need to lie down and rest a minute."

"Is there a way to get to the house from here?"

Flossie rubbed her head. "I think the shortcut is just ahead."

"Can you make it to the house?"

"No."

"Then let's just get to the shortcut."

"Just to the shortcut," Flossie mumbled as she took a step when Nettie took a step and pulled Flossie with her. "This is the shortcut." Flossie tried to sit, but Nettie jerked up on her belt.

"Let's just get to the house," Nettie said.

"Just to the house." Flossie took a step.

By the time they stepped into the driveway, tears from the excruciating pain of strained muscles soaked Nettie's coat collar. She called out, "Bella."

Bella raced out of the back door.

"I knew you'd find her."

"Tell your granny I need help to get Flossie inside."

Bella ran into the house and returned with Estelle.

After Estelle took away Flossie's weight from Nettie, Nettie collapsed on the ground, and Bella gasped.

"Help your granny; I'll be right behind you."

Bella quickly signed, and Estelle nodded and then half-carried Flossie to the house.

"Granny has Miss Flossie." Bella helped Nettie to her feet.

"I'm fine; I just wore out," Nettie said.

"Your legs are bleeding."

When Bella opened the back door, Nettie groaned, "I want to clean up before Percy gets home, except I hear his car."

"We can do it. You rinse off your legs, and I'll grab a pair of trousers for you."

"And a blouse, socks, and shoes." Nettie's eyes twinkled as they went inside. "Meet me in the kitchen. Go."

Bella raced up the stairs while Nettie hobbled into the kitchen and pulled off her coat and dress. After she tossed her coat, dress, and shoes into the pantry, she soaked a dish cloth then rinsed off the blood on her legs and dried them. While she tossed the dish cloth and towel into the closet, Bella returned with her clothes and helped her dress.

"Granny took Miss Flossie to the living room," Bella said.

"Let's go. I'll put on my socks and shoes there."

When Nettie and Bella went into the living room, Estelle raised her eyebrows at Nettie.

Bella quickly signed, "Percy is here."

Estelle nodded and then signed, "Flossie has a knot on her head."

Nettie signed, "She told me her head hurt."

Bella signed, "I'll get some ice, Granny."

When Bella returned with ice wrapped in a towel, she handed it to Flossie. "Here's an ice pack for the bump on your head."

Flossie put the ice pack on her head and glared at Nettie. "Estelle is letting me rest. She isn't mean."

The back door slammed.

Nettie nodded. "Good. Why does your head hurt?"

"That man hit me on my head after I climbed into his car. He said you were in a crash. Are you okay?"

"I wasn't..."

"What's going on? What's wrong with Flossie?" Percy asked.

Nettie signed, "Star, can you take care of Flossie? I have to talk to Percy."

Estelle nodded.

"Let's go into the kitchen, and I'll tell you. Estelle and Bella will take care of Flossie."

After they were in the kitchen, Percy asked, "Before you say anything, are you okay?"

"Yes. Can I tell you everything from start to finish, with no interruptions?"

"No."

Nettie glared at him.

"I'll make you a cup of tea." Percy turned on the burner to heat the water in the tea kettle. "Do you want any crackers or cookies?"

Percy headed toward the pantry.

"No, thank you. Do you want to sit at the table, or would we be more comfortable in the dining room?"

Percy frowned. "Why do I feel like I need a little fortification in my tea to get me through what you're about to tell me?"

Nettie shrugged. "It's your suspicious side; let's sit in the dining room."

After they carried their tea to the dining room, they sat together at the end of the table near the kitchen.

Percy sipped his tea then set down his cup and sighed. "I'd rather have Estelle's coffee; tell me what happened to Flossie."

"After you dropped me off at the driveway, I came into the house by the front door and immediately went to my sewing room to study the senator's schedule and his telephone script. I used them as a template, but changed the schedule around to minimize the time you would be on the road and rewrote the script so it's in your voice. I have your schedule and script ready for you to review."

"That's great. Are we going to do that right after you tell me about what happened to Flossie?"

Nettie sighed. "Okay. I went to the kitchen, and Estelle and Bella told me a man came to the house and told Flossie we'd been badly injured in a crash. She left with him after he offered to take her to the hospital where we were supposed to be."

Percy slammed his fist on the table. "That shouldn't have happened. We have to have a code word, so it doesn't happen again."

Nettie furrowed her brow. "You're right; we should have thought of that earlier when Bella came to live with Estelle and Oliver. Bella told me the man had a scar on his face. Her description of the man who took Flossie was the same as the man who attacked Theresa."

Percy's tone was clipped. "I have to talk to Ira. Is that all?"

"I had a feeling I'd find Flossie in an abandoned building. Oh dear, I left Oliver's car at the barn."

"We'll take care of it, but why did you take Oliver's car and where did you find Flossie?"

"I borrowed the car to look for Flossie; Estelle gave me permission. At first I thought Flossie would be at the abandoned house, but she wasn't. Flossie told me about the shack near the barn, so I went to the barn and searched for the shack."

"I'd like to hear all the details you left out..."

When Nettie glared at him, Percy continued, "I know you, doll, don't waste your breath denying it. We can argue later, but I have to talk to Ira right away. I'll drop you off at the barn, so you can bring back Oliver's car, and then I'll go into town. Ira will know who the man with the scar is, and who he works for."

"I'd really appreciate the ride; I'm not sure I'm up to another battle through blackberry bushes today."

After they were in the car and on their way to the barn, Nettie said, "I forgot to tell you about the hole."

"What are you talking about?"

"There was a hole that look freshly dug; it reminded me of a shallow grave."

Percy side-glanced at Nettie. "I'll follow you back to the house to be sure you don't have any problems with Oliver's car. Sometimes it's temperamental."

Nettie narrowed her eyes. "Now you're the one leaving out details. I'll take you up on your offer to argue later."

After Nettie climbed out of the car, she used all her strength to slam the passenger door to let Percy know how annoying he was. Unfortunately, the door latch didn't catch because the heavy door swung so slowly, and there was no satisfying slam. Percy reached over and pulled the door closed. Nettie pursed her lips as she stormed to Oliver's car.

After she sped down the barn driveway with Percy on her tail, she slid into a turn onto the road, accelerated out of the slide, and floored it. Percy stayed within inches of her bumper.

When she neared her driveway, she tapped her brake.

As she turned, Percy beeped his horn and shouted as he continued toward town, "Good run, doll. Thanks!"

Nettie mumbled, "He thought I was playing."

After she parked, she shook her head. *He got away without looking at the schedule or script. I slipped up on that one. How can he be so completely infuriating and clueless?*

. When she reached the house, Bella met her at the back door.

"Mr. Willis is waiting for you in the kitchen. Granny is in the living room with Flossie who requested tea and cookies."

"I don't want Flossie to take advantage of your granny, but I'm glad she's better," Nettie said.

Bella smiled. "She won't get away with it for long. Granny said she'll spoil Flossie a little today because she's happy Flossie is okay."

"We all are; maybe Mr. Willis has good news too."

When Nettie went into the kitchen, Willis sat at the counter with a cup of coffee and a plate of cookie crumbs. He pointed at the plate. "I was going to save you a cookie so you could join me in my pity party, but I got carried away. The torpedoes beat us to it. They bought up all the moonshine and paid for two months of additional product in advance, with bonuses for extra product."

Nettie narrowed her eyes. "It's time to play dirty. They want a war? I'll be happy to oblige; we'll smash their torpedoes, and I'll personally sink their ship with the kingpin on it."

Willis raised his eyebrows. "I'm not sure what you said, but you made it sound easy; I'm in."

"We can't let Percy in because he has to focus on his campaign."

Willis stared at her. "How are you going to pull that off?"

"If Ira takes care of the torpedoes, Percy will be more willing to focus on his campaign, and he'll be following a tight schedule."

"Won't he become the kingpin's target?"

"Cliff and Laird will have his back."

"Laird, the deputy?"

"Laird's going to be Percy's photographer and will be traveling with him."

Willis nodded. "So, what are we going to do?"

"We're going to steal the whiskey."

Willis stared at her. "A heist?"

"Sure! The grandest flim-flam of all times."

"That's going to take an army."

"You'd think so, wouldn't you? Does anyone know where they plan to store all this product?"

"Only the kingpin knows, according to the moonshiners and their torpedo contacts." Willis smirked. "However, there's an old cotton gin six miles north of town in the middle of nowhere that has been undergoing renovation for some rich city fella recently. It's been a topic of conversation among the farmers who sit around the pickle barrel at the hardware store every morning because no one plans to grow cotton this year with the price of cotton so low. The farmers concluded the city fella must have fallen for a scam that claimed cotton prices are going to shoot up."

"I'll bet it's our kingpin, because that's the perfect cover for a warehouse." Nettie raised an eyebrow as she tapped her finger on the counter in thought. "It also might explain why Percy became a threat when the talk of him running for lieutenant governor erupted. The kingpin has to be nervous about his warehouse being in Percy's home territory."

Willis nodded. "Now the kingpin not only has to focus on shutting down your operation, but also stopping Percy's campaign. He has to keep Percy from being elected because all the kingpin's political eggs are in the incumbent's basket. The incumbent's campaign will probably drop into a dirt-smearing campaign, but Percy can handle that."

Nettie smiled. "So, we are the target of the kingpin. He didn't expect any resistance to filling his warehouse at a discount price, so you forced him to buy moonshine at a premium price, and he definitely can't deal with an honest politician at the state level."

Willis rubbed his chin. "Yes, but he's got whiskey, and you don't, so you're out of business. How would that stop Percy's campaign?"

"He'll send the torpedoes after me. If they are successful, the kingpin expects Percy to drop his campaign and rush home to defend me."

Willis nodded. "That's exactly what Percy would do, except Ira will stop the torpedoes."

"I want to see the warehouse, but I'd have to leave right away. Is Oliver around? I'd like for him to keep an eye on Estelle, Bella, and Flossie while I'm gone."

"I'll brief him, and we can leave as soon as he's in the house."

After Willis left, Nettie grabbed her soiled clothes from the pantry and rushed to the living room.

Bella tapped Estelle's arm and pointed at Nettie.

Nettie signed, "Willis and I are leaving on some business. Oliver will be working in the house if you need him."

Estelle raised an eyebrow and signed, "We'll stay inside."

"Thank you," Nettie signed.

As Nettie turned, Bella jumped up. "We'll wash your clothes; don't forget your warm coat."

Bella took the clothes before Nettie could protest and headed to the laundry room.

Nettie glanced at Estelle, who smiled and signed, "She was worried you might get cold."

Nettie returned her smile and signed, "Estelle, we need a code word, so Bella knows if someone claims to have a message from us, it's not phony. What do you think?"

Estelle furrowed her brow and then smiled as she signed, "Star."

Nettie chuckled. "That's perfect. No one would ever guess it. Star is our code word."

She raced up the stairs for her warm coat and to change her shoes for boots.

After Oliver came inside, he said, "My project for the day is the dumbwaiter."

"Flossie and I planned to move the hospitality room to my sewing room, so the dumbwaiter doesn't have to be done right away," Nettie said.

"We can move the hospitality room to the main floor whenever you like, but I still want to finish the project," Oliver said. "It will be in operation before the weekend if it's needed."

On her way out, Nettie picked up her walking stick and smiled. *Oliver hates an unfinished project.*

As she climbed into Willis's work truck, she said, "I assumed we wouldn't park at the gin."

Willis chuckled. "I forgot to mention we'd have to hike through the woods, but I see you figured that out."

After they'd gone five miles north of town, Willis slowed. "If the gin sign is still up, you might see it down the road on the right."

When Willis slowed even more as he went past the road, Nettie narrowed her eyes as she inspected both sides of the intersecting road for the gin's sign.

"I see it. I would have left it up too."

Willis slowed down even more. "There should be a driveway along here somewhere."

Nettie pointed. "Is that it?"

Willis turned. "Looks like a cow path, doesn't it? The farmhouse burned down twenty years ago."

Nettie clung to the dash and her arm rest while the truck rolled from side to side and bucked as Willis drove through the brush and high weeds until he came to a brick chimney in a clearing.

"Kind of like riding a bronco, wasn't it? What do we want to learn?" Willis asked.

"Their level of security, number of doors, any signs of activity or weakness."

As they neared the gin, they stopped and listened to men arguing.

"Can you hear what they're saying?" Willis asked.

Nettie nodded. "The delivery door is locked, and they don't know what to do. Nobody has a key or knows who's in charge. This is ripe for a heist."

Willis smiled. "Do you have any scratch on you?"

"Always." Nettie pulled out a wad of bills from her wallet and gave it to Willis.

"Stay low." Willis strode into the woods to his truck.

A few minutes later, Nettie's eyes widened as she heard Willis's truck pull up at the gin.

His door slammed. "I was afraid of this. That old drunk gave you the wrong address. This location won't be ready for another week."

The men grumbled, and a few voices were angry.

Nettie crept closer to the edge of the woods as the men settled down. *Willis has taken control.*

Willis said, "I don't blame you one bit for being mad, and I can guarantee you this won't happen again. Here's something for your trouble, and here's the correct address for your delivery. You'll get another bonus for your time when you get there."

A few minutes later, the last truck rumbled away.

"Come on, Nettie. We have to beat them to the barn. I know a short cut."

Nettie stepped out of the woods, and the two of them rushed to Willis's truck.

As Willis sped down back roads toward the barn, he said, "I picked the lock on the delivery door and looked inside. There were only a few barrels of whiskey in them. I left the door unlocked. After we get to the barn, I'll give you my shotgun. Stand near the barn where the drivers can see you when they unload."

"Aren't we worried they'll recognize me and tell where they dropped off the whiskey?"

"The men work for the bootleggers; they'll report back that you paid them extra to deliver the whiskey to you, and the bootleggers will love it. When the kingpin complains to the bootleggers he didn't get his delivery, the bootleggers will tell him their drivers delivered the whiskey on time at the gin, but no one there to receive it, so they left it."

Nettie grinned. "That's going to cause a ruckus between the bootleggers and the kingpin."

Willis chuckled. "Won't it, though? You'll be the bootleggers' favorite customer."

"I love it; I don't need the shotgun because everybody knows I carry a derringer. This saves me all that time and effort in finding the kingpin. He'll come after me."

Willis's face paled. "I didn't put that together. What do we do?"

Nettie rubbed her hands together. "Whatever else we can think of to distract the kingpin's attention from Percy."

When Willis turned at the barn driveway, Nettie pulled out her lipstick and applied her signature red to her mouth. She smacked her lips together while she put away the tube. "Does my hair look okay?"

Willis laughed.

Chapter Ten

When they heard the first truck rumble up the driveway, Nettie said, "Tell the drivers to unload the whiskey and stack it next to the barn. If you'll keep a tally of how many barrels or cases were on each truck, I'll pay them their bonus after they unload."

Willis strode to the driveway and directed the drivers where to park and unload.

After the first driver backed his truck to the barn, he hopped out to unload. When he saw Nettie, he grinned. "Hey, Miss Nettie. It's always a pleasure doing business with you."

After he unloaded and Willis showed Nettie the total, Nettie gave the driver his bonus and shook his hand. "Thank you for your help."

"Yes, ma'am. You treat people right, and we appreciate you."

After the last truck was unloaded, Willis said, "If you'll take my truck to the house and send Oliver here to help me, it won't take long for us to put away our plunder."

Nettie chuckled. "Whiskey pirates has a nice ring to it, doesn't it? Do you think it would help if we let Ira in on what we're doing?"

Willis exhaled and scratched his head. "Ordinarily, I'd say no, but under the circumstances, I think Ira can use the information to undermine the torpedo leadership."

"I trust Ira too."

"After Oliver and I have stored our new stash of moonshine, I'll go into town to let Ira know what we've done so far while you come up with our next steps."

When Nettie arrived at the house, Bella opened the back door for her.

"We've kept the doors locked because Pappy is working upstairs. Mr. Willis's truck isn't as loud as the rest of them, but I heard it when you turned at the driveway," Bella said.

"I'm glad you're keeping the doors locked. How's Flossie doing?"

Bella grinned. "She's tired of being hurt and is arguing with Granny about taking it easy."

Nettie smiled. "She's back to normal, then. I have to talk to your pappy, and then I'll come back down to the living room."

Nettie found Oliver putting away his tools in the meeting room.

He wiped his brow with his handkerchief before he closed his tool box. "I've done everything I can until Willis can help me with the last steps to put it into operation. Is he back?"

"No, he's at the barn. He needs your help to store our latest delivery. I drove his truck here; you can take it back."

Oliver raised his eyebrows. "Another delivery? That was fast."

"Willis will fill you in."

As they headed to the stairs, Oliver said, "I'll bet the story about this delivery is a doozy."

When they reached the living room, Oliver kissed Estelle and hugged Bella, and then left.

Estelle signed, "Flossie is all yours; I have work to do."

After Estelle and Bella left, Flossie said, "It's about time you rescued me from that devious tyrant. Every time I tried to get up, Estelle would bring me another snack. She knew I was too polite to turn down anything she cooks or bakes."

Nettie nodded her head. "Always watch out for the quiet ones."

Flossie burst out laughing, and Nettie smiled.

After Flossie caught her breath, she asked, "What can I do to help?"

Nettie raised an eyebrow. "I have a schedule for Percy's campaign and a script for his telephone calls. I could sure use a second pair of eyes because he'll just glance at them and say they're fine."

"Bring them on." Flossie leaned back and put her feet on the footstool next to her.

"Let's go into my office."

Flossie narrowed her eyes. "Are you just tricking me into giving up my invalid status?"

Nettie raised her eyebrows. "Your choice."

Flossie groaned as she slowly rose from the sofa. "You're just mean."

When Nettie turned on her heel and strode to her sewing room, Flossie exhaled and followed her.

Nettie picked up the schedule from her desk then narrowed her eyes. "Do you feel well enough to hold a sheet of paper and read?"

"Ha, ha." Flossie snatched away the schedule and furrowed her brow as she read. "This fourth stop is backtracking. Is that on purpose?"

Nettie stood next to Flossie and studied the schedule. "This is awful; I should have remembered I automatically put things in order. This schedule is completely predictable; by the third stop, the kingpin will have his thugs waiting for Percy. We have to mix this up."

"I'm pretty random; why don't I take a shot at it?"

After Flossie renumbered all the stops, Nettie studied it.

"This is perfect; it's so random, it makes my head hurt. I only have one change."

After Nettie switched two numbers, she pulled out the map and traced the revised route with her pencil. "What do you think?"

"It makes my random heart happy," Flossie said.

Nettie drew arrows on her schedule. "I'll fix it before I give it to Percy. What about the script?"

Flossie furrowed her brow as she read and then sat in the office chair at Nettie's desk while she studied the script. "This is very good, except it sounds like you, not Percy. Can I spend a little time on it?"

"I'd appreciate it. I can sort through my fabric to select what I'll take into town this week while you do," Nettie said.

While Nettie folded pieces of fabric and put them into her tote bag, Flossie mumbled while she crossed out and rewrote sentences.

After thirty minutes, Flossie dropped her pencil on the paper and leaned back in her chair. "I think I've caught the essence of Percy on paper. See what you think."

Nettie read the revisions. "This is excellent. Your changes are so natural I could have sworn I've heard Percy use these exact words when he has talked about running for lieutenant governor."

Flossie raised an eyebrow. "I know. I've been tagging around behind him since I could walk."

Nettie laughed when Flossie hooked her thumbs in her belt and swaggered around the room and stopped at the door to catch her breath.

Nettie joined Flossie at the door and put her arm around her. "Well done, Flossie. I'm convinced you're a Percy expert. I'll help you to the living room."

After Flossie sat on the sofa and put up her feet, Nettie went into the kitchen.

Estelle pointed to Buster. Bella said, "We think Buster needs to go out, but Granny wouldn't let me go out by myself."

"I'll grab my coat, and you put on yours, and we'll take Buster outside," Nettie said.

When they went outside, Buster trotted to the front of the house, and then stopped while he sniffed the air. He growled then barked.

"What is it?" Bella asked.

Buster's bark became more insistent.

Nettie furrowed her brow then deeply inhaled. "I smell smoke."

Bella pointed past the woods toward the road in front of the barn. "The wind's coming from that direction."

Nettie scanned the horizon where Bella pointed. "You're right; I don't see anything, do you?"

When two sharp, explosive sounds came from the same direction as the smell of smoke, Bella asked, "Were those gunshots?"

"Could have been, but it's more likely a car backfired. Why don't you and Buster run inside and get warm? I'll be there in a few minutes."

Bella ran to the back door with Buster on her heels.

The hair on the back of Nettie's neck rose when she heard the roar of a speeding car heading toward their driveway. *It's too soon for the kingpin to show up, but we still need a plan for torpedoes. Flossie and I can ambush them, but Estelle and Bella have to be safe.*

She hurried toward the back of the house and then breathed a sigh of relief as the car zoomed past their driveway and continued toward town.

When Nettie strolled inside, Bella and Buster met her in the hallway.

"The wind is picking up; I need a cup of hot tea."

"Granny put on the kettle because she said it would be colder today," Bella said.

While she sat in the kitchen and sipped her tea, Nettie signed, "There may be trouble for us because Percy is running for lieutenant governor. We're his most vulnerable spot; there could be an attack on the house."

Estelle signed, "The speakeasy is our tornado shelter; we would be safe there."

Oliver joined them in the kitchen.

"Willis has the updated numbers for you, Nettie, if you'd like to record them," Oliver said. "He went to your sewing room because that's where he thought you would be."

When Nettie hurried down the hall, her eyes widened at the drops of blood that led to her sewing room. She rushed to the room and opened the door. Willis held a fabric scrap against his left upper arm. The fabric was soaked with blood.

"It's just a graze, but it's bleeding like crazy."

Nettie cut away his shirtsleeve at the shoulder then folded a piece of fabric into a compress. She examined the wound. "You're right; it is just a graze, and the bleeding has slowed down."

While she wrapped the compress onto his arm with a wide strip of cloth, Willis said, "We heard someone driving up the driveway, and it sounded like they stopped at the shack, so I went to investigate. Two guys had stacked small limbs against the front door of the shack. They must have found the limbs in the woods because they were still damp from the dew. They lit them off, but it wasn't much of a fire. I yelled, and one guy fired at me, and I returned his fire. The second guy jumped into their car and raced away."

"Did either of them have a scar on his face?"

"I didn't get a good look at the man who abandoned his partner."

"What about the guy you shot?"

"He didn't have a scar on his face. He had eagle talons tattooed on his arm. Oliver and I will take care of him."

She ripped more strips of cloth to secure the compress; after she secured the dressing, she said, "I'll make you a sling, so you won't reopen the wound."

"That would be too restrictive; I'll be careful."

Willis threw his coat over his shoulders before he grabbed up the bloody shirt sleeve and the rest of the blood-soaked scraps of cloth. "I'll drop these into the burn barrel and take care of them later."

Nettie pointed to his coat. "I can repair the rip in your sleeve."

Willis tossed his coat over the back of the visitor's chair then strode out of the room and called out, "Break's over, Oliver. I'll meet you out back."

Nettie grabbed a scrap of fabric and hurried to the bathroom to dampen it. After she wiped up the blood from the floor in the hallway and in her sewing room, she rushed outside and dropped the rag into the burn barrel.

When she returned to her sewing room, she found a scrap of fabric that matched Willis's coat. After she repaired the small tear in the coat's liner, she created a patch for the coat sleeve and sewed it on with tiny, invisible stitches.

Nettie put on her coat and went to the kitchen with Willis's coat over her arm.

Flossie kneaded bread while Estelle stirred a pot of soup on the stove, and Bella washed dishes. Bella tapped Estelle's arm.

Nettie signed, "Willis forgot his coat."

"They're at the barn. You can take it to him; we'll be fine," Estelle signed.

Flossie nodded then brushed away the hair that had fallen onto her forehead with the back of her flour-covered hands.

When Bella snickered, Flossie asked, "Did I get flour in my hair? It's the latest look."

After Flossie strolled to the sink and tapped a floured finger on Bella's chin, Bella giggled. "Now, I've got the latest look too."

Nettie bit her lip and furrowed her brow.

Flossie said, "Estelle said we'd be okay, and we will. I locked the front door earlier, and we'll lock the back door behind you."

Nettie nodded as Bella followed her to the back door.

"People don't understand Miss Flossie is fierce," Bella said.

Nettie paused. "You're right; even I forget sometimes. Keep an eye on her for me, though."

Nettie hiked along the path through the brush and woods to the barn. When she reached the building, all the doors were locked, and no one was there. She continued down the driveway to the shack and exhaled in relief when she saw both of their trucks.

When Willis came around from the front of the shack, he frowned then waved. "What are you doing here, Nettie? Is something wrong?"

"I brought your coat."

Willis wore a red plaid flannel shirt as she strode up the driveway to join Nettie before she reached the sack.

"Thanks. We're going to be here a while. You probably don't want to stand around in the cold, so we'll see you later at the house."

Nettie narrowed her eyes. "I'll be fine. What's going on? Are you burying your attacker?"

Willis exhaled. "It's more complicated than that. I walked down and on my way, I heard them arguing. The two guys were ordered to call attention to the bodies in the shed with a fire."

Nettie cocked her head as she furrowed her brow. "Bodies?"

Willis nodded. "They brought a body here and expected to find Flossie's body in the shack. You don't want to go into the shed, Nettie. Helen has been dead for two days."

"Who did they expect to be blamed for the deaths?"

"They didn't care who; their purpose was to cause a scandal that implicated Percy after two women were found dead on Percy's property and someone tried to burn their bodies. We thought we'd bury both bodies, but I'm useless for digging, and it would take Oliver all night to dig two graves."

"Did they have Helen wrapped in anything?" Nettie asked.

"Her body was wrapped in a tattered section of canvas that looks like a sail."

"Let's take her body to the old launch by the river and drop off your attacker on the edge of the overgrown parking lot."

"I can do it alone after Oliver helps me put the bodies in the back of my truck."

"Oliver can return to the house to work on the dumbwaiter, so I can go with you."

Willis cocked his head. "I don't see how you can help; I can take care of this."

"Not without me," Nettie said.

Willis rubbed his forehead with his fingertips. "Is this one of your feelings? I'll be in trouble with Percy if he finds out you went with me."

Nettie glared at him. "No, this isn't one of my feelings. Percy can't be involved in this at all; if we mentioned anything about it to him, he'd want to fix it or shield me."

"You're right; I'll talk to Oliver, and we'll load the bodies into the back of my truck."

"Good; we don't have any time to waste because we have to be back at the house before Percy returns."

Willis spoke quietly and briefly with Oliver. After the two bodies were loaded into the back of Willis's truck, Oliver strode toward the barn.

On their way down the driveway, Willis said, "After the stop at the abandoned marina, I want to go to the sheriff's office and report seeing a possible body. I don't like the idea of leaving anyone out where predators could drag them away. The best way to shield Percy is for you to be at home. The risk of not making it back in time is too high."

Nettie exhaled and furrowed her brow. "You're right, and I like your idea of reporting only one body so the sheriff's office can find the other. Why would you have gone to the marina in the first place?"

Willis smiled as he turned at the Wyndhams' driveway. "Everybody knows I carry a fishing pole in the back of my truck, so no one would be surprised the marina is one of my favorite spots to fish and think."

Nettie smiled. "Maybe I'll throw a few sticks and small limbs into our burn barrel."

"That's an excellent cover if anyone else reports the smell of smoke, and thanks for the great repair job you did on my coat. It wasn't a large tear, but it was obvious enough to draw attention to my upper arm."

"I have to ask where did the red flannel shirt come from?"

"Oliver told me Estelle worries he will get caught in a rain shower, so she makes sure he has a change of clothes in a bag in his truck."

After Willis dropped Nettie off, she strolled to the back door, and Bella met her outside. "Pappy told me Mr. Willis might bring you home later, but I thought he meant much later."

"We finished up earlier than we expected. I have to collect a few sticks and limbs for the burn barrel so we can set it on fire. Want to help me?"

"That sounds like fun; what are we really burning?"

Nettie chuckled. "You're learning. We're really burning what's already in the burn barrel because it's getting too full."

Bella side-glanced at Nettie. "That was a Miss Nettie answer."

"It certainly was. You're getting good at interpreting clues."

"I still have a ways to go before I'll be at your level." Bella's mouth twitched into a smile, and her eyes lit up. "But I'll get there."

Nettie nodded. "It won't be long."

After they had flames dancing and smoke curling up from the burn barrel, Nettie and Bella stood back to admire their fire skills at work.

After the fire became smoldering ashes, Nettie said, "Dump our bucket of water over the fire, then go inside. I'll be there in a minute."

After Bella doused the ashes, she said, "Mr. Percy's car just turned at the driveway. I'll let Granny know you'll be in soon."

When Percy parked and climbed out of his car, Nettie raced to him, and he caught her up in his arms. She buried her face in his chest.

"How did it go with Ira?" she mumbled.

Percy stroked her hair. "Ira told me he wants to stop the kingpin, but the only way that's going to happen is if we work together."

Nettie slipped her arm through his as they headed inside. "He's right, you know. While he scatters the thugs, you can focus on your campaign, and I'll take care of the business. After we review your schedule, you can read the remarkable telephone script Flossie wrote for you."

"I thought you were going to write my telephone script."

"I did, but Flossie edited it for me to pick up on your tone. It sounds just like you."

When they were inside, Percy said, "I'll have to tell Estelle I'm home."

Nettie smiled. "I'll bring the schedule and the script to the kitchen. She'll have coffee and a snack ready for you."

When Nettie placed the documents next to his plate, Percy put down his scone and reviewed the schedule. "There's a lot of backtracking on here. Is that on purpose? Where are you going to join me?"

"The backtracking is new. The original schedule was a smooth, logical loop, but I realized we don't want the kingpin to guess where you're going next, so Flossie helped me make it random. You don't need his reception committee waiting for you." Nettie pointed to Percy's next-to-last stop. "The senator recommended here for a last or next-to-last stop. You'll be warmed up from visiting the smaller towns, and this is your opponent's core. We won't contact them until two days before our planned arrival date because we don't want to tip off your opponent. We'll hit them hard with your high energy and charisma and top it off with your flapper wife, who is a complete opposite of your opponent's lower key, more traditional wife."

"Won't they be resistant to such a drastic change?"

"The senator thinks your opponent's core has been taken for granted, and they are more than ready for a change, especially if the change is not a dull copy of your opponent. By the time we get there, word will have gotten around about your soaring popularity with voters, and people will show up just to see for themselves."

Percy chuckled. "I agree that if you're there, it won't be dull."

"Now that we've agreed on your schedule, you can make a few telephone calls today. Here are your revised scripts. After I wrote six unique scripts for you, Flossie revised them so they'd feel more natural to you. You can pick one and stick with it, or use a different one for each call. It's up to you."

After Percy read them, he said, "I'm very comfortable with the scripts. Listen to this."

Nettie closed her eyes while he read all six scripts aloud. "You sounded like you were just talking; that's absolutely perfect."

"Good. Let me hear your scripts."

While Nettie read, Percy chuckled. "They do sound exactly like you. Why don't I get to say anything funny?"

"Because the only time you joke around is with close friends. It wouldn't fit on the telephone because you like to watch your friends' reactions. You enjoy seeing people laugh."

Percy stared at her. "And you don't?"

"Not really, so I'm surprised when I say something and people think it's funny."

"Since the schedule shows my first meet and greet is this Friday, I'll have to be there on Thursday, right? Should I go into town and make a few calls?"

Nettie nodded. "I hope we can confirm as many dates as possible today and finish up tomorrow with any loose ends. I'll go with you and make overnight reservations for you and Laird after you confirm the dates. Is anyone else going with you?"

"Yes, I meant to tell you Smitty volunteered to go with me, but what about Cliff and his sister?"

"I have a copy of your schedule that we can drop off with Cliff after you confirm the dates. I suspect they would prefer making their own reservations."

When Nettie strolled into the telephone business office, the manager's big smile faded when he saw Percy had followed her inside.

Nettie cleared her throat to keep from laughing at the hapless man. "Is the offer still open for us to make calls today?"

"Yes, ma'am, and we have your telephone scheduled to be installed on Tuesday right after lunch. I put in an order for a private line for you. It might not be available right away, but I knew you'd like that. I'll show you to the office you can use to make your calls."

The manager extended his right arm to put around Nettie's waist, but Percy stepped between the two of them and the manager smacked the back of his hand on Percy's cane. The manager jerked back his arm and rubbed the back of his hand as he mumbled, "First door on the left."

"Thank you," Nettie said. "We appreciate your wonderful customer service."

After they closed the door, Percy grumbled, "Customer service, my foot."

"Your timing with your cane was the cat's meow." Nettie's eyes twinkled.

"It was, wasn't it? I thought about whacking his shin, but that would have been too obvious."

"You make the calls, and I'll take notes."

After the first call, Percy said, "That wasn't nearly as awful as I thought it would be. I understand why the senator suggested I use a script."

"I've recorded them as confirmed, and I'll write letters this evening for you to sign."

At the end of two hours, Percy said, "I feel like I ran a marathon."

"You were smooth. We have only one follow up call for you to make tomorrow besides the one we're saving for later. I'll call your contacts tomorrow and ask if they have any recommendations for places for you, Smitty, and Laird to stay. Let's drop off Cliff's copy of the schedule."

On the way to the boarding house where Cliff and his sister lived, Percy asked, "Why are you calling the contacts for recommendations?"

"I realized it will help them feel more involved with your campaign if we ask them where you should stay."

"What if they're polite and suggest I stay with them?" Percy frowned.

"I'm sure most of them will, but I'm highly skilled at the polite dance and will let them off the hook."

Percy exhaled. "I knew that."

"The three of you will probably have dinner with your hosts, though."

"That's okay with me." Percy parked in front of the boarding house. "All three of us? I don't think Smitty would want to go to a dinner; I don't know about Laird."

"Smitty will want to go because you need someone watching your back, and Laird should go because he may see an opportunity for some candid photos the local newspapers can print."

"Will you talk to Laird for me?"

"I don't mind telling Laird the plan, but you have to be there. You'll have to get used to talking to Laird, or you'll be awkward in all the photos."

Percy reached for his door handle. "Aren't you getting out?"

"Here's the copy of the schedule for Cliff. I want to jot down a few more notes, so I'll wait in the car."

"I won't be long."

"Take all the time you need. I have to clarify some of my notes or I won't understand them later."

While Nettie worked on her notes, a large box truck she didn't recognize drove past her then pulled in front of their parked car. Nettie slipped her hand into her beaded bag, pulled out her derringer, and casually placed her notes over her right hand to hide the pistol.

When Laird climbed out of the truck and headed toward her, she smiled and returned her derringer to her bag.

She rolled down her window as he approached her.

"Is that your truck?" she asked.

"Sure is. We planned to put the old wagon on the back of a truck, but it made more sense to put a new engine into the old box truck that's been sitting on the dealer's lot for ages. It didn't take me long to gut the wagon and set up the box truck. I have more room inside and a reliable vehicle to drive. Smitty helped me with the work. He said since we'd be working together it didn't hurt to get better acquainted."

"I'm glad you stopped, because Percy and I would like to review the schedule with you. Are you available to come to our house for dinner tonight?"

Laird furrowed his brow as he bit his lip. "Well, I'm not sure about..."

Nettie interrupted him. "I know Flossie would enjoy seeing you."

Laird's eyes lit up. "I wouldn't mind seeing her either."

"Good; then we'll see you at six. Don't dress up; we're only fancy on Friday and Saturday evenings when we host the supper club members."

"Thanks, I'll be there at six."

Nettie smiled as Percy came out of the boarding house.

Percy climbed into his car. "You look pleased with yourself. What's going on?"

"Laird and Smitty put a new engine into a box truck, so Laird's all set. I invited him to have supper with us tonight, so we can talk, and you can be not scary."

"You're no fun." Percy side-glanced at Nettie.

Nettie punched him on his upper arm. "I'll show you how fun I can be tonight if you behave."

Percy chuckled. "You win, but isn't that bribery of an almost state official?"

Nettie shrugged. "Sounded like it to me."

Percy exhaled. "Are there any laws you won't break?"

Nettie glared. "Of course, there are. Have you ever known me to wear white after Labor Day?"

Percy laughed. "You got me there."

Chapter Eleven

After they were home, they went into the kitchen.

While Percy rubbed Buster's round belly, Estelle smiled and signed, "Oliver and Willis are upstairs working on the dumbwaiter."

Percy signed his thanks then headed toward the stairs.

Nettie signed, "I invited Laird to have supper with us this evening. He'll be here at six."

Estelle smiled as she signed. "Flossie will be happy; you'll find her in the living room. She's dusting. I have chicken and dumplings for tonight's supper, and there is an apple pie in the oven, so you will have plenty of food."

"Will you, Bella, and Oliver join us?" Nettie signed.

"Thank you, but I already have our supper in my oven."

"Chicken a la king is Pappy's favorite and mine too," Bella signed. "I helped Granny make it. We wanted to surprise Pappy."

"I'm sure he'll be very pleased. I'll let Flossie know we're having company."

Bella and Buster followed Nettie to the living room.

"We're having company for supper this evening," Nettie said.

"I'm almost through cleaning the living room. I didn't plan to dust the dining room sideboard today, but I'll get on it. How many do we expect?"

"One," Nettie said.

"What's wrong?" Flossie dropped onto the sofa. "You can tell me; I'm ready for the worst. Is it the police? What time?"

"Six o'clock, but it's not really a dinner party, it's more of a meeting."

Flossie exhaled. "That doesn't sound good. Should I make myself scarce?"

"You could, but Laird said he was looking forward to seeing you."

Flossie squealed, "You invited Laird to supper? He'll be here at six?"

She threw down her dust cloth and raced to the stairs.

"Do you think she's mad at me?" Nettie asked.

Bella shook her head. "No, ma'am; Miss Flossie was tickled to hear you invited Deputy Laird."

"I thought so, too. What do you think about Deputy Laird?"

"I think he and Miss Flossie have been seeing each other longer than they let on."

"Why do you think they've kept it a secret?"

"They're afraid Mr. Percy wouldn't approve, but I don't think Mr. Percy would welcome any young man who was interested in Miss Flossie, because she's like his little sister."

"Men are funny sometimes."

"That's what Granny says too."

Percy appeared in the doorway. "Where's Flossie?"

"She's getting ready for dinner."

"Why so early? Never mind; come into the kitchen. We have something to show you."

When they were in the kitchen, Percy threw open his arms. "See anything different?"

Nettie slowly scanned the room while Bella giggled.

"I'm obviously missing something, but I can't see what it is." Nettie raised an eyebrow, and Bella pointed to the far cabinet.

"Is it the cabinet where we store old pots?" Nettie strode to the cabinet and opened it; her eyes widened. "All the shelves are gone."

She craned her neck and looked up. "Are those ropes along the side? I can't tell where they go; it's too dark up there."

"Lower away," Percy called out.

The dark top of the cabinet slowly came down until Nettie said, "It's a box with a door. You've fixed the dumbwaiter."

When the box stopped, Percy said, "Open it up."

Nettie opened the door on the box, and inside was a hammer.

She laughed. "Thank you for the hammer."

"You're welcome; it was all we had to send down," Willis called out.

Estelle smiled as she handed Bella a plate of cookies. Bella gave the plate to Nettie, who put it inside the box next to the hammer before she closed the door.

"How do I send it?" she asked.

"We haven't set that up yet. They'll pull it up. Right now, it needs someone at the top to lower and raise the dumbwaiter, but Oliver will fix that tomorrow."

"Back to you," Nettie called out, and the box slowly lifted out of her sight into the dark. When she heard a soft thud, she knew it had reached its destination.

Percy laughed when Oliver called out, "Y'all are the cat's pajamas. Tell Estelle."

Bella tapped Estelle's arm and signed the message from Oliver. Estelle signed, "A cat wearing pajamas would be funny."

Bella hugged her granny then signed, "But it would be a very special cat."

Estelle smiled as she returned Bella's hug.

Nettie ran her fingers over the cabinet. "Percy, the dumbwaiter definitely has potential beyond its original purpose. I can't think of any examples right offhand of how we might want to use it, but I have a feeling when we need it, we'll be glad it's here."

Percy furrowed his brow. "I'm not sure I followed that, but if you're happy, I'm happy."

"Will you give Laird a chance tonight? You need people you trust around you."

Percy exhaled. "You're right. I have to trust the men who are supporting me, especially while I'm traveling." Percy furrowed his brow and then rose to leave the kitchen.

"Where are you going?" Nettie asked.

"I have to talk to my experts."

When he went up the stairs, Bella peered at Nettie. "Are Pappy and Mr. Willis his experts? I thought you were."

Nettie smiled. "I'm not an expert at everything."

When Percy walked into the hospitality room, Willis and Oliver were putting away their tools.

Percy pulled out a chair and sat at a table. "Nettie invited Laird to have supper with us tonight."

Willis and Oliver exchanged glances.

"Makes sense to me," Oliver said. "Isn't he going to be traveling with you as your campaign photographer? Don't you need to discuss your itinerary and expectations with him? Are you having second thoughts about him?"

"He and Flossie have been seeing each other for a while. Are you worried about trusting Laird with your campaign or your cousin?" Willis asked.

Willis and Oliver joined Percy at the table.

"He's a deputy sheriff," Percy said. "I don't think Nettie understands how dangerous he is to her business."

"Everybody knows Nettie is a brilliant businesswoman; the sheriff appreciates how much Nettie has done for the community and has given Laird time off to support your campaign. She wouldn't have invited him if she had any concerns," Willis said.

"Nettie invited him here so you could get to know him and trust him, right? How can we help?" Oliver asked.

"It takes time to trust a man; how can I say I trust him after only one evening?"

"You could ask him what he thinks about Nettie's business. If he tells you what he thinks, and you believe him, then he trusts you. If he tells you he doesn't know anything, then you fire him because he's doesn't trust you enough to tell you the truth," Oliver said.

Percy rubbed his chin.

"If you really want to clear the air after that, follow up with telling him you've always been responsible for Flossie and ask him what his intentions are," Willis said.

"I agree," Oliver said. "If the two of you can't talk man-to-man, how can you trust him?"

"I don't have the luxury of months to get to know him; this is the best way to go." Percy rose from the table. "Thanks."

"Any time," Willis said. "But you'd have done something similar even if we hadn't talked."

"Maybe so, but this is going straight to the point, which is more Nettie's style than mine."

Willis chuckled. "We just cut out an hour of small talk, didn't we?"

Percy's eyes twinkled. "Maybe I'll tack on an extra hour of small talk to annoy the women in my life."

Oliver laughed. "You do like living on the edge, don't you?"

Percy shrugged. "Just following orders; Nettie said I have to get to know him."

Percy smiled as men's laughter followed him down the stairs. On his way to the kitchen, Percy noticed Nettie's sewing room door was open. He peered inside and smiled at his young wife who had her head down while she composed a letter. Nettie sniffed without looking up. "I smell a brilliant man in my sewing room."

Percy chuckled. "You left out the handsome part."

"No, I just don't care to state the obvious." Nettie fluttered her eyelashes. "Do you feel better?"

"Much better; I had to take some time to gather my thoughts."

"What's your plan?"

"I'd like to go for a walk with Laird and have a private chat. Should I do that before or after we eat?"

"That's up to you. If you take your walk before we sit down to eat, you'll have cleared the air, but you might feel rushed. If you wait until after we eat, it will be dark and colder, but you can take all the time you need."

"I think I'll do both."

"Flossie's going to think you're monopolizing Laird to annoy her."

Percy winked. "That's my bonus."

"I've revised the letter." She handed him her draft.

After he read it, he returned it to her. "I like that; it's from both of us."

"Thanks. I'll have Flossie review it while you and Laird are on your walk."

"I forgot to tell you I talked to the mayor today. We talked politics, of course, but he's really worried about his wife and Doctor Doughtery. He's convinced the doctor is a dope peddler."

"Should I step in?"

"He was hoping you would. He doesn't have anything he could take to the sheriff to support an official complaint."

"Flossie's been a little peaked lately; we'll see what the doctor has to say."

Percy smiled. "I'm really sorry I can't go along."

Nettie raised her eyebrows. "It must be close to six o'clock. I hear a car coming up the driveway."

Flossie squealed, "Laird is here!"

Percy shook his head as she clattered down the stairs. He peeked out the door. "Good; she stopped and took a breath. I was afraid for Laird because she would have knocked him down."

"Close the door and give them some privacy," Nettie hissed.

Percy motioned for her to shush as he watched. When he closed the door, he said, "You were right. They need their privacy."

"What are they doing?" Nettie rushed to the door, but Percy blocked it.

"Get out of my way, you big meany," Nettie growled.

"Shh, they'll hear you," Percy whispered.

"Are you going to join us in the living room after your meeting is over?" Flossie called out.

"Let's meet in the kitchen; we'll be there in a few minutes," Nettie said.

"Where are we eating?" Percy asked.

"In the kitchen. It will be cozier. I'll take my letter and ask Flossie to review it."

When they joined Flossie and Laird in the kitchen, Flossie said, "Estelle left me a note. I'll drop in the dough for the dumplings while we enjoy our appetizers."

"Sweet tea or coffee?" Nettie asked.

"Coffee for me," Percy said.

Laird nodded. "Sounds good to me."

When Nettie passed Laird on the way to the stove for the coffee, a chill ran down her spine. Her hand shook when she reached for the pot. *Something's off with Laird.*

She turned to Percy. "Would you pour the coffee? I made a large pot, and it's too heavy for me."

When Percy picked up the pot, he side-glanced at her.

She quickly signed, "Be careful. I have a feeling about Laird."

He nodded as he poured four cups. "The pot is heavy, but we'll certainly have plenty of coffee."

After Nettie put the four cups on the table, Percy asked, "Can we hold off on supper? Laird and I have a few things to discuss."

"The living room is all yours," Nettie said. "Flossie and I have a few things we have to catch up on too."

"What do we have to catch up on?" Flossie asked after the men left.

"First, I have a letter I need for you to read and revise."

Flossie read the letter. "This is from both of you. That's genius." Flossie sat down at the table, and Nettie handed her a pen.

Flossie mumbled as she read, and then went back and furrowed her brow as she marked up the letter with changes.

Nettie read over her shoulder. "This is fantastic; thank you."

"What else?"

"The mayor is worried about his wife; he thinks Doctor Doughtery is drugging his patients and wants me to check him out. I think the mayor hopes I'll run the quack out of town."

"What are we going to do?"

"At first I thought you could go in because you haven't been feeling well, but I'm worried about the mayor's wife's behavior. I'm convinced he's giving her laudanum."

Flossie gasped. "That's dangerously addictive."

"So, what's our best way to put him out of business?" Nettie asked.

"If we shut him down, won't he just go somewhere else? That wouldn't be right. What if he was under surveillance, and you, as one of his biggest fans, give him a heads up so he can disappear before the feds catch up with him?"

"That's really far-fetched, but we're on the right track," Nettie said.

"We need to scare him out of town."

"Let's break into his office tonight and smash everything we can find. He'll be more receptive to the information the syndicate is after him when he goes into his office tomorrow."

"A midnight raid." Flossie rubbed her hands together then cocked her head. "What about Percy?"

"He can't know anything about this. He's a light sleeper, but I frequently get up because I can't sleep, so he'll roll over as usual and be fine."

"So, if I change clothes and wait for you in the living room, we'll leave after Percy goes to sleep."

"That would work." Nettie furrowed her brow. "I'd like to ask Oliver if we could use his truck."

"I'll do that right now." Flossie dashed out the door.

Nettie picked up the schedule from the counter where she had put it and folded the paper into quarters so it would fit in her pocket.

A few minutes later, Flossie returned. "It's getting colder, so we'll have to dress warm. Oliver said his truck was at the barn, but we're welcome to use it. He gave me the keys."

"The barn? That's perfect."

Flossie wrinkled her nose. "I'm glad you think so; I'm not crazy about maneuvering that path in the dark."

"Willis keeps a flashlight and a bat behind the bar in the speakeasy. We can use the bat to break the bottles and display cases; I'm certain Oliver has a crowbar in his truck. We'll go in, smash everything, and get out."

"I'll be right back." Nettie returned from the speakeasy with the flashlight and the bat. After she stuck the bat into the pantry behind the aprons and the flashlight behind the flour, she said, "We'll be fine."

After Percy motioned toward the sofa, Laird sat down, and Percy sat in his leather chair.

"I heard the good news that you found yourself a truck that will work for you," Percy said. "I'm glad you've joined my team as our campaign photographer because I need people around me I can trust."

"Thank you, sir. It's a great honor to serve with you."

"Call me Percy, and the honor is all mine. Tell me what you know about my wife's business."

Laird studied Percy's face before he spoke. "Your property was in foreclosure when you and Nettie first married. She began a subscription supper club, but she paid off the mortgage with her income from her exclusive speakeasy. Nettie has expanded her operation and is highly respected for her unselfish willingness to help others. She has created jobs and paid off loans for farmers and businesses to stop foreclosures."

Percy tilted his head. "Where did you hear all that?"

"The sheriff told me Nettie's business was not up for discussion around here. Everyone is very protective of her."

The sheriff wouldn't have shared that much information with a new deputy. His source was someone else. Percy nodded. "When we were first married, I tried to advise her until I saw how brilliant she was."

Laird smiled. "The sheriff spoke highly of both of you when I started working for him. He said you were smarter than most men he's known because you weren't jealous of your wife's talents."

Percy chuckled. "I was pig-headed for a while, but I finally caught on."

"How did you do that?" Laird asked.

"Stay out of Nettie's way and stick with her plan." Percy rose. "Are you starving? Estelle's cooking is the best."

When they went into the kitchen, Buster trotted to Percy, who scratched the puppy's ears. Flossie dropped the last ball of dough into the boiling broth that included chicken and vegetables while Nettie set the table.

"We can eat in fifteen minutes. Are we going to toast the beginning of your campaign? We have apple cider from the farmers' market," Nettie said.

"I'll heat the apple cider," Flossie said.

"While we wait, why don't we go over the schedule?" Percy signed, "The original copy."

Nettie smiled. "Good idea."

She returned from the office with the draft of the first schedule. While Percy explained the schedule to Laird, Flossie put their hot apple cider in front of them.

Laird furrowed his brow. "The only stop I don't understand is why you're going to your opponent's hometown."

"Nettie said the same thing, but we're making a big loop. It's not too far out of the way to make it my first stop. Maybe you're right after all, honey, and we should take it off the list."

Nettie smiled. "You could always do a special trip later, if you felt strongly about it."

Laird nodded. "You'll have plenty of time to assess whether it would be necessary."

Flossie giggled. "I love how you said that."

Percy side-glanced at Nettie who fluttered her eyelashes. Percy smirked then cleared his throat. "How much time do we have until the dumplings are ready?"

Flossie removed the lid from the pot and flipped over the dumplings. "Two minutes."

Flossie pointed to the cups of warm cider on the counter. "Aren't we going to have a toast?"

After everyone had picked up a cup, Percy raised his. "Here's to a clean, successful campaign."

"And to our next lieutenant governor," Nettie added.

After they finished eating, Percy and Nettie cleared the table and put away the leftovers while Flossie washed the dishes and Laird dried them.

"Cleanup went really fast with all hands on deck," Nettie said. "Flossie and I will put away the dishes so we don't get into trouble with Estelle for putting them in the wrong spot."

"We'll step outside so we won't be in the way," Percy said.

When he opened the front door, Percy asked, "Are you coming, Buster?"

Buster trotted to Flossie and sat for his after-dinner treat.

Percy chuckled. "Don't blame you one bit, Buster."

Before Percy turned to leave, he winced. Nettie furrowed her brow. *He overdid it today.*

After they were on the front porch, Percy said, "Flossie's my cousin, but she's like a sister to me."

"I know, and I should have talked to you sooner, but Flossie begged me not to. She was worried you wouldn't approve of us being together because of Nettie's business and my profession, but I would never do anything to hurt Flossie or Nettie. I'd like your permission to ask Flossie to marry me. If the timing's not right, I understand. I'll wait."

"How long have you and Flossie been seeing each other?"

"Two months. I know that's not long, but I want her to know I'm committed to her."

"Flossie's her own woman; you don't need my permission, but I'd suggest putting it off until after the campaign."

Laird frowned. "Does that mean I don't have your approval?"

"Now isn't the right time."

"I'm not sure what to do." Laird ran his fingers through his hair. "I realize Flossie is a modern, independent woman, but I'm old-fashioned."

"I completely understand. Welcome to my world." Percy shrugged.

"I feel like I should tell her something so she doesn't think I'm stringing her along," Laird said.

"Nothing wrong with telling her the truth."

Laird scowled as they went inside.

Flossie and Nettie were in the living room; Buster puppy-growled in his sleep at Flossie's feet.

Percy stopped at the doorway and furrowed his brow. "Sugar, we have to go over the schedule again. I'm having second thoughts."

Nettie put her hand on her chest. "Oh, no. It's not about the campaign, is it? Oh, mercy, I'm certain whatever it is we can adjust."

"You haven't failed me yet."

After they were in the sewing room, Nettie crossed her arms. "Why are we really here?"

Percy's eyes widened. "How'd you know?"

"When have you ever called me Sugar?"

Percy rolled his eyes. "I thought that would sound more urgent; is that why you were so dramatic?"

Nettie giggled. "It seemed to fit, Sugar."

The two of them held hands as they tiptoed to the living room and listened.

Laird said, "What I've been trying to say..."

Chapter Twelve

Flossie interrupted him. "It's something bad, isn't it? That's the third time you've said that. Did you decide not to work with Percy after all? You know he's counting on you. You're not a quitter. Are you sick?"

"Would it be okay if we spent more time together?"

Flossie gasped.

Nettie put her hand over her mouth to stifle her giggle as she and Percy tiptoed backward to the sewing room, then slammed the door behind them and hurried to the living room.

Flossie said, "Of course it is."

They reached the living room in time to see Flossie fling her arms around Laird's neck as he hugged her.

"What's going on in here?" Percy asked.

Flossie turned around, and Laird kept his arm around her waist. Her face was flushed and her eyes glistened. "Laird asked if we could spend more time together, and I said..."

Nettie interrupted her. "You'd think about it. Wise choice."

Flossie growled, "I said yes."

Nettie laughed as she hugged Flossie. "That's absolutely wonderful; I'm happy you'll be getting to know each other better."

"We might as well have a family meeting and include Laird," Percy said.

"Okay, what's our topic?" Nettie asked.

She and Percy sat in their chairs, and Flossie and Laird sat close together on the sofa.

"Is this coming Friday going to be business as usual?" Flossie asked.

"Yes, unless you hear something that would justify a change in plans," Nettie said. "Percy, I'd like to stay up this evening to write the letters to the towns you'll be visiting with your new revised schedule; if you'll sign them first thing in the morning, Flossie and I can take them into town to the post office and be back long before lunch."

"Why don't you write them first thing in the morning?"

"That would work if you don't mind hanging around until we're done," Nettie said.

Percy frowned. "I'm not sure I'm interested in waiting; it makes more sense if you want to write all of them tonight. Laird, I'd like a tour of your photography truck. Is that something we can do tomorrow?"

"I'd like that. Smitty and I plan to make a few more changes on the truck in the morning, and I'd appreciate it if you were there for our discussion."

Percy narrowed his eyes. "Are you being polite?"

Laird's eyes twinkled. "Heck, no; I'm trying to get on the boss's good side by including you in the plans for the truck."

Percy smiled. "I was a little worried about you, but you fit right in."

"I'd better go so y'all can get those letters written," Laird said.

Percy rose when Laird did. "I'll walk out with you to your truck." Buster followed them outside.

Flossie asked, "What's our plan again?"

"We knock out the letters then you go upstairs when I do."

Percy returned with Buster on his heels. "Flossie, I think it's great that you and Laird will be getting to know each other better."

"I knew that's what you'd think," Flossie said. "I don't see why Laird was so reluctant to talk to you. Thank goodness Nettie invited him to dinner so you two could get acquainted."

Percy exhaled. "It's been a long day. I'll lock up then call it a night."

"I shouldn't be too long," Nettie said.

"Can I help you?" Flossie asked.

"I'd love it if you'd read over the letters after I write them to make sure I didn't make any mistakes."

After Percy was upstairs, Nettie pulled out the estate's stationery and frowned. "I don't like this; we need stationery with Percy's name on it."

"What do you want on it? I have my calligraphy pens and could create it."

"That's a great idea."

"We don't want it to look old-fashioned, so I'll copy the style of the estate's stationery you designed the week after you and Percy were married."

Flossie tiptoed up the stairs. When she returned with her calligraphy set, Flossie had a change of warm clothes with her; she sat at the space on a work table Nettie had cleared for her.

After Flossie had created the first page of Percy's stationery, Nettie said, "That's perfect. I'll start writing."

Flossie added, "I'll do a dozen pages. We don't need that many, but they'll be nice to have on hand."

After Flossie finished the stationery pages, Nettie said, "Here's the list of names and addresses for the envelopes."

While Nettie continued writing letters, Flossie addressed envelopes then read each letter and paired up the letters and envelopes.

"That was fast." Flossie yawned as she read the last letter. "All we need is Percy's signature."

"I'll be down after I'm certain Percy is asleep." Nettie headed toward the stairs while Flossie strolled to the living room with her change of clothes.

When Nettie went into the bedroom, she smiled at Percy who sat in his chair with his feet propped up.

"Am I supposed to be asleep?" he whispered.

"Yes. Flossie and I are going into town to break into the doctor's office and smash his inventory and display cases."

"I like it, but I'm not supposed to know about it, am I? Why not?"

"Because we want to keep your reputation untarnished, and I don't want Flossie accidentally saying anything that would indicate you're involved."

"That's nice, but I have to watch your back. How can I go along?"

"We're taking Oliver's truck, but it's at the barn."

"Good; I'll ride in the truck bed. When should I leave so I can hide before you get there?"

"We'll leave right after you do, but be sure to dress warm for the ride. You'll get through the woods faster than we will because Flossie's nervous about going through the brush at night. When we go to the kitchen to pick up cookies for the trip, you can leave by the front door."

"Just don't let Buster out of the kitchen because he'll bark to go with me. Bring me some cookies too," Percy said.

"Now, how am I going to pull that off? Why would I want to drop cookies in the truck's bed?"

"I don't understand half the things you do; how am I supposed to know?"

Nettie glared at him then rolled her eyes. "Okay, I'll smuggle cookies to you, if you'll take a blanket for extra warmth."

"That seems excessive to me, but I won't argue and jeopardize my cookies." Percy opened their closet door and pulled out his drab green military blanket then stuffed it into a backpack. After he removed his favorite hunting rifle from the gun chest, he put on his khaki wool cap. "I'll get my warm jacket out of the coat closet when you get yours."

After Nettie added layers for warmth, she said, "Let's go."

When she opened the closet door, it creaked, and she glared at Percy and whispered, "I thought you were going to fix that."

He shrugged as he grabbed his coat and went out the front door. Nettie put on her coat then locked the front door and went to the living room.

"Flossie," she whispered. When Flossie didn't budge from the sofa, Nettie walked to the sofa and kicked it. "Hey, Flossie, get up or I'll leave you."

Flossie yawned and then stretched. "I needed a nap. What time is it?"

"It's eleven thirty."

"Are we going out the back door? The front door creaks sometimes."

"Good idea. We have to have cookies for a celebration snack; it's a tradition," Nettie said. "If Buster wakes up, pet him so he won't bark, and I'll put some in a bag."

Flossie kneeled next to Buster and stroked his back while Nettie put cookies into two sacks.

Nettie put one sack in her coat pocket. "Okay, let's go."

When they were outside, the flashlight's beam in the night mist created an illusion of creatures in the trees ahead, and the sound of the grass as it crunched under their feet added to the feeling of impending danger.

Flossie shuddered. "It's too damp and cold. Are you sure we should be on the road tonight? I need my scarf to wrap my face and put over my nose."

"You'll stir up Buster if you open the back door, and he'll bark. If you aren't going with me, wait here until I get back."

"It's too cold to stand around and wait. You lead."

"Okay, but you'll have to keep up with me."

Nettie strode to the woods with a grumbling Flossie close behind her.

"I can't see; you're going too fast," Flossie hissed. "You're going to make me run into a tree."

"We'll be warmer if we go fast; we're almost there."

Flossie hurried to the passenger door and hopped into the truck while Nettie dropped the sack from her pocket into the truck bed.

Nettie started the truck and headed down the driveway as a light fog rolled in.

"How long does it take for the cab to warm up?" Flossie shivered.

"Too long. We probably should have taken the brick inside earlier and heated it."

The fog thickened as they neared town, and Nettie slowed down as she peered at the road ahead.

Flossie asked, "What kind of tradition is it to celebrate with cookies? I never heard of that."

"It's related to the tradition of drinking a toast then throwing your glass into the fireplace except not as messy to clean up."

"I knew it had to be something. I like it, especially since we don't have to clean up the glass."

"Look in the glove box for goggles; there should be two pairs," Nettie said. "If we're going to be breaking glass, we should have eye protection."

Flossie pulled out the goggles. "These are more stylish than safety glasses."

The fog thickened as they reached the outskirts of town. Flossie peered at their surroundings. "How can you drive when you can't see the road? I can't even see the front of the truck, and on top of that, I'm frozen solid. Next time, I'll put the brick in the oven for an hour before we leave, or better yet, we can wait for a warmer night with no fog."

"I'm going to park next to the back door so we can make a quick getaway if we have to. Do you want the crowbar or the bat?"

"I'll take the bat," Flossie said.

"Put on your goggles and don't take off your gloves."

After she parked, Nettie put on her goggles and grabbed the crowbar from under the driver's seat. Flossie stayed close as Nettie pulled out a slender piece of metal from her beaded bag and quickly picked the building's door lock.

"How did you learn to do that?" Flossie asked.

"I like to read."

When they went inside, the storage room and the doctor's office doors were locked. Nettie unlocked them.

Nettie turned on the light in the storage room.

"Wow, this room is huge," Flossie said.

"Let's start at the back then you go to the right and work your way around the room, and I'll take the left side. Try not to leave any bottles intact."

After they smashed all the bottles in the storage room, Flossie said, "That was noisy; next time we should bring hearing protection. Now what do I do?"

"Find a big box. Dump all the boxes of hypodermic needles into them. Smash the display cases and whatever is in them. I'll check the doctor's office."

"Jackpot," Nettie called out from the doctor's office. "Invoices with names and addresses." Nettie glanced at more documents. Her eyes widened as she flipped through a journal she found in the doctor's locked desk. She shoved it down the neck of her shirt for safekeeping.

While Flossie smashed the glass display cases, Nettie found a large trash can. She emptied it onto the floor and dumped all the records into the trash can. Nettie carried out the box with the hypodermic needles and handed it to Percy.

After she dragged out the trash can, Percy hopped out and lifted the heavy container into the truck bed.

"I thought we could dump this box and the trash can of records in the sheriff's parking lot," Nettie said.

"Grab Flossie, and let's roll," Percy said.

Nettie went into the building. "You've done a great job. Bring your bat."

After Flossie climbed into the passenger seat, Nettie took off her goggles and handed them to Flossie. When she reached the parking lot next to the sheriff's department lot, she jumped out. "I'll just be a second."

She ran to the back of the truck. Percy handed her the box of needles. While she set down the box, Percy lowered the trash can to the ground.

Nettie hurried back to the driver's seat and slowly drove away in the thick fog. When she reached the main road, she clutched the steering wheel and maintained a steady speed.

"Oliver said we could park the truck in its usual spot near his car by his house," Flossie said.

"That's good news. After we get home, you can go to bed. I'll take Buster for a quick walk and make sure the house is locked. Are you going with me to mail the letters in the morning?"

"That means getting up early, doesn't it? Remind me I want to go with you when you wake me up."

After Nettie parked Oliver's truck in its usual spot, she hurried to the back door and unlocked it. Flossie rushed inside and went straight up the stairs.

Nettie opened the kitchen door. "Do you want to go outside, Buster?"

Buster danced to the back door; when Nettie opened the door, he dashed out to Percy and ran a tight circle around him.

Percy chuckled as he handed his wool blanket to Nettie and rubbed Buster's ears. "Good boy, Buster."

After they were inside, Percy locked the back door and checked the front door.

"Would you like a cup of hot apple cider?" Nettie asked.

"Sure would; what about you? I'll make it so I can stand next to the stove and warm up. I'm glad you insisted I take a blanket. The night air stung like there were ice crystals in the fog when we were on the road coming back."

Nettie pulled out the journal from her shirt. "Look what I found."

Percy flipped through the journal. After he poured the hot apple cider, he scrutinized the first ten pages. "Do you think the man Doctor Doughtery refers to as boss is our kingpin?"

"I'm absolutely certain the boss he mentions is the kingpin."

While Percy kept reading, Nettie smiled as Buster circled his soft rug then flopped down and almost instantly fell asleep.

Percy tapped the journal with his fingers. "I'd like to give this to Ira tomorrow. He's in the best position to use the information."

"I'd like to read it before you give it to Ira."

"Bring it upstairs; you'll be warmer reading in bed, and I don't mind if you read it aloud to me, as long as you don't mind if I snuggle you and fall asleep."

After Nettie climbed into bed, Percy rolled close, put his arm around her, and promptly fell asleep. Nettie smiled. *He sleeps with the innocence of an honorable man.*

When she read the last page, Nettie flipped back through the book. *I still don't know who the kingpin is, but Ira might. I'm positive the kingpin wants to stop Percy because our town has been his base for a long time.*

Nettie turned off her light, and the sleeping Percy pulled her closer.

Chapter Thirteen

When Nettie woke, she rolled over to warm her feet on Percy, but he wasn't there. She quickly dressed and raced down the stairs.

When she went into the kitchen, Estelle was pulling a coffee cake out of the oven, and Bella sat at the counter with her art notepad.

Nettie peeked over Bella's shoulder at the drawing and smiled. "That's Buster. Very well done, Bella."

"He's easy to draw because he's cute." Bella beamed.

Estelle signed, "Percy and Oliver are out back checking the garden. We had a hard freeze last night."

When Percy and Oliver came into the kitchen, Percy kissed Nettie's neck, and she giggled.

Oliver signed, "It was smart to pick the tomatoes and peppers yesterday. We would have lost them, but the cabbage is fine."

Estelle signed, "I'll pick cabbages this morning and start a batch of sauerkraut before I can the tomatoes and peppers."

"Flossie and I are going to the post office this morning to mail letters," Nettie signed. "Do you need anything from town?"

"A book," Bella signed.

Nettie glanced at Estelle and raised her eyebrows. Estelle smiled and nodded.

Before Bella dashed out to catch the school bus at the end of the driveway, she signed, "Thank you."

Nettie went upstairs with a cup of coffee. When she tapped on Flossie's bedroom door, then went inside. "Flossie, you wanted to go with me into town. I have a cup of coffee."

Flossie sat up in bed. "You're the best."

"I know. Get dressed and come downstairs so you can have a cup too. Estelle just pulled a coffee cake out of the oven."

"Why can't I have that one?" Flossie grumbled.

"Because you'd forget to get dressed. See you in a minute."

Nettie bit her lip to keep from laughing when Flossie threw her pillow at her, and it landed halfway to the door.

When Nettie went downstairs, Percy was waiting for her in the hall. "What's your schedule like today, sweetie?"

"My number one priority is to mail the letters this morning so I can be home when the telephone is installed. If I have time, I would like to visit with Theresa and Marian. After the telephone is installed, I'll call all the contacts to see how they are doing and ask if they have any recommendations for accommodations for you, Smitty, and Laird."

"All I have is to talk to Ira and see Laird's truck. Did you spot anything in particular I should mention to Ira?"

"I got the impression from the journal that Doctor Doughtery and maybe the thugs have no loyalty to the kingpin because his power is based on fear. I'd be interested in knowing whether Ira agrees. If it's true or even partially true that his power is eroding, Ira can take advantage of that weakness. With Ira's help, we could be in a perfect position to collapse the kingpin's organization in South Georgia."

Percy shifted his weight to lean on his cane. "We need more coffee. I just realized we have a transportation conflict."

As they strolled together to the kitchen, Nettie said, "We can always draw straws. Short straw gets the car."

"I have an option that is less risky for me because you always win. Oliver planned to work on the dumbwaiter this morning, so maybe he'll let us use his car. I'm sure he'd rather keep his truck here in case he needs any supplies from the hardware store."

"After I have another cup of coffee and a piece of coffee cake, I'll ask him," Nettie said.

"I love your priorities, darlin', but if he's outside, I'll look for him." Percy polished off two pieces of coffee cake and downed his second cup of coffee.

When Flossie stumbled into the kitchen, Percy had already left to find Oliver in the vegetable garden.

Estelle poured a cup of coffee for Flossie and pointed to the coffee cake in the pan on the kitchen table.

Flossie nodded as she sat at the kitchen table with her cup. After Flossie served herself a piece of coffee cake, she glared at Nettie while she picked up her fork.

Nettie refilled Flossie's cup and joined her at the table. When Buster whined at Flossie's feet, she smiled as she reached down and stroked his soft ears.

"Buster is amazing, isn't he?" Nettie asked.

"He's the best boy," Flossie cooed as she rubbed his belly and polished off her last bite of coffee cake.

Percy burst into the kitchen. "Okay, you can take our car, and Oliver said I could use his car." He left as abruptly as he entered.

"Good morning, Percy." Flossie giggled.

"Man on a roar, right? Are you ready to go? We have a tight schedule ourselves," Nettie said.

Flossie grumbled as she rose from the table. "I have to get my coat. Why is everybody in this family always in a rush early in the morning?"

"The main reason you and I are in a rush is that we're getting our telephone today," Nettie said.

"Where will we put it? If we put it next to the sofa in the living room, I can put up my feet while I listen in on the party line conversations. What is it you say when you want to make a call and someone has the line tied up?"

"You aren't supposed to listen in on other people's conversations. It isn't polite. If you pick up the telephone and you hear someone talking, you quietly hang up and wait a few minutes before you pick up the receiver again. The telephone has distinct rings for each household, but we only answer on our ring. The installer will tell us which ring is ours," Nettie said. "Grab your coat. I want to be at the post office when it opens."

"We won't see anybody, will we?" Flossie drained her coffee cup.

"I'm not sure what you're asking, but I plan to check on Theresa and Marian to see how they are doing."

"That's not what I meant. Are we going to inspect Laird's truck?"

Nettie stared at her. "I hadn't planned to, but maybe we should."

"Give me five minutes. I have to change."

"Your five minutes turns into thirty. I'm leaving now; you can go with me or stay here." Nettie put on her coat and strolled to the back door.

"Hold your horses; I'm coming." Flossie threw on her coat.

When they were on the road, Flossie asked, "Can we cruise by Doctor Doughtery's office to see if anything is going on?"

"After the post office."

When they reached the post office, Flossie groaned. "Look at that line. There's no reason for both of us to wait. I could mail the letters while you check on Theresa."

"Your sudden interest in efficiency is impressive," Nettie said.

"I'm always impressive. Hurry, give me the letters; the two women coming this way with packages are notorious for rehashing a month's worth of gossip instead of taking care of their business and letting other people do the same."

Flossie jumped out of the car with the letters and dashed to the post office door. She took the steps two at a time and darted inside in front of the two women with packages who had reached the top step.

Nettie rolled her eyes. *Flossie certainly can move when she feels like it.*

Nettie parked in front of Theresa's fiber shop. When she went inside, Theresa was waiting on a customer. She smiled and waved to Nettie.

Nettie returned her smile and wandered to the back of the shop. While she ran her fingers over the soft fabric and examined the colors of the florals, the shop bell rang.

Nettie peered around the corner at the two women Flossie had passed at the post office as they plopped their packages on top of a fabric-covered table.

"You won't believe what happened," one woman said. "That Flossie bust into line in front of us at the post office, so we left."

"She thinks she's so high-and-mighty because she's Percy Wyndham's cousin," the second woman said.

"Flossie and Nettie are good friends of mine," Theresa said.

"Everybody knows that, but nobody's figured out why." The first woman snorted. "So, you must know if Flossie has a new boyfriend. Is she seeing that new deputy? I heard he has a wife and family living in a one-bedroom shack with no running water. Percy must have hired him to be a photographer because he heard about the family."

The second woman added, "Men stick together, don't they? Leave it to Percy Wyndham and his poor judgement when he hired a man who isn't even from around here just because he fooled the sheriff into making him a deputy."

"Horsefeathers!" Theresa growled. "Curb your tongue in my shop or get lost. I am a staunch supporter of Percy Wyndham, and Nettie and I go way back."

"Well, I never," the first woman said.

"Well, maybe you should," Theresa growled.

The front door slammed so hard, the bell crashed to the floor.

"Did you hear all that nonsense, Nettie?" Theresa called out.

Nettie sighed as she joined Theresa at the front of the store. "They're always spouting off. I hate to see you lose their business on my account, but I do have a question. Maybe she should what?"

Theresa snorted as she climbed on a stool to rehang the bell. "Take a long walk off a short pier. They're gossipy dead beats who never buy a thing. I kick them out two or three times a week, but they keep coming back."

Theresa chuckled, "Not that I have anything against gossip, mind you."

Nettie smiled. "Sounds like you're feeling better. Your sense of humor is definitely back."

Nettie peered at Theresa's face. "It looks like the swelling on your face is finally going down, but you definitely have two black eyes. How's your arm?"

"Doc told me the swelling would be down enough by tomorrow so I could go to the hospital to have a plaster cast put on my arm. He said he has never kept specialty supplies like that on hand."

"What can I do for you?" Nettie asked.

"I expected a delivery of fabric tomorrow, but it came early. The deliveryman was nice enough to put the boxes on my utility cart, but it's a little awkward for me to get the bolts out one-handed. Do you have time to help me put the bolts on the table next to my cutting counter? If I lift one end and you grab the other, we could empty the boxes."

"Let's do it."

While they stacked bolts of fabric on the table, the bell on the door jingled, and an elderly woman called out, "Yoo-hoo! Where are you, Theresa?"

"I'm at the cutting counter. Look around if you like; I'll be right with you."

"I can finish up," Nettie said. "There are only a few more left."

"Thanks." Theresa hurried to the front. "What can I help you find?"

"I need some red lace; my sister told me my Christmas apron was dowdy, so I'd like to dress it up."

"Were you thinking of a lace trim, or did you want a lacy overlay?"

"Ooo; a lacy overlay ought to give that old sourpuss something to complain about. I used two and three quarters yards when I made the apron, so two yards would be more than enough to make a lacy overlay."

"I have something you may like. If you'd like to sit in the comfy chair next to the cash register, I'll bring it to you to see what you think."

When Theresa returned to the front, she asked, "How's this?"

The woman tittered. "That's perfect; it looks like naughty lingerie."

Theresa chuckled. "I'll cut two yards for you; I'll be right back."

While Theresa cut the fabric, the woman said, "My friend told me somebody broke into that fancy doctor's office last night and smashed his entire stock of that so-called magic snake oil medicine he's so proud of. He must have been apoplectic when he saw it. My sources said he was so angry, he left town. I don't understand why he didn't just have his place cleaned up and restocked. With the prices he charged, he certainly could have afforded the cost of a few hours of janitorial services."

Theresa placed white tissue paper over the fabric then neatly folded it. "I agree with you about his prices; they're too steep for me."

After the woman paid for her purchase and left, Theresa joined Nettie. "That was a shocker, if it's true."

"I agree; I briefly met Doctor Dougherty once, but he didn't seem like the type to walk away from such a lucrative practice."

"There must be more to the story, or maybe there is no story." Theresa chuckled.

Nettie smiled. "Hard to say. Is there anything else I can do for you before I leave?"

"No, I appreciate your help; thanks for stopping by."

Nettie pulled in front of the post office and parked as Flossie came out. Flossie waved then rushed to the car and hopped in.

"You won't believe what I heard. Somebody broke into the fancy doctor's office and smashed all the bottles of magic cure-alls."

Nettie smiled. *Theresa's elderly customer with the naughty lace was making her rounds this morning.*

"Are we going to see Laird's truck next?" Flossie asked.

"I want to visit with Marian and her mother first."

"Drop me off at the boutique, then come pick me up there or at the drug store, depending on how long you are."

After she dropped off Flossie, Nettie went past the restaurant and narrowed her eyes when she saw the banker and Doc Jackson go in together. On a whim, she pulled into the restaurant lot and parked in the back.

When she went into the restaurant, she glanced around the main room.

A server who carried a pot of coffee stopped. "Were you looking for someone, Miss Nettie?"

"I thought I saw Doc Jackson come in."

"He and Mr. Cartwright wanted a quiet place to chat. They're in the small dining room that we only open for the lunchtime overflow. Do you want me to tell him you're looking for him?"

"No, that's fine. I was just going to say hello."

The server nodded and continued on her rounds with the coffee pot. Nettie headed toward the ladies' restroom and then diverted to a small hallway off the dining room where she could listen.

All she heard were hissed words until Cartwright said, "I'm packed and ready to leave."

A chair scraped.

"You need to calm down, Cartwright," Doc Jackson said. "All this panic and blubbering will only draw attention to you, and that's not good for your health, is it?"

Nettie darted to the ladies' room and quietly closed the door. *What an odd conversation.*

She heard the back door slam.

"Hey Doc," a man called out in the main part of the restaurant, "you got time for a friendly card game this afternoon at the legion hall? The action starts at two."

Doc Jackson chuckled. "I might have to rearrange my social calendar, but I can probably make it."

Nettie waited a few minutes, then left the restroom. As she strolled toward the door, she scanned the room.

Johnny sat alone at a table in the far corner. He saluted her with two fingers then motioned for her to join him.

When she reached his table, Johnny rose and pulled out a chair for her.

The server appeared out of nowhere with a cup and a coffee pot. "Coffee, Miss Nettie? We have fresh scones; do you want blueberry or cinnamon?"

"Coffee sounds wonderful." Nettie sat down.

"We'll have one of each," Johnny said.

After the server left, Johnny said, "You can have first pick, or we can both have half of each."

"I'll take half of the cinnamon scone," Nettie said.

"A server told a guy sitting at the counter the blueberries were freshly picked yesterday at a local blueberry farm. I don't think I've ever had a scone with fresh blueberries. How's your day going?"

"Peachy; so why am I sitting here?"

Johnny chuckled. "I'm surprised you let me practice my small talk as long as you did. I don't suppose after our chat is over you'd be willing to leave the table in a snit."

Nettie smiled. "It's my best skill; again, why am I sitting here?"

The server placed two small plates, two forks, a knife, and a plate with the scones between them before she refilled their cup and dashed away to fill more cups.

Johnny cut both scones in half. Nettie slid one half of the cinnamon scone onto a plate with a fork, then broke off a piece with her fingers and took a bite.

While they ate, Johnny said, "My boss isn't happy because an independent player with a vicious gang is trying to take over Georgia politics and put you out of business, which puts my boss out of business."

Nettie furrowed her brow. "I don't understand how my business has anything to do with your boss."

"You have a good relationship with your suppliers, and so does my boss. If you folded, he would have to divert resources to pick up your deliveries before someone else did, which means he'd be less involved in the political arena during the upcoming critical pre-election weeks."

Nettie cocked her head. "How can I help?" She took another bite of her cinnamon scone.

"Percy's opponent has succumbed to flattery and promises of big bucks and has deserted us after all the years we have worked together. According to informants, the independent player intends to assassinate Percy, but I think that's a diversion."

"An assassination attempt on Percy is a diversion?"

"Yes, because I think the true target is you, Nettie," Johnny said. "If you're out of the picture, your business will fold, and Percy will be completely devastated and drop out of the lieutenant governor's race."

Nettie said, "Percy has Smitty and Laird..."

"Laird's with the Fed; he's a plant," Johnny said.

Nettie nodded. "Good guy or bad guy?"

Johnny choked on his coffee.

After he caught his breath, he said, "Nobody but you would have asked that question. His assignment was to undermine Percy's campaign, but I have a feeling he'll go rogue, and Percy will have a dedicated team member at his side along with Smitty."

"So, what are you going to do?"

"My boss wants me to shadow Percy."

"Good." Nettie rose. "Are you ready for my dramatic exit?"

Johnny nodded. "It's more important for me to shadow you."

Nettie hissed. "Don't do it. Stick with Percy."

She slammed her chair against the table as she rose and then stormed out of the restaurant.

As she started her car, she smiled. *That felt good.*

When she stopped in front of the boutique, Flossie came out with a pink sack with the boutique logo on it.

"I found the cutest dress." Flossie closed the car door. "Now can we go see Laird?"

"Oh, yes," Nettie said.

"I had a terrible time trying to decide which dress to buy..."

Nettie was lost in thought and wasn't listening. *How do I convince Johnny to stick with Percy? I have a strong feeling he knew more than he was saying. What was it?*

When she pulled into the alley behind the boarding house where Laird lived, Nettie furrowed her brow as she interrupted Flossie. "I thought they'd be working on his truck here."

Flossie tapped her forehead with her fingers. "I forgot to tell you Smitty's brother has an old shop they're using. It has all the tools they need, and it gives them a roof over their heads so they won't be slowed down by bad weather. It's just a few blocks from here. I can get us there."

After Nettie parked in front of the old shop with a broken window and missing shingles on the roof, she narrowed her eyes as she scanned the area.

"It doesn't look like much, does it?" Flossie said. "Maybe Smitty's brother is well-stocked with tools."

"It's probably better than nothing; I thought Percy would be here, but I don't see our car."

Flossie jumped out then stared at Nettie. "Aren't you coming?"

When they went inside, Laird beamed when he saw Flossie. He strode to her and hugged her. "It's nice to see you, honey; we've gotten a lot of work done this morning on the engine. Smitty thinks we'll have it running like we want by this afternoon. I'll give you a tour after we finish the inside; we're hoping we'll have all the work done by tomorrow. It doesn't look like much yet."

"Where's Percy?" Nettie asked.

"He left a while ago. Ira stopped by, and they talked for a few minutes. Percy left not long after Ira did."

"Flossie, our time's getting tight. I have to drop by to see Marian."

"Would you like to stay here, Flossie? It's not very exciting to watch, but you're more than welcome," Laird said.

When both Flossie and Laird stared at Nettie, their eyes reminded her of Buster when he was hoping Estelle would drop a snack of chicken for him while she cooked.

Nettie smiled. "If you'd like to stay, Flossie, it's not too much out of my way to pick you up."

"That would be lovely." Flossie smiled at Laird; he returned her smile.

"I'll be back soon." Nettie hurried to the door.

When she opened her car door to climb in, Flossie called out, "Take your time; don't rush on my account."

Nettie chuckled as she drove to Marian's mother's house. *I wonder if Percy and I were ever that annoying.*

When Nettie pulled in front of the small white house, she admired the neatly trimmed lawn and the pansies and chrysanthemums that gave the front of the house a homey, welcoming pop of color.

When she raised her hand to knock, the door flew open, and Nettie was greeted by an aroma of enticing cinnamon.

Marian smiled. "Ira told me you might be coming by today, so Mama and I have been watching for you. Mama made pumpkin bread early this morning. Do you want hot tea or coffee?"

"Hot tea sounds wonderful, and I smelled the pumpkin bread when you opened the door."

Marian giggled. "We can't hide anything from you."

They linked arms as they strolled together into the kitchen.

Chapter Fourteen

"Mama, you remember Nettie, don't you?"

A black and white kitten with white front paws meowed as she strolled into the kitchen and rubbed against Nettie's legs. Nettie reached down, and the kitten smelled her hand.

Marian's mother was at the sink, washing dishes. She turned and smiled at Nettie. "Of course, I remember our sweet friend. How are you doing? Would you care for some pumpkin bread? The pumpkin came from my back yard. I decided it needed pumpkin seeds on top, so you'll be the first to try my latest creation."

While she scratched the kitten's ears, Nettie said, "It sounds delicious; I just had breakfast, so I'd like half a slice."

Marian said, "The kitten appeared at Mama's back door last week. She set up a yowl until Mama let her in. Mama said Mittens waltzed right in like she owned the place."

After Marian served their hot tea and pumpkin bread slices, her mother said, "If I may be excused, my favorite radio show comes on in five minutes."

"Enjoy." Marian smiled.

"Thank you for the pumpkin bread," Nettie added.

Mittens scampered after Mama.

"Mama's convinced Mittens likes the same music she does because Mittens sits on her lap and purrs while they listen to the radio. The two of them are already practically inseparable. Would you care for more tea?"

"I'm fine," Nettie said.

Marian glanced toward the hall and waited until the sound of the radio drifted to the kitchen. "Our house fire was no accident. Ira wanted me to stay with his folks in Alabama too, but I couldn't leave Mama alone. Do you remember the mayor's assistant, Helen?"

Nettie nodded as she sipped her tea.

"We all thought she'd left town when the mayor fired her, but a fisherman found her body down by the old boat ramp."

"That's terrible," Nettie said.

"It is." Marian exhaled. "But worse than that, Ira believes the head of the group that wants a monopoly on the whiskey and plans a takeover of the state government is a resident of our town. Ira called him a 'sleeper.' I didn't know what that meant, but Ira explained it's someone who goes undercover for years to develop a respected reputation to avoid discovery. Ira wanted me to tell you; he didn't go to Percy because Percy would drop his campaign. Ira said he'd do whatever you need to stop the group."

"I've been calling the sleeper the kingpin, but I didn't know he was embedded in our community. Thanks to Ira and thank you for telling me. The biggest thing Ira can do is to stop the thugs who are attacking people like Theresa, and I suspect, threatening others."

"He expected you to say that, but he said he wants to do more."

"Could he spare someone to shadow Percy? Somebody Percy knows and trusts, but wouldn't be a part of his team."

"A shadow." Marian furrowed her brow. "Percy knows he's there, but no one else does. I'll tell Ira; I'll bet he could. Do you want to know who the shadow is?"

Nettie smiled. "I want to know everything, but I'm not sure how smart it would be; that's up to Ira. I trust his judgment."

"He'll be tickled to hear that." Marian returned Nettie's smile.

Nettie rose. "Thanks for everything; I hate to run off, but you know how it is."

Marian nodded. "Indeed, I do."

When they reached the door, Marian hugged Nettie. "I pray for you and Percy all the time. Be safe."

A small smile crept across Nettie's face when tears welled up in her eyes on her way to pick up Flossie. *Gramma used to kiss my forehead and tell me she prayed for me all the time. It's so sweet to hear her words again, but I can't tell Marian she reminds me of my grandmother.*

When Nettie reached the shop, she tapped the horn twice, and Flossie and Laird strolled out of the shop holding hands.

Nettie narrowed her eyes. *Laird better treat Flossie right; if he doesn't, he better hope Percy gets to him before I do.*

On their way home, Flossie went on about how wonderful Laird was, but Nettie tuned her out. *I have to talk to Willis to see what our follow-up is after our whiskey heist.*

"Hey, Nettie." Flossie's voice changed in tone from swoony to bossy. "You better slow down if we're turning in our driveway."

Nettie slammed on the brakes and slid into the driveway.

"You have to teach me how to do that." Flossie glanced back. "Those skid marks are the berries!"

Nettie rolled her eyes. "I hope Percy doesn't notice them. If he does, I'll tell them you had your first driving lesson."

"Oh, please do! Do you think I could be a rum runner? No, that's a boat bootlegger, isn't it? I get seasick. Bootlegger drivers rip up roads at night, don't they? I could drive while the creatures of the night hunt, and then you'd have to let me sleep until noon."

Nettie rubbed her forehead and then exhaled. "We'll start your driving lessons the day after the election."

"That's perfect timing."

"Do you think Laird will approve of you being a bootleg whiskey driver? You know, with him being a deputy sheriff and all."

Flossie furrowed her brow. "I guess he'll have to adjust, won't he? Or should I be an undercover bootleg driver?"

"I like the way you think." Nettie exhaled when she parked the car. "Let's go inside."

As they strolled to the back door, Flossie asked, "You're going to put the telephone in the living room, aren't you? That's the most comfortable place for it to be."

"That would make sense except we don't want our guests to be disturbed or eavesdropping on Friday and Saturday nights."

"You're right. What are you thinking?"

Flossie opened the back door, and Buster snarled and barked as he rushed down the hallway. He skidded when he saw Flossie and slammed into her feet. Flossie leaned down, and Buster rolled over for a belly rub.

She giggled as she obliged him. "Buster is working on his guard dog skills. Have you decided where you're going to put the telephone?"

"We'll put the telephone in the sewing room so we'll have privacy especially for calls on Friday and Saturday nights."

Flossie snorted. "I hate it when you're logical, but I can make it work."

"Installing the telephone on the main floor means we won't be moving my sewing room upstairs. Are you okay with the hospitality room staying where it is?"

"Of course, the telephone is much more convenient for me downstairs," Flossie said. "When we were setting up the hospitality room, I found a loveseat in the storage area. I'll move it to the sewing room and add a few throw pillows so I can be comfortable while I check to see if the telephone is in use."

"You will not be lounging in my sewing room listening to the party line, so forget about adding a loveseat," Nettie growled. "If you find a chair and a small table for the telephone that will fit in the corner opposite my desk and be out of my way, we can talk."

"It won't be as comfortable, but there is a Queen Anne chair and all kinds of end tables in the storage room." Flossie sighed.

"Show me the chair so we can put it where we want the telephone before the installer shows up."

After they made their way to the back of the storage room, Flossie pulled away a white sheet and pointed to the chair. "Don't you love how the intertwining, deep green ivy and pale sage green background complements the pale creamy pink camellias?"

"It really is pretty. Let's carry it downstairs," Nettie said.

After they placed the chair in the corner that was near the door, Flossie said, "Isn't it perfect?"

"It really is. See if you can find a small table for it. A drawer would be nice so we could keep a pad and pen available to take notes," Nettie said.

While Flossie raced upstairs to find the perfect table, Nettie went into the kitchen and made herself a cup of hot tea. While she sipped her tea, she heard Willis's truck roar up the driveway. She put on a pot of coffee. Willis strode into the kitchen just as the coffee finished percolating.

"Do I smell a fresh pot?"

"I heard you coming up the driveway and thought you'd like a warm up."

Willis poured himself a cup then joined Nettie at the counter.

"I heard our heist had the desired effect; the syndicate scrambled to find more whiskey and were unsuccessful. The suppliers apologized and blamed the weather for this year's poor corn crop. So, what's our next step?"

Nettie smiled. "I was going to ask you that. We have a plan for Percy's campaign, and Ira is tracking down the thugs. We've hit the syndicate in the wallet hard. What if word got out that their gambling ring was skimming off the top?"

Willis shrugged. "I don't know. Everybody knows the house wins. How big of a surprise would it be that the house also cheats?"

Nettie furrowed her brow. "Not much at all when you put it like that. It needs to be more personal. How do we expose the kingpin?"

"What if word got out that somebody talked?" Willis asked.

"I heard Helen's body was found by a fisherman; what about the man who attacked Flossie? Has his body been found? Maybe he talked."

"I found a table; come up and I'll show you," Flossie yelled down.

Nettie exhaled. "Think about it."

Willis drained his cup and rinsed it while Nettie headed to the stairs.

Flossie met her at the top and pointed to a small square table with a drawer. "It's taller than a bedside table; it might have been in the foyer for calling cards to be dropped off. Isn't that what people used to do?"

"Something like that. I think it will fit in just fine next to your chair. Do you need any help?"

"No, it's light as a feather. When is the installer supposed to be here?"

"The manager said right after lunch."

Flossie smirked as she picked up the table. "Can we eat lunch right now, so the installer can show up?"

Nettie followed Flossie down the stairs. "I don't think it works like that, but you're welcome to try. There's a fresh pot of coffee on the stove. I'm waiting for Percy to come home before I heat the leftovers."

When they reached the bottom of the stairs, Nettie said, "Perfect timing. I hear a vehicle in the driveway. If it's the installer, I don't want you following him around asking a lot of questions; you'll only slow him down."

Flossie wrinkled her nose at Nettie. "Fine. I pulled everything out when I was looking for the right size table. I'll reorganize the furniture upstairs to make the time go faster. Will you call me when Percy gets here so I can have lunch with you?"

"I'll do that."

After Flossie went upstairs, the back door opened.

Nettie rushed to greet Percy, but she furrowed her brow when she saw his uneven pace and how heavily he leaned on his cane.

She took Percy's coat from him and hung it up. "How are you doing, sweetie?"

He put his arm around her. "I wore myself out by standing all morning in the cold shop. Laird offered me a chair, but it looked rickety, and the seat was grimy, so I passed."

"I have a pot of coffee on the stove, and I planned to heat the leftover chicken and dumplings for our lunch."

"Sounds good. I'll sit at the table to keep you company."

Nettie grabbed his wheelchair and followed him into the kitchen. "I'll put your wheelchair near you in case you'd like to give your leg a rest this afternoon."

Percy's smile was weak. "I'm sure I'll feel better after a warm lunch."

"Shall I heat the coffee or would you rather have hot tea?"

"Hot coffee, please."

After she turned up the burner under the coffee pot, Nettie strolled to the stairs and shouted, "Fifteen minute warning for lunch."

She returned to the kitchen and poured Percy a cup of hot coffee.

"Is the photography truck ready to roll now?" Nettie asked as she pulled out the leftovers and put the pot on the stove.

"As far as I'm concerned, it is. Laird may keep fussing with it and moving around equipment. I don't blame him for wanting it to be just right because he's the one who will be practically working and living in the truck for the next four weeks."

"Has your impression of him changed?" Nettie asked.

"I think he's the best photographer we could have found, but I reserve judgment on him personally; it takes me a while to really warm up to somebody. I'm glad Smitty will be by my side. He told me he was my butler, and I told him he was fired."

Nettie laughed as she stirred the chicken and dumplings. "What did he say to that?"

Percy chuckled. "My old friend Smitty looked me dead in the eye and told me he wasn't fired unless you said he was fired. I told him he had me there."

"You two are a mess." Nettie dished up chicken and dumplings into bowls then joined Percy at the table.

Percy selected a small piece of chicken with his fingers from Flossie's bowl and blew on it before he said, "Sit."

Buster sat and stared intently at Percy.

"Good boy." Percy gave Buster the piece of chicken.

Flossie dashed into the kitchen and sat down.

"You almost missed out, Flossie." Percy pointed at Buster, who stared at Flossie's bowl while he licked his chops.

"It does smell good, doesn't it, Buster? You're such a good boy." Flossie cooed.

Flossie blew on a spoonful of broth and chicken with a bit of dumpling. "I didn't quite finish organizing the storage room because I ended up pulling out everything and starting over with pushing the large items to the back and pulling the smaller items to the front, so it will be easier to see what we have. I had an interesting morning. Laird told me his mother and father were on the Titanic and were lost at sea when he was in high school. They had gone to visit his mother's relatives in England and were coming home. Isn't that tragic? His father's parents took him in. He told me they're Swiss and are kindhearted people, and he'll take me to meet them after the election."

When Percy glanced at Nettie and winked, she smiled. *He knows I'm going to check the Titanic passenger list.*

After they ate, Nettie said, "Flossie, if you want to get back to organizing the storage room, I'll take care of the dishes."

"You wash, I'll dry," Percy said.

"Are you sure?" Nettie asked after Flossie headed toward the stairs.

"There's not that much."

"Okay, but I'll be in trouble if Estelle catches us."

"We'll be safe; Bella will come busting in first."

While she washed dishes, Nettie said, "I could use your advice on something you're not supposed to know anything about because you'd worry."

"I worry about you all the time anyway, so it won't matter."

"I didn't say you'd worry about me."

"What else do I have to worry about?"

Nettie exhaled. "I want to flush out the kingpin. Do you think spreading a rumor that word got out that somebody talked would work?"

"It would if you had a snippet of truth to go along with it so it didn't look like idle gossip."

"You're right, thanks."

"What are you going to do?" Percy narrowed his eyes.

"Find a snippet of truth and then embellish it just enough to make it juicy." Nettie kissed his cheek. "Thanks."

"You'll keep me updated, right?"

"Sure will." Nettie paused and listened. "A truck is coming up the driveway. Maybe it's our installer."

"Where are we putting the telephone?"

"In my sewing room; we'll be able to make private calls, or at least as private as they can be on a party line."

"Your admirer at the telephone company said he'd put in an order for a private line, but no line is truly private because the local operator has access to the line. When I made the calls in the telephone office, I'd pick up the telephone, which alerted the telephone operator. She said number please, and I told her."

"The operator could listen in on a private line?" Nettie asked.

"They theoretically could, but I think they're too busy."

"How do you know the operator didn't listen in on your calls?"

"I guess I don't." Percy frowned. "Now, I have something to worry about besides you."

"See what Ira thinks; he knows everybody."

Percy nodded as he used his cane to rise from his chair. "Either he'll ease my mind, or we'll be talking about how to do damage control. I'll let the installer in."

Percy led the installer to the sewing room, and Nettie followed them.

Percy pointed at the green chair. "That's where we want it."

The installer nodded. "I appreciate you have your spot selected, and all set up. I've spent an hour waiting while folks decided, then half the time I had to go back and move their telephone a week later. Not that I mind, but it throws my schedule off for new installations."

"That's a shame," Percy said.

"Thank you. I won't be long. After you're all hooked up, you'll get a call from Miz Myrtle to check out your connection, and she'll answer any questions you have. You probably already knew you're getting a private line. Most people think a private line is like a confidential line, but it isn't. Miz Myrtle will go into all that with you."

While the installer worked, Nettie went upstairs to check on Flossie.

Nettie coughed when she stepped into the hospitality room. "Are you cleaning, Flossie?"

Flossie came out of the shadows and flopped down on a soft chair. "It's all your fault, Nettie. First, you wanted a chair, not the sofa, and I had to pull everything out. And then, you wanted a table. It took me forever to find that little table, which is absolutely perfect, isn't it?"

"It really is, and the patina on the wood is beautiful. You must have polished it with linseed oil and a lot of elbow grease."

"I did, thank you; it was hard work, but I loved how it turned out. It looked so nice that I had to polish the rest of the tables. I'm almost done. I still have a few small tables and chairs to put away, but everything is polished, brushed, or dusted."

"While Percy is on the campaign trail, we might want to do some shopping in the storage room. It wouldn't hurt for us to update some of our rooms, especially the hallway, our two spare bedrooms, and the living room."

"That would be fun, wouldn't it? We could surprise Percy when he gets back." Flossie wrinkled her nose. "Except he's not much into change. I'll let you handle selling him on how brilliant we are."

Nettie chuckled. "That will be easy because we are. The installer is here. He said we're getting a private line."

"Oh, no!" Flossie fanned her face with her hand and then sighed. "It's my fault; I had my heart set on a party line, and I jinxed us."

"You still have Friday and Saturday nights. I can't imagine anyone who can eavesdrop on as many conversations at once as you can."

"It is a special skill, isn't it?"

"Percy appreciates it, and so do I. There's no way Percy and I could keep our fingers on the pulse of our members if you weren't there."

Flossie giggled. "Don't go spreading that around; you'll ruin my reputation as a flapper."

Nettie's eyes twinkled as she pushed her lips together, motioned a quick zip across her mouth with her forefinger and thumb and then mimed throwing away a key.

"The installer's done," Percy called up from the bottom of the stairs.

Flossie dashed toward the stairs, but Nettie raced past her and beat her to the sewing room.

Percy stepped back to keep from being trampled. "Sometimes you two act like you're ten."

"Sorry, Grandpa." Flossie feigned a duck from an imaginary swing from Percy.

"Awright, youse guys, break it up here." Nettie mimicked a tough guy accent.

The telephone rang, and Flossie dived for it, but Nettie beat her to it and picked up the receiver as Flossie crashed into her chair.

"Hello."

"Hello, Nettie, dear. This is Myrtle at the telephone department. Did the installer tell you that y'all have a private line?"

Flossie smashed her ear against Nettie's as she tried to listen in. Nettie pushed her away.

"Yes, ma'am, he did."

Flossie sat on the edge of the chair and leaned against Nettie. Nettie elbowed her, and Flossie gave her a little space.

Percy snorted.

Myrtle continued, "When you want to call someone, you pick up the telephone. When I answer, you give me the number, and I will contact you. Most of the time, I stay on the line until your call goes through before I hang up unless I'm super busy. I'm going to be real quiet. Tell me what you hear."

Nettie listened to a low buzzing. "I hear a buzzing sound."

Flossie moved close then held up a thumb, and Nettie nodded.

"That's wonderful. My nephew who is an engineering genius added that to my line. Despite what everybody thinks, I can't work twenty-four hours a day, seven days a week. I'm such a slacker." Myrtle chortled.

Nettie chuckled to be social. "I'd never thought about that; so I can tell if someone from the telephone office is on the line when I am because I'll hear the buzzing."

Flossie clasped her hands over her head like a prize fighter, and Percy smiled.

"That's right, Nettie. You'd be surprised how many people can't hear it. I blame it on the jazz music. Have you noticed how loud those trumpets are when they blare out the call of their tribe?"

When Nettie's mouth quivered involuntarily and threatened to break into a smile, or worse yet, a laugh, she cleared her throat. "Yes, ma'am. Thank you for telling me about the buzzing, and you are brilliant for asking your nephew to add it."

Myrtle tittered. "You're too sweet; thank you. You let me know if you need any help with your telephone or anything else. It's been a pleasure talking to you."

Myrtle disconnected, and Nettie listened. *Silence. Myrtle really is a genius.*

"Do you think I'll hear the buzzing, or is my hearing loss from the gunfire in France worse than I've thought?" Percy asked.

"It might be, but we should check you and Bella. If Flossie and I are not around, maybe Bella will be," Nettie said. "It's nice to have backup."

"So, what's your schedule this afternoon?" Percy asked.

"I have the follow-up calls to make, and I'd like to go to the library if I have time. What about you?"

"I'm meeting Ira at the bank; we're going to pay off his team's home loans. I'm doing my best to get our bank account as low as we can."

"Willis and I have a Golden Star tonic meeting later this afternoon at the beauty shop. He told me after this, I have to find a different place to hold meetings if I want him to go along," Flossie said. "Maybe I'll talk to Theresa."

Percy chuckled. "I don't blame him. If we're not back when you leave, Flossie, let Oliver know no one will be at the house with Buster."

"I'll do that; I'm sure he'll take Buster to his house to keep Estelle company, and Bella will love seeing Buster when she gets home from school."

Chapter Fifteen

After Nettie called the contacts for Percy's first three stops, she slipped her library books that were ready to be returned into her book tote.

"Your first three contacts insisted you stay with them, which we expected. When I call them back tomorrow, they expect to tell me where Laird and Smitty will be staying. I'm ready when you are."

On the way to town, Percy asked, "You're doing more at the library than just returning books, aren't you?"

Nettie shrugged. "I need more books, and I might do a little research."

Percy suddenly slammed on the brakes when a deer darted across the road in front of him. "I always worry there's a second deer."

Nettie nodded. "Drop me off at Theresa's shop. I can walk from there to the library."

When Percy stopped in front of the fabric shop, he said, "Ira and I will go to the restaurant to grab a cup of java after we finish up our business at the bank. Do you want me to pick you up at the library on the way?"

"No, I'm dressed warm enough, and I need the walk to clear my thoughts and work up to running with Bella; she's fast."

"I should have known you had a hidden agenda; you always do." Percy chuckled. "Of course, I still don't know what it is."

He put his hand on her shoulder to stop her and kissed her. "See you later."

When Nettie went into the fabric shop, it was quiet. "It's me," she called out.

"I'm in the back," Theresa said.

"What's up?" Theresa stood on a ladder as she tugged on a bolt one-handed. The fabric teetered on the shelf and then dropped onto the floor.

Nettie shook her head. "That was impressive. Where do you want it?"

"Next to the cutting board. I have a few ladies coming in later this afternoon, and I'm pre-selecting fabric for them. What are you doing?"

"Checking up on you and making sure my twenty percent of your business is being run right."

Theresa burst out laughing. After she wiped away her tears, she said, "My eighty percent is doing great. Your twenty had a rough day."

Nettie laughed.

"Do you have a little time? Would you like a cup of hot tea? I ordered an electric hot plate from the Sears and Roebuck catalog and keep a pot of water on it, so I can have my hot tea whenever I feel like it. It's been a timesaver to have on-hand. I had hot soup for lunch today, and it was a delicious treat on our early wintry day."

"Hot tea sounds wonderful." Nettie removed her coat then carried the bolt of fabric to the table next to the cutting table.

While they sipped tea in the back of the store, Nettie asked, "Are you sleeping okay?"

"Not bad. The hospital gave me some pain pills to take at night so I could sleep, but I'd rather be able to hear if someone is trying to get inside my house. I'm taking aspirin at bedtime because Doc told me that's what he takes, so I figure it's good enough for me."

"I don't have his medical training, but you need to eat something when you take the aspirin."

Theresa smiled. "I know how much you read, so if you think that's wise, that's good enough for me."

Nettie chuckled. "I do read a variety of books, which reminds me, I have books to return to the library. Thanks for the tea."

Theresa strolled with her to the door.

Nettie paused. "I almost forgot to mention that you might hear from Flossie about a meeting place for her group, but I don't think I was supposed to tell you."

Theresa chuckled. "I'd heard they were meeting at the beauty shop today. It would be a pleasure having them here, but I'll be appropriately surprised when Flossie drops by to ask."

Nettie buttoned up her coat, pulled up its collar, and put on her gloves before she went outside. She put her head down as she trudged against the brisk wind, holding her tote with the books with both arms across her chest like a shield.

When she reached the library, she tugged open the door, but the wind whipped it out of her hands and blew it wide open. An elderly man caught her before she fell and pulled her inside while the young librarian pulled the door closed.

The young librarian exhaled. "That gust snatched that door away from you like it was a trap it set for you, didn't it?'

"Thank you for rescuing me," Nettie said.

The elderly man chuckled. "Most excitement I've had since that old gent set another man's mustache on fire because of a stolen cigar. I'm still not clear on which one of them was the thief."

"Set a man's mustache on fire? When was that?" the young librarian asked.

"About twenty years ago. Seems like it was yesterday." The elderly man exhaled as he sat at the nearest table. "I need to catch my breath; it's been ages since I moved that fast."

"Did that happen here?" the librarian asked.

Miss Charlotte, the head librarian, came out of her office. "Did what happen here?"

"We were talking about a man who set another man's mustache on fire twenty years ago," the young librarian said.

"It was in a hospital in New York. Ask Doc about it. According to the New York newspaper that reported it, he was the one who put out the fire," the man said.

The young librarian narrowed her eyes. "You remember an article from a New York newspaper you read twenty years ago?"

The man glared. "I'm more likely to remember something from twenty years ago than something that happened yesterday. It just goes with the territory."

He turned to Nettie. "Don't believe the rambling of an old man; you must always check things for yourself."

"I'll do that." Nettie rose and carried the books to the librarian's desk.

After she added her books to the stack of others that had been checked in, Nettie said, "I told Bella I'd bring her a book, and for me, do you have any books about the Titanic?"

Miss Charlotte said, "I know just the book for Bella. A young lady returned it earlier, so it's still on the cart to be shelved."

Miss Charlotte pulled a book from the cart and signed it out to Nettie.

Nettie slipped it into her empty book tote.

"As far as the Titanic, we don't have anything about its last voyage, if that's what you're interested in."

"I'm interested in the manifest; you know, a list of cargo and passengers' names."

"I'll tell you where you can find that, young lady," the elderly man said. "The newspaper office would have it in their archives. They printed the list of the crew and passengers not long after the incident. People everywhere went to church and prayed for the lost and the survivors, and the pastors stood in the pulpit and read each name and their age."

The man gazed out the window as he drifted back in time to the church and the solemn moment.

A woman sat next to the man and patted his hand. "Sad times."

He peered at Nettie. "I was sorry to hear your friend Theresa was attacked by a man with an eagle talon tattoo."

Nettie exhaled. *This might be my opportunity to start a rumor.*

"Thank you; we're not sure which one of them it was."

The woman gasped. "I didn't know there was more than one man with a tattoo like that. Are we being invaded by a gang? Does the sheriff know?"

"I'm sure he does because I heard one of them went to the fed and told them who the leader was," Nettie said.

The elderly man raised an eyebrow. "I heard the leader is from around here."

Nettie nodded. *I think I have an ally.*

She nodded. "I heard the same thing."

The woman quickly glanced around. "We need to watch for him, don't we? Do you think he has the same tattoo?"

The elderly man leaned back in his chair. "He might, but I doubt it."

The young librarian glanced up from her desk. "I saw a man with a tattoo at the grocery store. I thought there was something off about him."

"You can't judge a man by a tattoo," Miss Charlotte said.

While the discussion about tattooed men became heated, and speculation about their leader continued with additional details, Nettie picked up her book tote and quietly left.

As she kept her balance while the wind pushed her forward, she smiled at the memory of the man who helped her establish the rumor so quickly.

When she reached the newspaper office, she stopped a moment in the alcove and took a breath before we went inside.

"What are you doing out in this weather, Nettie? I'm surprised you didn't blow away." The publisher chuckled.

She smiled. "Actually, I am too. I'd like to write a short story based on a historical event. I thought you might have some ideas."

"That's exciting; I'll be happy to publish your story in the paper after you finish. Did you have any historical events in mind?"

"I didn't until I was at the library earlier and someone mentioned the Titanic. I'm sure the disaster has plenty of stories about it, so I was thinking about writing about someone before the disaster. Like who they were and how they came to be on the ship on its last voyage."

"That's a brilliant twist; I published a list of the manifest that included all the passengers. Were you thinking about writing about someone who was lost or survived?"

"I'm not sure. Maybe if I spent some time studying the passengers and where they were from, a story would pop out at me."

The publisher nodded. "Spoken like a writer who is genuinely serious about her craft. Hold on; I have quite a few copies of that old edition. I'm happy to give you a copy. There were a few follow-up articles two or three years later from the New York newspaper I included in later editions. I'll give you copies of them too."

When the publisher returned with a stack of newspapers, Nettie smiled. "This is wonderful. I love to read; I'll get them back to you next week."

"You're welcome to keep them if you'd like to have them for reference as you write. I'm rarely asked for old editions, and except for the newspapers with the Titanic manifest and the Wright Brothers' flight and the announcement of President McKinley's assassination and the end of the Great War, there's no reason for me to keep over two copies of any paper."

While Nettie put the neatly folded newspapers into her tote bag, he exhaled. "I guess I just assigned myself the job of culling out newspapers this afternoon, since there's not much else to do in this weather."

Nettie smiled. "While I was at the library, I heard a really interesting story that a New York newspaper had printed about a man in a hospital setting another man's mustache on fire. Do you know anything about that?"

The publisher guffawed. "I know who told you that. He and I still laugh about it. I might still have a copy of that paper, or at least the clipping. Are you going to work that into your story about the Titanic? That would be swell. I'll see if I can find that story."

Ten minutes later, the publisher reappeared with a stack of old newspapers and a box. "I not only found that story, but I found several others you might enjoy reading for inspiration." He wrapped the box with twine so Nettie could carry it.

He beamed as Nettie added the stack into her book tote and picked up the box by the twine.

"Thanks for everything."

"Anytime, Nettie. I'm happy I could help."

Nettie braced for the wind that pushed her after she stepped outside and headed toward the restaurant that was two blocks away.

Nettie smiled when she reached the parking lot. *Percy's car isn't here. I'm here first; I win.*

When she went inside, she put the box and her tote on a chair at a table that was the farthest from the front door and pulled off her gloves. The server called out, "Coffee or hot tea, Nettie?"

Nettie smiled as she removed her coat and put it on the back of her chair. "Hot tea, please."

The server brought her a large mug of hot water with a tea bag and lemon wedges on a saucer. "Chef made blueberry cobbler to counter that icy blast of wind we're getting today. It's still warm from the oven and comes with a side of vanilla ice cream."

"That sounds perfect."

The server returned immediately with a bowl of steaming cobbler and melting ice cream. Nettie took a big. "Mmm; this is delicious."

Percy came inside before her second bite. When he scanned the restaurant for a table, his eyes widened when he saw Nettie. He strode to her and kissed her cheek before he sat down. "They told me at the library you'd already left earlier. How long have you been here?"

"Not long; I stopped at the newspaper office and picked up a few older editions."

She pointed to the box and patted her tote bag. "I have some interesting reading ahead of me this afternoon."

The server brought Percy coffee and cobbler. "If you don't want the cobbler, someone else will."

Percy chuckled. "Chef's cobbler is almost as good as Estelle's."

"I take that as a compliment," Chef shouted from the kitchen.

When Ira came into the restaurant, the server raced him to Nettie and Percy's table with a cup of coffee and a bowl of cobbler.

When she reached the table and set down the cup and bowl, she said, "I saw you drive up, Ira. Chef bet me I couldn't beat you to Nettie's table."

She shrugged as Ira shook his head and sat down. "We catch our fun when we can around here."

Ira took a large bite of a perfectly balanced combination of cobbler and ice cream. "Hot and cold. Mmm."

After he sipped his coffee, Ira said, "I heard interesting news at the gas station. The man who attacked Theresa was part of a big gang, and the feds are closing in on the gang leader who lives here."

"Wow; that's big news." Percy glanced at Nettie, who took a bite of cobbler.

Ira nodded. "If I were the leader of a gang like that, I'd be worried one of those thugs would break rank, and I guess one did."

Nettie raised her eyebrows when a stranger sitting at the counter whispered to the man sitting next to him. The first man rose and dropped a fin on the counter, and the two men left. *Big tipper.*

She nudged Percy's knee with hers, and he nodded.

Ira lowered his voice to a near whisper. "Our town visitors appear to be evacuating."

Percy's eyes twinkled. "Easy come; easy go."

When Johnny came into the restaurant, Ira covered the side of his face as he rubbed his forehead. Johnny slightly nodded at Nettie and she returned the nod.

After Johnny sat at the counter, Ira whispered, "You know him?"

Nettie nodded.

Ira exhaled. "He's the number one hit man for the largest syndicate in Chicago. I can't be here."

Ira sauntered to the men's rest room that was only a few steps away and then out the back door.

Percy took another bite of his cobbler. "We do have eclectic friends, don't we?"

Nettie furrowed her brow. "I don't understand."

Percy nodded and signed, "Later."

After Nettie and Percy finished eating, Percy carried the box, and Nettie carried her tote as they strolled together to their car.

As Percy drove toward home, he said, "Ira and I got to the bank just in time. Only the manager and the head teller were left, and he was packing up his things."

"He fired everyone?"

"That's what I think. We paid off the loans for Ira's team; Ira has all the signed paperwork, and I have a receipt that shows you have a bank balance of one hundred dollars; at least you did when we left. The banker locked the front door behind us and hung up a sign that said closed."

"He shut down the bank?"

"We were glad we got there when we did."

Nettie asked, "Why did Ira have to leave the restaurant when Johnny came in?"

"He was sitting with us; he doesn't want any of the Chicago crowd to think he's gone rogue. Your reputation as a maverick is firmly established, so Ira can't be closely associated with you. It's okay if he's helping me because I'm the best man to beat the incumbent who has worn out his welcome with the Chicago bunch. They're tired of the incumbent's incompetence and erratic behavior and being taken for granted. They know where I stand, and while they aren't willing to support my campaign, my opponent should be careful to not alienate them further, or they will."

Nettie furrowed her brow. "I thought Johnny was with the Atlanta mob."

Percy shrugged. "I did too; maybe he keeps track of what's going on in Georgia for the Chicago mob."

She stared at the passing fields. *Doesn't seem all that plausible to me. He makes Ira nervous; I won't drop my guard.*

Nettie watched a crow chase a hawk. "Is there a way I can nip at the incumbent's tail feathers to fluster him more?"

Percy laughed. "Please don't."

When he turned at the driveway, Percy said, "Laird's found another woman."

"What?" Nettie screamed. "Turn around. I'm going to shoot him between his eyes. Twice."

Percy exhaled. "Sorry, honey. It sounded hilarious in my head, but I guess it wasn't as funny as I thought. A dog wandered into the shop yesterday and stayed. Laird had left one of his jackets at the shop, and she dragged it under the photography truck and slept on it there. She's a scruffy-looking girl and was a little wary of me at first, but she was friendly after Laird told her I was okay. Laird thinks she's a border collie and golden labrador retriever mix. He has an appointment to take her to the vet this afternoon and to a groomer afterward for a bath."

"What's her name?" Nettie asked.

"He wants Flossie to name her. This whole dog thing has actually caused Laird to rise a little higher on my trust scale."

"I have the passenger list for the Titanic, so if his parents are listed, I'm okay with him."

After Percy parked, Nettie hopped out with her box and book tote bag and peered at the back door. "There's a note on the door. I'll bet Flossie is gone, and Buster is at Estelle's house. I'm really torn between wishing I could be there when Flossie meets Laird's new dog and wanting to tear through the newspapers to see if Laird's parents were on the Titanic."

While Percy went to Estelle's for Buster, Nettie hurried inside. After she hung up her coat, she rushed to her office and set the box on the floor and pulled out the newspapers from her tote bag.

When she found the newspaper dated April 28, 1912, she was overcome by a deep sorrow as she gazed at the artist's rendition of a sinking ocean liner and the blazing headline:

RMS Titanic Tragedy: 706 Survive 2,240 Souls Perish

Tears slipped down her cheeks as she read through the lists, looking for a couple with Miller as their last name. When she reached the end of the third class list, she felt her heart thud. *No Millers.*

She started over with the first class list and read slowly; after she finished the second class list, she put her head in her hands while she sobbed.

Percy came into the sewing room with Buster dancing alongside. He rushed to Nettie who had tears streaming down her face; he pulled her up from her chair into a hug. "I'm so sorry, sweetheart. You didn't find them, did you?"

"No, and I really thought I would; it broke my heart to read all the names and feel how excited they must have been to sail on Titanic's maiden voyage."

Percy stared at the newspaper. "Didn't Flossie say Laird's grandparents on his father's side were Swiss? Look at this." He pointed to a line. "Aldrich and Lidia Müller."

Nettie's eyes widened. "I totally missed that. Müller is German and would have been translated as Miller in English when Laird's parents immigrated. They must have had passports from Switzerland."

She stared at the first names. "They used almost all the letters in both of their first names when they named Laird."

"Are you convinced?" Percy asked.

"Maybe, but he could be telling Flossie the truth about his parents but still be working against us for the fed, couldn't he?"

"I suppose, but I like Laird, and I don't think he would do anything to jeopardize the campaign."

Nettie narrowed her eyes. "You're more trusting than I am. Wouldn't it be nice to ask Laird what his parents' names were? Why don't you do that? You're smoother than I am."

Percy snorted. "No kidding, but this is your show. You need to get to where you're satisfied."

"What about you?"

"I'll wait and then agree with you."

Nettie rolled her eyes. "I've made the calls for this weekend and the next two for next week. I'd like to make a few more calls before the afternoon is gone. Do you want to listen to the telephone while I make the first one to see if you hear the buzz when Miss Myrtle picks up?"

Percy nodded as he sat on the soft chair next to the telephone table and invited Nettie to sit on his lap. He wrapped his arms around her and nuzzled her neck, and she giggled.

"This is serious stuff, lady. What's wrong with you?" Percy growled.

Nettie laughed. "This isn't going to work."

Percy exhaled. "Okay, I'll behave."

"I doubt it." Nettie picked up her list of names and telephone numbers she'd left on the small table.

"Ready?" She picked up the telephone and leaned close to Percy so he could hear.

Miss Mrytle said, "Number please?"

Nettie peered at Percy who shrugged; she patted his arm as she recited the number.

When the contact for the third town answered, Nettie rose, so Percy could vacate the chair for her. While he sat in the chair at her desk, Nettie introduced herself to the contact then ignored her script as they chatted.

After she hung up, Percy asked, "Didn't you completely dump your script?"

Nettie sniffed. "My script was a guideline to be sure I covered all the points. You're confirmed for three nights with your host on Thursday, Friday, and Saturday nights. There may be an additional event on Sunday afternoon, which will add a fourth night, but they'll let me know so I can adjust your schedule for your visit that follows. Same schedule for Smitty and Laird with nearby neighbors. Cliff and his sister are scheduled to be there early next week, so if there is anything off, one of them will get in touch with you. How can we let Cliff know we have a telephone?"

"I'll get word to him," Percy said.

"How are you feeling?" Nettie asked.

"Health or campaign wise?" he asked.

"Yes."

Percy chuckled. "Healthwise, I have to remember to sit a bit to rest and walk to stretch my legs since you won't be around to glare at me. I'm getting excited about the campaign because you're lining up everything for me. All I have to do is listen and talk to the people, which I love doing. The only part I don't like is being away from you."

"I'm not fond of that either, but I'll have to come up with a plan to shift household chores away from Flossie so she can focus on her tonic business. She'll want to continue helping with our Friday and Saturday membership dinners, but she's also been helping Estelle and has taken over a majority of the everyday housekeeping chores. I'll have to hire someone else fulltime to work Mondays through Fridays."

"I'm sure you'll find someone."

"Transportation is our biggest obstacle," Nettie said.

"Hire Bella to be the driver."

Nettie laughed. "Bella would love it, but you'd lose status as Estelle's favorite because I'd tell her it was your idea."

When Percy rose to leave, Nettie said, "I'll talk to Estelle about Bella. We should have her on the payroll anyway with most of the money going into a college fund and the rest for her to learn how to manage money."

"Why don't you talk to Estelle about a fulltime position while you're at it?" Percy left the room.

Nettie stared at the closed door and then put on her coat.

When she passed the living room on her way to the back door, Buster was squeezed in next to Percy on the sofa. Percy had stretched out, and his eyes were closed. Buster opened his eyes then closed them.

Nettie shivered when she went outside and was slammed by a freezing gust of wind that took away her breath. *Buster made the right choice.*

When she reached the front door, she knocked, and Bella answered.

The inviting warmth of the living room fireplace and the intoxicating aroma of baking bread greeted Nettie.

"Come in; I told Granny it had to be you. We're in the kitchen." Bella led the way. "I'm finishing up my homework, and Granny is baking bread."

Nettie took off her coat. "I could smell the bread; it's cold outside. I picked up a book at the library for you, Bella."

Nettie pulled out the book from her tote bag and gave it to Bella.

Bella squealed. "Thank you so much! I can't believe the library had this book. Agatha Christie is the new author that everyone is talking about. I'm almost through with my homework; I can't wait to read it."

They strolled together to the kitchen. While Bella resumed her studies, Nettie drank hot tea and ate a slice of warm bread slathered with butter while she caught Estelle up on the news, including the latest with Flossie, Laird, and Laird's new dog. She asked Estelle about working extra hours during the week.

Estelle signed, "I can do laundry on Mondays and cook enough for you and Flossie for two days; on Wednesdays, I can dust, vacuum, and cook another two-day meal because that's really all you need. We already spend Fridays and Saturdays getting ready for our guests."

Nettie smiled as she signed, "You're right, and Bella has taken over as your sous chef, hasn't she?"

Nettie explained her idea for paying Bella, and Estelle sniffed back tears.

"That's wonderful," Estelle signed. "Thank you."

Nettie swallowed the lump that had risen in her throat then signed, "We'll come up with a way to make sure her college money is secure."

Estelle nodded. "I like the idea of Bella learning to manage her own money. Will you teach her how to budget?"

Nettie nodded then signed, "Percy and I appreciate all you do for us."

Estelle signed, "Family isn't always blood-related."

After they hugged, and Nettie hugged Bella, Nettie put on her coat and left with a warm loaf of bread under her arm.

Chapter Sixteen

When Nettie opened the back door, Buster greeted her with his backend wiggling as furiously as his tail. Nettie removed her coat then sat on the floor with him and rubbed his ears and face while she cooed, "Good boy, Buster."

Flossie called out from the kitchen, "I just got back; come have tea with me. I've got news for you."

While Nettie sipped her hot tea, Flossie said, "My big news is that Laird has a dog. She's a beautiful girl; we took her to the vet who said she's a border collie and lab mix. He vaccinated her for rabies and told Laird to feed her pumpkin seeds and applesauce to treat her worms. The vet said some people give their dogs apple cider vinegar and garlic instead of applesauce, but the vinegar would upset her stomach, and who would want to give their dog garlic breath?" Flossie giggled.

Flossie refilled her cup and joined Nettie at the table. "She's so skinny, I don't think it wouldn't hurt for her to put on a little weight, either, but Laird said it's better for her if she puts on the weigh slowly. He's really smart.

We named her Peaches; she likes her name. I suggested Linda at first, but Laird said his mother's name was Lidia, so I decided that was too close; when I said 'Peaches,' her cars perked up."

Nettie smiled. "I'm not sure I've ever heard of a dog picking out her own name; she must be exceptionally smart."

"She is; after the vet, we took her to a groomer, and she got a bath and her nails trimmed. She's tan and cream with a creamy white chest, and her muzzle is white. We didn't know how white her coat was until after her bath, though. She is such a girly-girl. The groomer put a pink bandana on her, and she loves it. When Laird took it off to put on her pink collar, she whined, so he put it right back on. Isn't that funny?"

"Peaches sounds like a wonderful dog."

"She really is; I love her to pieces. She'll travel with Laird. I don't think he has a choice because she sticks to him like glue. His boarding house doesn't allow dogs, so he'll shower and have his meals at the boarding house, but stay with her at the shed in the wagon until they leave on Thursday. The sheriff has a friend who is working on the truck at his farm. I don't exactly know what he's fixing, but Laird said something about a cracked fuel line, or maybe he said clogged." Flossie shrugged. "I didn't really pay attention because I was talking to Peaches. Laird will get his truck back tomorrow. He's planning to spend his nights with her in the truck while they're on the road."

Nettie cocked her head. "Why don't I make some calls? There might be a possibility of dog-friendly homes where they could stay."

She rushed to her sewing room with Buster and Flossie on her heels. When she called the first contact, she explained the situation with Peaches. "I just don't want Laird's host to feel like their hospitality is not appreciated."

The man said, "Give us a chance to make some calls; maybe we can work something out. We'll call you back tomorrow."

After she hung up, Nettie called all the contacts for the upcoming two weeks.

"What's the verdict?" Flossie bit her lip.

"They all understood and will get back to me. Even if they don't find a dog-friendly place for them to stay, at least Laird's hosts won't be offended that Laird is sleeping in his truck."

"I'm going to fry cube steaks and make gravy. How does rice sound to you?"

"Perfect; what can I do?"

"Talk to me while I cook unless you have something urgent."

While Flossie prepared the cube steaks for frying, Nettie told her about the plans she made with Estelle.

"That's brilliant; I've been worrying about how I could do everything. Do you want to hear about my meeting?"

"Oh, yes."

"I expected at least eight people to show up, and we had twenty people who are very interested in the business. I talked to Theresa, and we'll meet every day at her shop at two o'clock. After we are more organized, we won't have to meet as often. I told Laird about our new Golden Star tonic business, except I didn't go into specifics about the ingredients. He's very supportive and excited for me."

Nettie smiled. "That was smart to skip mentioning the ingredients. He's a good guy, and we don't want to put him in an awkward position."

"Exactly. Do you want to warn Percy we'll be eating in about twenty minutes?"

When Nettie strolled into the living room, Percy was awake, but still stretched out on the sofa.

He sat up. "I feel a lot better after that nap. What did I miss?"

"Flossie's home, and she named Laird's dog Peaches. She also told me she first picked Linda for the dog's name, but Laird told her his mother's name was Lidia. How's that for smooth?"

Percy laughed. "That's great news, and a relief for me."

"Peaches will be traveling with Laird, so I called our contacts to let them know Laird would be sleeping in his truck with Peaches. All of them said they'd call me back tomorrow."

Percy reached for her, and she sat next to him. "You're brilliant."

"One more thing." Nettie told him about her conversation with Estelle.

Percy kissed her cheek. "I should nap more often."

Nettie giggled. "We'll be eating in twenty minutes."

While they ate, Flossie talked about how pretty and smart Peaches was and how wonderful Laird was.

"I need to meet Peaches before y'all leave," Nettie said.

Percy nodded. "I'm sure that can be arranged. There must be something we need in town that we can pick up tomorrow."

"We need apples," Flossie said. "I'd like to can small jars of applesauce for Peaches."

"Sounds like a plan," Percy said.

After they ate, Nettie shooed Flossie out of the kitchen and washed dishes while Percy dried them.

"Do you hear that? Flossie's vacuuming," Nettie said.

"It's her nervous energy; she's excited about Peaches, and she had a great day." Percy grinned. "Of course, you wouldn't know anything about that nervous energy thing, would you?"

Nettie snorted and hurried to her sewing room to organize the newspapers then put them away.

When Nettie returned to the living room with a book she hoped to finish, Flossie was reading a book about how to manage a business, and Percy and Buster sat in front of a roaring fire in the fireplace. She sat in her yellow chair and read.

When Percy kissed the top of her head, she opened her eyes. "I think I dropped off."

"You did, and I didn't want to wake you, but Flossie's gone to bed. Buster and I have been out for our last walk of the night, and we locked up."

Nettie yawned. "I think I'm ready for bed."

Percy helped her to her feet, and they went upstairs together.

After she changed and climbed into bed, Nettie asked, "Do we need another blanket on the bed?"

"I'll throw an extra blanket on the bench at the foot of our bed, so it will be handy if we need it."

Nettie crawled into the bed and shivered at the crisp, cold sheets. "I forgot to heat some water for our hot water bottles."

Percy turned off the light and climbed into bed. Nettie put her cold feet on his back, and he jumped.

"I should have expected that," he mumbled.

Nettie closed her eyes.

Nettie gasped and opened her eyes when she heard a dog whine then howl.

She shook Percy. "Something's wrong."

Percy groaned and rolled to sit up.

Flossie stood in their doorway. "I had a nightmare."

Nettie jumped out of bed. "Get dressed. We have to go into town."

Flossie rushed to her room.

"Now?" Percy swayed as he got out of bed.

Nettie threw on the clothes from the previous day. "You don't have to go if you don't want to."

Percy dressed before Nettie reached the top of the stairs. The three of them threw on their coats and raced to the car. Buster had slipped out with Percy but stopped for a quick break. Before Flossie closed her door, he jumped inside.

"Buster jumped into the car," Flossie said.

"Go," Nettie said.

On the way to town, Percy asked, "Where are we going?"

"To town," Nettie said. "Did you hear that? A dog howled."

Buster howled in the back seat.

"I've never heard Buster howl before." Percy pushed the accelerator to the floor.

When they reached town, the dog howled again, and Buster answered with a howl. "I heard it," Percy said. "Hang on. I see fire a block away."

Percy skid to a stop near the shop where Laird's wagon was stored. One side of the shop was engulfed in flames. The sides of the building slowly darkened as the fire moved across the roof and the sides of the shop. Nettie ran to the shop with Buster at her side.

Percy grabbed her arm and pushed her down. "Stay back."

He ran into the smoky building on the side opposite the flames. Buster barked and followed Percy.

Flossie helped Nettie up; Nettie followed Percy and Buster into the building as the flames.

"You people are crazy," Flossie screamed. Buster ran out of the building and barked at Flossie.

"Okay, okay. I'll follow you."

Buster led Flossie to the side of the building that was in flames. A section of the tin roof had fallen against the door frame at an angle and had created a shelter from the direct flames. Buster's bark was answered with a weak bark. Flossie ran to the space left by the tin roof, but it was narrow and filled with smoke. Nettie joined her.

"I'm smaller." Nettie held her breath and crawled into the space. The thick smoke burned her eyes. When she couldn't hold her breath any longer, she breathed in smoke and coughed then was answered by a weak whine. She felt something furry; she wrapped her arms around it and pulled it toward her. *I'm stronger than I look.* She coughed, pulled, and tugged until something grabbed her legs and dragged her out while she held onto the dog.

Flossie shouted, "Move out of my way. The building's going to collapse, and I have to get Peaches out."

Nettie let go of Peaches and rolled to the side out of Flossie's way. She screamed when she was snatched to her feet.

"I've got you," Percy said. "I found Laird; he'll be okay. He had gone back into the fire to find Peaches."

Percy carried Nettie, and Flossie carried Peaches while Buster trotted alongside Percy. When they reached the car, Flossie set Peaches down next to Laird as the roof collapsed and the wagon inside burst into flames.

Men appeared from nowhere with buckets of water. A bucket brigade quickly formed to douse the flames so they wouldn't spread to any nearby structures.

When Nettie coughed then shivered uncontrollably, Percy carried her to the passenger seat. "I'll talk to the sheriff then get everyone in the car. We'll go home so we can get warm."

Percy put Buster on Nettie's lap, and she hugged the puppy. "You're a hero, Buster, and you're warm."

Percy quickly returned and sped with his passengers to the house.

While he parked, Oliver ran out of his house.

"What happened?"

"The shop where Laird's wagon was stored caught fire. Can you help him into the house?"

Oliver opened Laird's door and helped him out.

"I'll carry Peaches," Flossie said.

Percy picked up Nettie. "I think I can walk."

"That's nice. You can walk to the shower when we're inside. I'll bring you a change of clothes."

Percy unlocked the back door, and Buster ran inside. He carried Nettie to the downstairs bathroom next to the guest bedroom. "Take a shower; scrub good and wash your hair. Smoke is toxic."

While Nettie showered and dressed, Percy went into the kitchen where everyone had gathered, including Estelle, who was making pancakes to go with the coffee.

Percy said, "Flossie, you're going to be next. Do you need me to pick you out a change of clothes?"

Flossie snorted. "I was the only one who didn't go into the smoke. Laird should go next."

"I'll get a change of clothes for you, Laird," Oliver said. "They'll be a little big for you, but we're the same height, so you won't have high waters."

When Nettie came out of the bathroom, Estelle signed, "How are you?"

"Exhausted."

"Have a blueberry pancake." Estelle pointed with her spatula at the plate with butter melting on a single pancake.

Nettie smiled and cut her pancake into small bite-sized pieces then poured syrup over it.

Flossie joined Nettie at the counter and sipped her cup of coffee.

While Laird showered, Flossie narrowed her eyes at Percy. "You're next, hero. I'll go last. Maybe I can coax Peaches to go into the shower with me."

"That's a good idea if you can pull it off." Percy grinned.

"I just might; you don't know."

Nettie signed, "Estelle, would you find a piece of pink cloth so Peaches will have a fresh bandana?"

Estelle smiled and left for the sewing room. Flossie hurried upstairs and returned with a change of clothes.

Estelle met her in the hallway with a piece of pink fabric with tiny white roses on it.

"That's perfect," Flossie signed and then took the fabric into the kitchen.

Nettie signed, "I love what you picked, Star."

"What do you think, Peaches?" Flossie asked.

Peaches looked at Flossie. When she gazed at the pink fabric, she smiled.

"I agree; it's beautiful."

"You win, Flossie." Percy went upstairs and showered.

When Laird came out of the bathroom, Nettie asked, "How are you feeling?"

"Much better; I don't think I'll ever take breathing for granted, though."

"Same for me," Nettie said.

Percy came downstairs. "Okay, Flossie. It's shower time for you and Peaches, so Peaches can have her new bandana that doesn't stink like smoke."

"You heard the man; let's go, Peaches."

Peaches followed Flossie to the bathroom.

After he finished his third pancake, Laird said, "Flossie and Peaches have been in there quite a while."

"Girls take their time," Percy said.

Oliver signed for Estelle, and she laughed.

Oliver signed as he spoke, "If you good folks don't need us, we'll go home and get some sleep. We'll see you in the morning."

Estelle waved, and they left.

Nettie said, "Laird, we have a spare bedroom downstairs, if you'd like to use it. It's not as large as our guest bedroom upstairs, but I'm a little worried about Peaches and the stairs since this is a new place for her."

"Downstairs is just fine for us. Where does Buster sleep?"

"In the kitchen or in our bedroom."

"Maybe it will be better if he sleeps in the kitchen because it's close to us. I don't know whether Peaches is housebroken," he said.

"This is the best place to find out, but I'll bet she is," Nettie said.

When Flossie came out of the bathroom, Peaches trotted alongside her. "We don't have any dry towels left, but the floor's not so wet anymore. Where's Peaches' bandana?"

"Here it is, honey," Laird said.

Percy waggled his eyebrows at Nettie, and she coughed to keep from laughing.

Flossie tied on the bandana and stroked Peaches' back. "Girl, you are gorgeous."

Peaches raised her head and posed so everyone could admire her bandana.

"I don't know about anyone else, but I'm ready for bed," Percy said.

Flossie kissed Laird. "See you in the morning."

She went upstairs, and Peaches followed her.

"I guess you'd better take the upstairs guest bedroom, Laird, so Peaches doesn't have to go up and down the stairs to keep track of everyone," Nettie said.

Buster followed Peaches.

"I guess we can all go upstairs to bed. I'll be right up after I check the doors," Percy said.

While Nettie showed Laird the guest bedroom, Flossie and Peaches joined them.

"Peaches might stay with me, but she needs to know where you are, so she can return the favor and rescue you, honey," Flossie said.

After everyone was settled and all the lights were out, Percy whispered, "How did you hear Peaches howl?"

Nettie snuggled close to him. "Mmm. You're warm. I read howls can carry as far as ten miles if conditions are right. The conditions were just right."

Chapter Seventeen

Nettie woke to voices drifting up the stairs along with the enticing aroma of freshly perked coffee.

She rushed to dress but groaned when she lifted her arm up to put on her shirt. She sighed. *I need coffee.*

When she went into the kitchen Laird toasted her with his cup, and Peaches trotted to her. Nettie rubbed Peaches' ears then Buster's belly while Flossie poured her coffee.

"Where's Percy?" Nettie asked.

"Smitty picked him up; the sheriff wanted to talk to him. What's on the schedule for today?" Flossie asked.

"Lots of laundry, and I'll pack Percy's things for his trip. What about you?"

"I have my meeting this afternoon, so I'm available to help with whatever you need until then. What do you think about Peaches staying here instead of going on the road?" Flossie asked.

"I think it's a wonderful idea, but that's up to her and Laird."

Flossie turned to Laird. "Told you."

Laird gazed at Peaches and Buster who had snuggled together on the floor near the warm stove.

Laird furrowed his brow. "She'd be more comfortable here than being by herself all day in the truck while I take photos, but will she think I abandoned her?"

"Not if you tell her you'll be back," Nettie said.

"What can I fix you for breakfast, Nettie?" Flossie asked.

"Cinnamon sugar on toast."

"Good, I'll join you then we can start on the laundry."

"Laird, you're welcome to stay here until you leave for the campaign rallies," Nettie said as Flossie handed her a plate with cinnamon sugar on toast.

"Percy already said that," Flossie said, "but Laird..."

"I wanted to wait to be sure it was okay with you, Nettie."

"If you stay here, you'll be with Peaches, and you'll know she'll be safe with us when you're not here," Nettie said.

"I still can't believe you went into the burning building and dragged out Peaches, Nettie. You don't outweigh her by much, if at all," Laird said.

"I'm stronger than I look." Nettie sipped her coffee.

"No kidding," Laird mumbled.

"Did you want to go into town this morning, Laird?" Nettie asked.

"I can wait until Percy returns and catch a ride with Smitty."

"That makes sense. Finish your toast, Nettie, so we can get the laundry going. Do you want to start with Percy's clothes or the towels?"

Nettie popped the last bite of her toast into her mouth. "Percy."

She headed upstairs with Peaches and Buster following her. After she gathered the dirty clothes from her room, Nettie carried the basket downstairs, and the dogs followed her.

"You two are going to get a lot of exercise today because it's going to be busy around here."

When she went past the living room with her basket on the way to the utility room, Flossie and Laird were in a deep discussion.

Before she ran the water into the washer, Flossie called out, "We'll do the laundry. I know your arms must be tired. I'll be there in just a second."

Nettie shrugged then checked the kitchen. *Flossie already cleaned it. I can read some of the old newspapers. I've earned some reading time.*

She set aside the newspaper edition that was dedicated to the Titanic. *I need a little recovery time before I can read it again.*

She read each newspaper from page one to the end before she went on to the next one. After she read a newspaper dated four years earlier, she furrowed her brow. *Why did the editor give me this one? There's no historic event of any type. Am I missing something?*

Buster whined at her, and Peaches looked at her expectantly.

"A walk sounds like a good idea. I'll put on my warm coat."

After she put on her coat, she stopped at the utility room. "The dogs and I are going for a walk. We'll be close if you need us."

Flossie and Laird jumped then stepped away from each other. Laird's cheeks were red.

Flossie cleared her throat. "Take your time."

When she took the dogs outside, Buster and Peaches raced in a big circle then romped in the yard. Nettie strolled around the yard then stopped to look at the clear sky. *The day is beautiful, but it's still cold.*

She stamped her feet to keep her circulation going. *I missed something in that four-year-old edition. I can feel it.*

"Ready to go back in?" she asked.

Buster and Peaches raced to the back door. Peaches stayed two steps ahead of Buster and kept checking for him over her shoulder. Nettie smiled. *Peaches didn't outrun Buster even though she could have. She's teaching him how to be in a pack.*

When they were inside, Peaches and Buster trotted to the living room and flopped down on the rug in front of the fireplace. Nettie gazed longingly at the warm, crackling fire then continued to her sewing room.

When she picked up the newspapers, a single page fell to the floor. She read the headline, "Armistice signed at 11:00 AM on November 11. The Great War Has Ended."

She set the page on the table and found the newspaper from four years ago. When she reached page three, she found a small paragraph under the recipes. "We welcome H. "Doc" Jackson from New York and congratulate him on his retirement after thirty-five years of service to the medical community."

Interesting, but I hoped I'd find the mustache story. I'll have to look in the box of clippings.

Nettie went to the laundry room, but Flossie wasn't there.

She put on her coat and went outside. When she turned the corner, she smiled at Flossie and Laird as they laughed and flirted while they hung clothes on the clothesline.

Nettie went back inside, hung up her coat, and went into the living room. After she sat in her yellow chair near the fireplace, she leaned back and soaked up the warmth of the fire and the calm from her chair before she returned to her sewing room to go through the box.

When Flossie and Laird came inside, Flossie came to the sewing room. "Percy's not back yet?"

"Not yet. Do you remember when Doc moved here?"

"Vaguely; I was in high school. The adult world was boring."

Nettie nodded as she continued going through the box. "That makes sense."

"Why are you asking?"

Nettie shrugged. "Do you need any help with the laundry?"

"No, we'll have the last load on the line in two shakes, and before you ask how long it will take for everything to dry, we might have to pull in the towels and hang them on the rack in the laundry room before dark, but Percy's clothes will be dry by early afternoon."

"Good. That gives me time to iron and pack his clothes before supper."

Flossie lowered her voice. "When I came to your room last night and said I had a nightmare, I dreamed we were at a lake and a baby was in a boat by itself. You jumped in to swim to the baby, but the lake was on fire. I started your car and was going to drive out to save you and the baby, but I don't know how to drive." Flossie sniffed back a tear.

"We'll make that a priority," Nettie said.

After Flossie left, Nettie continued going through the box. She grinned when she found an article with the headline, "Flaming Mustaches."

She quickly scanned the article and smiled. *The man in the library remembered the story exactly as it was written here.* Nettie furrowed her brow at the ending paragraph. "The flaming crisis was averted when hospital orderly Horace "Jack" Jackson doused the fiery mustache with a cup of leftover coffee. At his retirement party, his friends presented him with an over-sized coffee mug with the words "In Case of Fire" printed on it."

Nettie stared at the words 'In Case of Fire.' *There's no crime in assuming a new nickname, but I need to know more.*

Nettie hurried to the living room where she heard Flossie and Laird whispering. When she stepped in the doorway, Flossie quit talking mid-sentence.

"I'm going into town. Percy should be here soon; tell him I don't expect to be gone very long," Nettie said.

Nettie put on her coat and grabbed her beaded bag before she rushed out to the car and drove to the library.

The parking lot was fuller than usual, so she parked at the far end near the trees.

When she went inside, the young librarian said, "Nice to see you again, Miss Nettie. Is there anything I can help you find?"

Loud laughter erupted from the meeting room.

The young librarian smiled. "Today is the monthly meeting for our retired readers. The restaurant always caters lunch for us, so our meetings are very well-attended."

Nettie returned the smile. "I'd like to thank the elderly man who helped me yesterday. Is he here? I thought he might be a regular."

The librarian furrowed her brow. "He said he was just passing through. We don't get many lone tourists his age, but he certainly was interesting, wasn't he?"

A woman rushed into the library with her hand on her chest. "I just heard the news. Have you heard? The bank is closed. I went to the bank to withdraw money to send to my mother, and there was a sign on the door that said closed. So I went to the gas station and heard they found the bank manager's car in the lake south of town. He must have fallen asleep or had a heart attack because his tire tracks went right off the road and into the lake." She sat down at a table, and the young librarian rushed to get her a cup of water.

Nettie quietly left. Before she reached her car, Doc pulled in next to her and climbed out. He smiled as he strolled to the back of his car.

He smiled. "I was hoping to catch up with you today."

Nettie fumbled with her bead bag, and he tensed and put his right hand near his coat pocket.

Thanks for the tip, Jack.

She pulled out her keys, but left her beaded bag open.

"It's cold out here; would you like to grab a coffee at the restaurant to chat?" she asked.

He shook his head. "I won't take much of your time. You've been a real thorn in my side since you married Percy."

She shrugged. "I'm not sure I see how that could be, but I apologize, Jack."

His face paled. "What did you call me?"

A car raced through the parking lot and skid to a stop with the squeal of brakes. The thug with the scar across his face jumped out with a pistol aimed at Nettie.

"I told you I found her, boss. Do you want I should bump her off?"

"No, you fool. She's mine." Doc reached into his right pocket, but before he could raise his pistol, Nettie shot him in the middle of his forehead as a second shot rang out, then a third and fourth followed.

Doc crumpled, and the thug with the scar dropped.

Percy, Smitty, and Johnny stepped out of the woods and strode to the parking lot. The elderly man stayed near the trees and waved; Nettie smiled and returned his wave.

Percy strode to Doc and kicked him in the head then grabbed Nettie and hugged her. "I was afraid things might heat up, so we thought we'd back you up in case there was trouble. It's cold out here. Let's get you some hot tea."

Nettie cocked her head. "Who is the man near the woods?"

Johnny exhaled. "My dad. He came out of retirement when he heard Horace Jackson was here and what was going on. He's a retired doctor from New York."

Nettie smiled. "He's amazing."

Johnny glanced at Smitty. "I've got this, Sarge."

Smitty nodded and disappeared into the woods while Percy led Nettie to the passenger seat of their car.

On the way home, Nettie asked, "Why did Johnny call Smitty Sarge?"

"Smitty was a First Sergeant in the marines. Turns out he took Johnny out on his first combat mission."

"Are we sure Doc was the kingpin?"

"Johnny is, and that's good enough for me."

"So what's next?"

"We have an election to win."

Chapter Eighteen

FOUR WEEKS LATER

Nettie smiled at Percy in his tuxedo as he stood in their dining room while the roomful of his closest supporters cheered and clapped. *He looks so sexy in his tuxedo.*

A woman approached Percy. When she laid her hand on his arm, she glanced over her shoulder at Nettie and sniffed. Nettie raised an eyebrow, and the woman jerked back her hand like it had been burned. Percy smiled at Nettie and winked.

Flossie wore her black sequined dress with her black sparkly headband.

"You're looking spiffy this evening, Flossie," Nettie said.

Flossie giggled as she linked her arm through Nettie's. "We actually did it. Lieutenant Governor Percy Wyndham. As soon as Laird gets around to popping the question, we're going to buy the abandoned house down the road. You can be my project manager for the renovations."

Nettie smiled. "You know I'd love it, but the house needs you, not me."

Flossie smiled and hurried to Laird, who was scanning the room in his search for her.

Percy raised his hands, and a hush fell over the room. He motioned for Nettie to join him.

He put his arm around her. "Thank you, everyone, for your wonderful support, and we all know we wouldn't be here if not for my brilliant bride."

The room erupted with applause and cheers.

When the noise died down, Percy continued, "All our hard work has paid off, and you are appreciated. We have more ahead of us, but we're strong and will tackle it together."

The rest of the evening was filled with swapping stories and enjoying Estelle's delicious hors d'oeuvres on the sideboards.

After everyone left at the end of the night, Nettie, Percy, Flossie, Laird, Buster, and Peaches relaxed in the living room in front of the fireplace.

Nettie sat in her yellow chair and slipped off her shoes. "You were brilliant, honey. I'm so proud of you."

Percy pulled his chair closer to hers then kissed her open mouth before he sat down. "You're the brilliant one, darling; I'm the pretty face."

"Don't be silly, Percy; Nettie is brilliant and much prettier than you are. You're stuck with being just the Lieutenant Governor." Flossie giggled as she hung up her feather boa so Buster wouldn't take it apart then sat next to Laird on the sofa and kicked off her shoes. He put his arm around her and pulled her closer.

When Laird cleared his throat, Flossie furrowed her brow, and Nettie raised her eyebrows at Percy. He smiled and winked.

Laird pulled out a small box from his jacket pocket while Flossie cocked her head.

He dropped to one knee. "Flossie, you're the love of my life. Will you marry me?" He flipped open the small box with the ring inside.

Flossie squealed, and Percy covered his ears.

"Yes, yes, yes!"

Buster howled, and Peaches barked while Flossie tackled Laird and bombarded him with kisses.

After they were in their bedroom, Percy said, "I appreciate everything you've done, sweetheart, but I need to know, are bad guys and ambushes behind us?"

"Of course they are." Nettie bit her lip.

Did you enjoy Nettie's story? If you're ready for the next Nettie story, let Judith know! Leave a review with your favorite bookseller!

Meanwhile, are you ready for an exciting story at the Wyndham estate over a hundred years later?

ELUSIVE EMBEZZLER
Jenna is a young widow, an innkeeper, and an accidental crimebuster.

When Jenna Ross inherits a charming bed-and-breakfast inn from her deceased husband's family, she sees the opportunity as a path to heal her grief. Jenna and her golden retriever, Katy, move into the small cottage behind the inn.

After she finds the body of a guest that could damage the B&B's reputation, Jenna unknowingly steps on the toes of the killer as she instinctively follows her uncanny intuition and unravels the mystery.

Jenna clashes with both her critical landscaper and her annoying architect, but a man in her life would complicate everything.

Jenna is single minded: save the inn. The desperate killer is single minded: kill Jenna.

ELUSIVE EMBEZZLER is available on BARRETT BOOK SHOP and your favorite retailer!

Join Judith's eNewsletter mailing list and become the first to know about new books and book specials and read unpublished stories and exciting news! Judithabarrett.com/newsletter

Find more Judith A. Barrett books in the Barrett Book Shop! BarrettBookShop.com

More About the Author

Judith A. Barrett, award-winning author, lives on a farm in Georgia with her husband, two dogs, and chickens. She writes series for her readers: thriller, mystery, historical fiction, post-apocalyptic science fiction, and cozy mystery novels. Stories with a twist: not your typical characters from not your typical author!

Her motto: *You keep reading; I'll keep writing!*

When she isn't writing, Judith is meeting readers at arts and crafts festivals, working on farm chores, hiking or camping with her husband and dogs, or rocking on her front porch while she watches the sunset and wonders what will happen next in the current book she is writing.

Website JudithABarrett.com

VIP Readers Subscribe to her eNewsletter

judithabarrett.com/newsletter

Exclusive Discounts and Sales

BarrettBookShop.com

Follow Judith on her Blog: The Latest Twist is on her website!

Find your next book(s) and buy direct from the author at
the Barrett Book Shop!
BarrettBookShop.com
where you will find exclusive sales and discounts for
ebooks, paperbacks, and audiobooks!